ALSO BY DAVID LINDGREN

Trust but Verify

In All Good Conscience

Atahualpa's Gold

DAVID T. LINDGREN

iUniverse, Inc.
New York   Bloomington

Atahualpa's Gold

iUniverse books may be ordered through booksellers or by contacting:

iUniverse
1663 Liberty Drive
Bloomington, IN 47403
www.iuniverse.com
1-800-Authors (1-800-288-4677)

ISBN: 978-1-4502-5410-6 (pbk)
ISBN: 978-1-4502-5408-3 (dj)
ISBN: 978-1-4502-5407-6 (ebk)

Library of Congress Control Number: 2010912560

Printed in the United States of America

iUniverse rev. date: 9/28/10

O cursed lust for gold, to what dost thou not drive the hearts of men!

Virgil:
Aeneid

The following is a work of fiction and all characters, events and conversations are products of the author's imagination. Many of the places described in the book are real and would be recognizable to anyone familiar with the city of Quito. Political events may have been inspired by actual incidents but have often been reshaped to fit the plot.

dtl

Prologue

He was prodding them to keep moving though he knew they were exhausted and reaching the limits of their endurance. The wooden chests they were hauling were bulky and extremely heavy, filled as they were with gold, silver and other valuables; he had to let them stop regularly to rest. They were traveling now through thick, nearly impenetrable jungle where they had little alternative but to use the narrow, twisting trails made by the local Indians. Unfortunately, these same Indians represented their greatest threat at the moment since they were deeply suspicious of anyone venturing into their territory. They also had a frightening reputation; not only were they known as an aggressive warlike people but also for their grisly custom of shrinking the heads of any enemies they killed in combat. Clearly, then, they were a people to be avoided at all costs. Yet, he thought to himself, if his small group managed to slip into the jungle, hide the gold, and slip back out without being observed, the Indians would provide a form of protection against those who might come later to search for the gold.

His destination was an area of abandoned mines from which ironically gold had once been extracted. They tended not to be large, some little more than animal burrows, but they were perfect for what he had in mind. The waterproof chests would be placed in one of the smaller mines, the entrance of which would be sealed with rocks and brush. Whatever remaining evidence of their activities would be wiped out by the jungle's swiftly growing vegetation.

Assuming now that he could successfully avoid being seen, the Indians helping him transport and bury the gold represented the only individuals other than himself who would know the secret of the gold's location. It was unfortunate but they'd have to be killed, though unfortunate only in the sense he'd have to somehow account for their disappearance. But, there was no way he was going to let them pass along what they had been doing here. In fact, he would have to kill them immediately after their work was completed and let the jungle's animals dispose of their remains.

They had stopped for a moment to rest when he spotted a shadowy figure gliding noiselessly through the trees, or at least he thought he saw someone. Perhaps it was only his overactive imagination, but he couldn't take the chance; they had to get going. Fortunately, they were almost to the spot where he intended to hide the gold. He realized full well that even if he were able to evade the local Indians it was only a matter of time before others would be coming after him; they would claim the gold was theirs and they'd stop at nothing to get it. But he would never give up the secret of the gold's location; they'd have to find it on their own!

One

Adam was waiting for me as I approached the exit from the terminal. Towering over everyone around him, he was impossible to miss. Adam was well over six feet tall with the broad muscular shoulders of a swimmer, which he had been during his undergraduate days at Harvard. But it wasn't only his build that made him stand out; he also possessed the kind of good looks once favored by Hollywood before it decided audiences preferred the dark, unshaven look: unruly sandy-colored hair, blue eyes, a masculine, well-tanned face. Walking over to him, I had to laugh. He was dressed as if he had just stepped out of the pages of GQ magazine, a white cotton shirt open at the collar, tan chinos, brown loafers, and a sweater draped casually over his shoulders. When he saw me he gave me that wry smile of his, no doubt because of my jeans, Adidas, and faded New England Patriots Super Bowl Champions sweatshirt. The only thing I appeared appropriately dressed for was one of the old Kennedy-style, Hyannisport football games. On second thought I probably wasn't even dressed well enough for one of those.

"Michael, good to see you again," he said, extending his hand. "To say this is a surprise is clearly an understatement. This is your first trip abroad, isn't it?"

"My first to South America. Actually, my father took my mother and me to Europe for a couple weeks the summer after my sophomore year in high school. But, you are right to feel surprised at my being here."

Of course, I thought to myself, you can't possibly be more surprised than myself. If fate had only been a little less unkind I'd be in New York right now, working, searching for the perfect engagement ring for Rachel, and planning for our life together in Westchester. Instead, here I was walking past a sign that read, Welcome to Quito, Ecuador. Elevation: 9,213 feet. Walk slowly.

"I am glad to be here, and I really appreciate how quickly you responded to my asking you if I could come down. Now," I asked, nodding at the sign, "should I really walk slowly?"

Adam laughed. "You should, but you won't. Americans are always in a hurry, even when they're down here on vacation. That's why they're so easy to recognize. Most Ecuadorians walk at a very relaxed pace. So, anyway, how was your flight?"

He motioned me towards a monstrous black Mitsubishi Montero parked a short distance away.

"The flight was packed; I think every seat was taken, and worse, I was squeezed between these two huge Texans, who apparently worked for one of the oil companies down here. But, thank god for iPods; I was able to just plug myself in and listen to my music. So, in spite of everything, the time passed pretty quickly."

"I'm assuming what you're saying is you flew economy? Why on earth did you do that? Why didn't you at the least use some of your frequent flyer miles to upgrade to business class?"

"Because I don't have any frequent flyer miles and you know it; I don't go anywhere to earn them. I live in New York, I work in New York and my girlfriend lives in New York. Well, let me rephrase that: I live in New York, my *former* employer is located in New York and my *former* girlfriend lives in New York. But, I also don't have the U.S. government to pay for my travel so that I can accrue frequent flyer miles."

"Oh, please, Michael, with what you make you have no business flying economy."

"OK, you've made your point. I promise to fly business-class in the future," I replied with a laugh. "Anyway, I do want to say the view of Quito when you land at night is really incredible. That alone made the trip over here from Miami worthwhile, though I know, I know, the view would have been just as incredible from business class."

"It is a beautiful sight," Adam replied, with a smile that implied so you got my point. "Unfortunately, they're building a new airport outside the city so in the future you won't get that same view. It'll be more like flying into Dulles rather than Reagan National where if you happen to land from the northwest you get a spectacular view of Washington."

I stowed my luggage in the back, then clambered into the front seat of the Montero. "So where's the T-Bird you used to drive when we were in Hanover? Did you trade it in for this," I asked, fairly certain that he hadn't.

Adam and I had attended Dartmouth's Tuck Business School together, where we had become friends, in large part because both of us quickly realized business school was not really where either one of us wanted to be. Adam had come at his father's insistence, although he had wanted Adam to attend Harvard Business School where he had gone. As for me, well, I didn't even have that excuse; my parents were hoping I'd become an Ivy League professor. Instead I applied to business school because that's where all my friends at Wesleyan were headed. Some reason!

"Oh, I still have my T-Bird," Adam was saying, "but as much as I love Ecuador I would never bring it down here; it would be stolen in a flash. Car-jackings are fairly common and in spite of what Ecuadorians tell you, they're not all carried out by Colombian drug-dealers. That's kind of a local joke. Every time something happens like a bank robbery or a car-jacking Ecuadorians blame it on the Colombians. Anyway, I left it in Boston at my parents' house."

"But don't you have to worry about this car being stolen?"

"To be honest, I was commuting to work on a Suzuki 1200S motorcycle that I bought from a departing embassy employee when I first came down here. That's when the embassy was only about five minutes away. Unfortunately for me they've built a new one that's located to the north of the city. It's about a forty-minute ride through traffic now and for security reasons the embassy prefers I use the Montero. However, if for any reason you need to use the Montero I can always take the Suzuki; I love riding it."

"Well, thanks," I replied, "but I can't imagine trying to drive around this country by myself; I couldn't even ask anyone directions if I got lost, which I'm sure I would. But, who knows, something could come up so I appreciate the offer."

"You know, you'll be amazed how quickly you'll pick up enough Spanish to survive in this country. As for driving, believe me, if you can drive in New York or Boston you can drive down here. Come to think of it, Ecuadorians drive very much like Americans, so not to worry," Adam laughed. "Or, maybe you should worry."

We had left the airport parking lot now and were driving through Quito's well-lighted streets. I was amazed to see so many familiar names—McDonalds, Burger King, Pizza Hut, Tony Roma's, American Airlines, Mobil, Gap. It could have been some city in the US.

"This isn't quite what I imagined Quito would be like. I guess I expected more of a Spanish colonial city," I said, the disappointment clearly audible in my voice.

"Relax," Michael replied reassuringly. "What we're passing through now is the newer part of the city, but there's an older, colonial part as well; it's really quite beautiful, you'll see."

Before I had much chance to think about it further, Adam announced, "We're here."

I did my best to get a look at Adam's building but we were already descending a ramp leading to the garage. To my surprise, the cars parked there were all expensive models—Mercedes, Volvos, BMWs as well as several models of SUVs.

"I didn't realize people lived so well down here; look at the cars."

"Believe me, most people don't live like this. Of course, there are those with money but it's a tiny proportion of the population. And anyway, you come from Connecticut, the state with the highest per capita income in the US. I mean, every day you come in contact there with people who are wealthier than this. What's going to amaze you more is the poverty down here. You're going to have to quickly get used to young indigenous girls four or five years old with even younger siblings strapped to their backs out begging in the streets, or older men and women doing much the same. And, if they're not begging they're selling fruit or candy; it's not an easy life for them."

Adam's comments surprised me. They were not what I had expected to hear from him of all people, yet when I thought about it I concluded that was exactly the reason he had gone into this business rather than banking like his father had wanted.

An elevator had taken us to the first floor where for security reasons we had to get out. Adam introduced me to the security guard monitoring the building's front door explaining I would be living there for a while. We then got into another elevator where Adam pushed the button for the seventh floor. When the door slid open we stepped directly out into a large foyer with a beautiful marble floor and from which rooms extended on all sides.

"Just drop your bags here for a moment and let me show you around," Adam suggested.

We first entered his living room, which Adam had furnished in a contemporary style with an array of couches and armchairs in various shades of white and black, several different sized coffee and end tables in chrome and glass, and on literally every wall hung reproductions of abstract paintings by Pollock, Rothko, Kadinsky. In an alcove to the left, Adam had placed a home theater complete with a flat-screen television that had to be at least sixty inches across, a DVD player, and an impressive-looking sound system that was clearly capable of handling CD's judging from the scores of them visible on an adjacent black metal rack. A collection of DVD's was stored on a shelf under the TV. If the thought had ever crossed my mind how someone like Adam could survive living in a country like Ecuador, it never would again. As I should have expected, he lived very well.

My attention was drawn to a huge picture window at the far end of the room. Walking over to it Adam warned, "You won't see much out there tonight."

What I found was a thick blanket of fog that was obscuring everything but a few very faint lights.

"The fog is very common around here, so common, if fact, they refer to this part of the city as 'little London.' It was the reason I had encouraged you to book yourself on the early flight into Quito. Every now and then the later flight is unable to land because of the fog so it has to go on to Guayaquil and that can be a bit of a hassle. But wait until morning, the view of the valley and the Cotopaxi volcano is incredible. Cotopaxi, by the way, is the world's highest active volcano, though its summit is snow-covered. Anyway, shall we go into the dining room; we should get a nice view of the city from there."

The dining room was situated just to the right as one entered the apartment. Adam didn't turn any lights on so I could better appreciate the view from the large picture window there. I had only time enough to notice this room was furnished more traditionally and sparsely. Obviously it wasn't a room in which he spent much time. As I approached the window I was amazed to see Quito stretched out before me, a myriad of twinkling lights muted ever so slightly by the swirling fog.

"And in the morning you'll have another incredible view when the sky is a crystal clear blue and there's a dusting of snow on the highest peaks of the Pichinchas."

"These views are incredible even in the fog," I replied.

"Well, there are trade-offs to this location, and especially to this fog. While I'm not trying to alarm you, at least three small planes have crashed into apartment buildings on this street in thick fog in the past ten or so years."

He said all this with just enough of a smile that I actually thought he was kidding.

Noticing my reaction he quickly added, "No, I'm serious, aircraft have struck these buildings, the most recent of which occurred only a month or so ago. It was a small single engine type, though all together I think seven people were killed. In the morning when you look up to see Cotopaxi, if you look down to your right you'll be able to see the charred ruins of the building the aircraft hit; there was quite a fire."

"Well that's certainly going to make me sleep a lot better," I replied sarcastically.

"Not to worry, those small planes tend not to have instruments so they don't fly in at night," he chuckled. "Come on, let me show you the rest of the apartment."

Adam led the way through a swinging door that opened directly into a surprisingly modern-looking kitchen, all chrome and glass and white paint. In the center stretched a long black marble counter, above which extended a rack holding a variety of polished stainless steel and copper pots and pans. It was impressive though I had great difficulty imagining Adam spending much time here. I certainly never remembered him ever mentioning doing any cooking on his own.

"Through that door are the maid's quarters," he continued. "I don't have a live-in maid, only Consuelo who comes in twice a week so I've put my computer in there. To be honest I seldom go in there. I have a computer at work and I tend to use that one for most things."

All I could do as we walked about was to marvel at how huge the apartment seemed.

"Can you imagine how much an apartment like this would go for in New York?" I exclaimed. "It would cost a fortune. My studio apartment in the Village probably costs more than this."

"This apartment is not inexpensive, but you're right, it doesn't come close to what a comparable apartment in New York would cost, maybe not even what it would cost in Hanover," he laughed.

We exited the kitchen into a small hallway.

"The bedrooms are here. That's your bedroom there, mine's at the end of the hallway. Each one has its own full bath and the same view of the valley you see from the living room. So, let's go back into the living room, this way."

"I still can't get over how beautiful your apartment is; does everyone who works for the embassy live like this," I asked in amazement.

"Some live better, especially those higher up in the ranks. The embassy leases a number of very nice houses down here but those are generally offered to employees with families. Single guys like me are generally given a housing allowance; it doesn't cover the entire cost of an apartment like this but I'm more than willing to kick in the difference," Adam replied.

"And the furniture, it's all yours?"

"The larger pieces I bought down here. Depending upon where they send me next I may keep some of the furniture, the rest I'll sell. But, I do have to admit I really like this apartment and I even have cable TV, so who knows, we might even be able catch opening day at Fenway Park."

The Red Sox were one of the few things I knew Adam to be passionate about.

"Listen," he explained apologetically, "I realize it's rude not to sit and talk awhile but I have to get up really early in the morning. I have to fly down to Guayaquil; I'll be back late afternoon. And I promise you, tomorrow night I'll take you to this great restaurant in the old part of the city. We can relax, and you can fill me in on the details about Rachel and anything else that has been happening in your life since we left Hanover."

"Sounds fine to me," I replied. "To tell you the truth, I could use some sleep myself."

"Now, you should be able to find anything you need around here somewhere. There's plenty of food in the refrigerator, beer, wine, whatever, though it would probably be best if you didn't consume any alcohol for a day or so. As for tomorrow, take it easy. Don't try to walk too much until you've become acclimated to the altitude. Watch how the indigenous people move about. Oh, and one more thing. We're right on the flight-path of planes landing at the airport. They start coming in about six in the morning; it's better than an alarm clock," he laughed. "Pleasant dreams."

I didn't get to sleep for hours, or at least it seemed like hours. All I could think about was the possibility there might be a another small plane up there blindly trying to find the airport while heading straight for our building.

Two

Adam's warning about the aircraft didn't begin to prepare me for what happened the next morning. At exactly 5:45, according to the clock on a nearby table, I was literally shaken from my bed by the roar of an aircraft seemingly about to land on the very roof of our building. I sat up long enough to realize it was getting light outside before falling back against my pillow with a groan. I pulled the sheet over my face and tried desperately to get back to sleep, but it proved impossible. Over the next hour another half-dozen aircraft zoomed in over our building just as noisily. I couldn't imagine how Adam could put up with this every morning, though it did probably explain why he went to work so early.

The smell of freshly brewed coffee wafting in from the kitchen compelled me to finally drag myself out of bed. I took a quick shower, got dressed and went in search of Consuelo; I was sure Adam had told her I was about. I found her in the kitchen leaning over the sink scrubbing vegetables. She was a rather plumpish young woman with short dark hair and wearing what I assumed to be a maid's uniform—a black dress with white trim and a white apron. When I entered the kitchen she glanced over at me. Almost immediately her broad, swarthy face broke into a delightful smile.

"*Buenos días*, Mister Michael," she beamed.

"*Buenos días*," I replied, finding it all but impossible not to stare at the shiny gold tooth that adorned the front of her mouth.

"*Desayuño*.....breakfast," she nodded towards the table where she had laid out juice, coffee and a variety of fresh rolls she had must have purchased from a bakery on her way to work. At her use of the word "breakfast" I became instantly excited that Consuelo might actually speak

English, but alas my hopes were quickly dashed. Her knowledge of English proved to be about the same as my knowledge of Spanish, that is to say, nearly non-existent. Still, we did our best to carry on some semblance of a conversation, but after "Yes, I like my breakfast" and "Yes, I like being in Quito" we more or less gave up in favor of just exchanging smiles. And, for all those people who say how much French is like Spanish, I have to take exception. Nothing, absolutely nothing, in my three years of high school French proved of any use in communicating with Consuelo.

Feeling frustrated, not to mention full, I left the kitchen and wandered into the living room where I was immediately drawn again to the large picture window. In the daylight the view was breathtaking. The valley directly below was still partially shrouded in fog, though it was not so thick I couldn't make out the beautiful old Spanish-era church in the foreground. Beyond the valley opened into a much broader plain where a patchwork of fields stood out in stark contrast to the darker tracts of woods surrounding them. The peaks of the mountains that formed a backdrop to the scene were aglow with the first bursts of sunlight. The sky, which appeared fiery orange along the horizon, merged gradually into a pale, then deeper blue overhead. But what really caught my eye, as Adam had predicted, was the majestic snow-capped peak of Cotopaxi that seemed to loom up out of nowhere.

As I stood there mesmerized by the view, I heard the phone ring and since Consuelo was about I let her answer it. A second or two later I heard her shout, "Mister Michael, is for you, Mister Adam."

Picking up the phone in the living room, I said, "Adam, so what's up?"

"I'm calling you on my cell-phone from Guayaquil; I'm actually in a taxi at this moment. Just wanted to find out what you had planned for the day; we never spoke about it last night."

"Well, it looks like a beautiful day so I thought I'd go out for a walk and see a little bit of Quito. Any suggestions where I might go," I asked.

"You should probably walk down to the Mariscal district. It's very touristy but there are a lot of nice stores and restaurants there. I think you'd like it."

"Sounds good," I replied, "I think that's what I'll probably do."

"Well, just remember what I said to you last night; be careful as you wander about the city? Whatever you do, don't walk around plugged into your iPod. I realize everyone does it in the US but this is definitely not the US. If someone doesn't actually accost you for the purpose of stealing it, you're very apt to have your wallet lifted while you're tuned into the music. Look, just be aware at all times of where you are and what's going on around you. By American standards it's a very safe city, but you can never be too careful. In that regard remind me to tell you what happened to a friend of a colleague of mine. If nothing else, it will make you appreciate just how sophisticated some of this street crime has become. And, in this case, it happened right here on Avenida Gonzalez Suarez. Anyway, don't let me hold you up; I'll see you later."

"All right, will do; and thanks for calling, Adam."

I hung up the phone and was off.

I crossed the street in front of the apartment and headed down Gonzalez Suarez past the Colegio de la Immaculada, a Catholic girls school. It must have been recess for the schoolyard was alive with scores of identically-dressed young girls—plaid skirts, white blouses, navy blue sweaters---running, laughing, yelling. Their youthful exuberance was infectious and it made me feel just a little bit more upbeat. At the first corner I took a right onto Calle San Ignacio and after a brief downhill walk I approached Orellana, the street that my guidebook explained would take me to Avenida Amazonas. As I rounded the corner onto Orellana I was unexpectedly confronted with the most incredible view of Quito. The city lay stretched out before me, extending down the hill, across the narrow valley and up the lower slopes of the Pichinchas. The sky at that moment was a deep blue with just a few wispy clouds adorning the higher peaks. I had often heard people describe views as breathtaking but I had always thought of it as just another cliché. However, this particular view of Quito truly took my breath away.

Continuing down Orellana, I came almost at once to an intersection filled with the kind of entrepreneurial activity Adam had described. While there were no young children begging, there were several women dressed in their traditional black ankle-length skirts, white blouses and black fedora hats moving between the stopped cars selling fruit, candy, chewing gum; there was a man with only stumps for legs politely accepting handouts from motorists; and most fascinating of all was a young man with soot-covered hands and face standing directly in front of the stopped cars breathing fire. Well, he wasn't actually breathing fire but spewing mouthfuls of some kind of flammable liquid across a burning torch. The whole scene reminded me in a way of the Big Apple Circus my parents took me to when I was four or five years old. I must have stood there for a good fifteen minutes watching in amazement what these people were willing to do to earn a little money. I remember being introduced to the concept of the informal sector in business school but until now I had never appreciated how vibrant and extensive it could be.

A few minutes more walking and I reached Avenida Amazonas, one of the three main streets that ran the length of the Mariscal district. It was just as Adam had said, an area crammed with souvenir shops, restaurants, internet cafes, youth hostels and dozens of travel offices advertising trips to the Galapagos, the Amazon, and to various locations in the Andes.

The streets were crowded with young people, many of them tourists judging from their shorts, hiking boots, backpacks and very white skin. I found it interesting that so few of them appeared to be American. If the little flags many of them had sewed to their backpacks were a good indication, they were overwhelmingly from Europe. Watching them I felt almost envious of their youthful independence. At their age, and most of them, I guessed, were several years younger than me, I hadn't traveled anywhere, not even within the United States. What had I been thinking about in those days? I decided I had wasted a good deal of unnecessary time worrying about where I was going to graduate school. But why did I do it? It would have been so much more fun traveling around with guys like this, not to mention with the young women who were accompanying them.

During the course of the afternoon I wandered into a number of shops though more out of curiosity than with any intention to buy. Ultimately, I did purchase an alpaca sweater made in Peru; I didn't really need it since I had no shortage of clothes but I simply couldn't resist the price. It occurred to me that I should probably buy a dozen or so of these sweaters since I could sell them in New York at three times the retail price here. Of course, they'd also make nice great gifts for my friends, too.

I had been walking for hours when I realized I was terribly in need of a cold drink, and I was desperate for a bathroom. From where I was standing I could see a dozen cafes and bars, it was simply a matter of choosing one. The bar I finally settled on didn't really look much different than any of the others, at least from the outside—a single story, yellow stucco building with black ironwork over the windows. But, it did have one unique feature—its name.

El Café de Los Toreros.

Three

Coming in out of the bright sunlight, it took my eyes a second or two to adjust to the relatively dark interior of the café. But, when suddenly they did adjust, I was startled to find myself confronting a fearful apparition in the form of a massive bull's head. The creature must have been frightening in the flesh for its horns were at least six feet from tip-to-tip; as for its eyes, they appeared to be glaring at me with such hatred, I felt a shiver of fear just standing there looking up at him.

"Impressive, isn't he?" came a voice in heavily accented English from behind the bar.

"I'll say," I replied, shifting my gaze from the bull to the speaker. "I've never seen any animal with a head that huge, or that menacing."

"He was one of the fiercest bulls ever to fight in this country. But, you must pardon me; you look like you could use something cold to drink. What can I get you?"

"What I desperately need right now is a bathroom, do you have one?"

"Over there." He pointed to a door to my right.

"Thanks," I murmured, rushing off. "I'll be right back."

Returning from the bathroom I had my first opportunity to look around at the rest of the café. The walls were covered with photos of famous matadors, many of them autographed. There were also colorful posters of past bullfighting events, including one advertising a series of bullfights held in the city's Plaza de Toros during the previous December's Fiestas de Quito.

A cold beer was waiting for me as I slid onto an empty barstool.

"Thanks," I said, raising my glass to the bartender, who along with two other customers, was intently watching a soccer game on a large-screen television attached to the wall next to the bar. At that moment the three were completely oblivious to my presence. It was not until the action was momentarily halted by an injury on the field that the bartender wandered back to where I was sitting.

"*Buenas tardes*, or I guess I should say, good afternoon, since I suspect you're an American. I'm Carlos, the owner of this place," he said by way of introduction.

"Michael," I replied, grasping his outstretched hand. "It's a pleasure to meet you."

Carlos may have been a couple inches shorter than I but he had the rugged build of a middleweight boxer. His swarthy face was adorned with a head of thick black hair, which matched his eyebrows and moustache. But, it was his smile you noticed most. He possessed an almost perfect set of teeth, the kind one normally saw only in toothpaste commercials.

"So, Carlos, your English is quite good, where did you learn it," I asked, genuinely curious.

"Silver Spring, Maryland, just outside of Washington; I lived there for three years."

"Three years, so why did you come back here? Didn't you like living in the US?"

"I enjoyed my time there, and I made a little money, money enough to buy this place, but to be honest I missed Ecuador......the people, the weather...."

"And bullfighting? I'm sure you didn't get to see many bullfights in Silver Spring, Maryland."

"You're right about that, I didn't, and bullfighting is my passion. When I was a kid I dreamed of being a bullfighter. Ah the artistry! Bullfighting when done well is like a.....like a ballet. To me it's far more exciting than a football game, or soccer as you Americans call it. There is just something so very special about bullfighting. So what do you think about bullfighting? I've found very few Americans who share my enthusiasm; they seem to find it a rather savage, uncivilized sport, except for your writer Ernest Hemingway, of course; he was obviously fascinated by it."

"Yes, he was, and to be honest all I know about bullfighting is from reading his novels. I've never actually seen a bullfight myself," I explained, wondering what I might be letting myself in for.

13

"Well, if you're still in Quito at the time of the Fiestas, you must go to the Plaza de Toros and see a bullfight. I mean it, it's really quite a spectacle, and if I'm not mistaken, you seem to be just the kind of guy who'd like it. Believe me, there is nothing like it."

I really wasn't sure what he meant by "I was just the kind of guy." It made me wonder whether Adam was that kind of guy. I made a mental note to ask him if he'd ever gone to a bullfight; I'd bet he had. Wasn't there, in fact, something rather Hemingway-esque about Adam? I quickly rejected the notion deciding instead Adam was actually more like F. Scott Fitzgerald. Anyway, after glancing at some of the photos on the wall I concluded I wouldn't enjoy the sport, no matter how artistically the bull was dispatched. I was not, however, about to be so impolitic as to say that to Carlos.

Instead I replied, "If I'm still here in December I'll make it a point to attend a bullfight."

It was both an honest as well as a safe answer since there was virtually no chance in the world I'd still be in Quito come December.

Fortunately, I was saved from having to say more when the two men watching the soccer game literally launched themselves from their seats, yelling something I didn't understand but got the gist of.

"I guess their team just scored," I commented, as Carlos turned quickly towards the television.

"Ecuador just scored," he replied, watching the replay.

"Who's Ecuador playing," I asked.

"Brazil," he answered curtly. It was obvious he did want to be interrupted and I could quickly see why, Ecuador was winning and even with my limited knowledge of soccer I knew that beating Brazil would be a major upset.

While Carlos's attention was focused on the game I glanced around the café. In addition to the bar there were a half-dozen or so tables each with a green tablecloth and a couple of battered old chairs drawn up to them. Only one of the tables was occupied, at the moment, by a lonely-looking old man dressed in a tattered leather jacket and a faded fedora. He was hunched over a bowl of soup or something and seemed totally oblivious to the game on television. I couldn't help wondering how Carlos could make a living from this place; then I laughed. Was I ever going to stop looking at this country through the eyes of an economist?

Finishing my beer I asked Carlos how much I owed him.

While he considered the question he asked, "By the way I never even inquired what you're doing down here in Quito; it's not the first place Americans think of when they're choosing a place to vacation."

"I'm not really on vacation. Well, then again, I guess maybe I am. The fact is I broke up with my girlfriend; actually, she broke up with me. I just decided I needed to get out of New York and since I have a friend working down here I jumped on a plane and here I am."

"I'm sorry to hear about your girlfriend, but you made a good decision coming down here. My country is very beautiful and so are the women," he said with a big smile.

"To tell you the truth, Carlos, I don't even want to think about women for the moment; I'm actually trying to forget about them. So, what do I owe you?"

"My friend, it's on the house, which by the way is one of the few expressions I learned in the US I can actually use in public," he explained, laughing loudly.

"No, really." I was feeling guilty now. All I could think of was that severance package I had received for losing my job, and here I was accepting a free beer from a guy who probably made no more than a couple hundred dollars a week, if that.

"I do it for all new customers. After all, maybe I can get you to become as regular a customer like Francisco over there."

He smiled as I turned to look at the old man.

"He comes here regularly," I asked.

"Every day. He comes in shortly after noon, orders a beer and a plate of tapas, and sits quietly by himself over there for an hour or so, then leaves."

"But, he doesn't look like he has the money to come in here every day," I commented.

"He doesn't. However, he's assured me that one day very soon he'll pay me every cent he owes me."

"Has he told you how he's going to get the money," I asked, not certain whether Carlos was joking or not.

"Of course," Carlos laughed, "he claims to know the secret of where Atahualpa's gold is buried."

"Ata....what?"

"You don't know about Atahualpa's gold? No, I guess you wouldn't; most Americans have never heard of it. I bet your friend has, at least if he's lived here awhile. Ask him? You can tell me what you've learned about Atahualpa the next time you come in."

For some reason I left Carlos' place feeling strangely upbeat. I guess it was because I now knew someone here in Quito other than Adam I could actually speak English with.

Four

It was nearly five o'clock when Adam walked through the door. I was slouched in one of his easy chairs listening to my iPod and reading a copy of the Miami *Herald* that had been delivered to his door. As always he was immaculately dressed—an obviously tailored grey suit, white shirt, and a striped blue tie that matched his suit perfectly. How he could possibly look like that after flying to Guayaquil, putting in a full day of whatever it was he did, and then flying back to Quito was beyond me. I, of course, was in my wrinkled polo shirt, with my wrinkled chinos, and wearing flip-flops.

"I used to dress like that," I said laughing. "That is, when I had a job."

Actually, I had never dressed like that, or I should say, I had never looked like that, not with suits bought off the rack. But even if my suits had been tailor-made I still wouldn't have looked like Adam. There was just something about the way he carried himself. I guess that's what you get by being a Boston Brahmin and having what people call "old money".

"By the way," I remarked, putting my iPod away, "I was just reading in the Miami *Herald* here that Fidel Castro's younger sister actually worked for the CIA right after the revolution. I find that incredible. You can bet Fidel and his brother, Raul, were probably hoping, dare I say praying, that information would never get out; talk about an embarrassment."

"I've heard rumors of it for some time but I guess now it's become public knowledge. And, by the way, it's not only Fidel who's probably feeling embarrassed by it all, how about political leaders like Chavez and all the other disciples of Fidel here in Latin America. And, speaking of the CIA," he said, becoming suddenly more serious, "I should warn you to be careful as you move about Quito. In the past few weeks there's been a great deal of anti-American rhetoric emanating from the President's Office down here. In fact, one of my colleagues at the embassy was asked to leave the country a couple of weeks ago on the charge he was working for the CIA. Needless to say everyone working at the embassy is suspected of being a spy, and your association with me could cast some suspicion on you as well."

"So, what should I do," I asked, wondering whether he was being serious, which it turned out he was.

"There's really nothing you can do about it other than being careful," Adam replied. "Unfortunately, President Acosta is presently pushing a very populist agenda here in Ecuador and one aspect of it is enflaming public opinion against the US. Interestingly, most people here tend to be very pro-American under normal circumstances, but taking a cue from Venezuela's President Chavez, he's been fairly effective in casting Washington as an imperialist power that has a long history of interfering in Ecuador's internal affairs."

"So, what you're saying is that Americans have to be especially careful?"

"Not really. At least up to now Acosta's campaign has not translated into any violence against Americans down here, but just in case we've issued a warning to all tourists asking them to be extra careful; we are not suggesting that Americans refrain from visiting Ecuador. So, as I said, just be cautious as you move about the city. But enough of such talk; let me just get out of these clothes and I'll make us a drink. I'm anxious to hear what happened both with your job and with Rachel."

He headed down the hallway towards his bedroom.

I had hardly folded up the newspaper and put it away when Adam walked back into the living room.

"How about a Maker's Mark on the rocks," he asked. "I have a whole new bottle my folks brought down when they came to visit last month."

Adam had changed into what I guess he called casual—grey pleated sacks, blue oxford button-down shirt, and black tasseled loafers. I hoped he had dressed with dinner in mind, but with Adam, well, you never knew.

"Sounds good to me," I replied.

Handing me my Maker's Mark, he tapped it with his own and said, "*Salud.*"

"*Salud,*" I responded, taking a sip. The bourbon burned my throat going down making me cough.

"You still can't drink," he laughed, sprawling on the couch opposite me. "OK, now let's hear about what happened to your job; we can talk about Rachel over dinner."

"Ah, my job. Well, as you remember, I was like you in not wanting to work on Wall Street or for some large corporation so I took a job with a small computer-software firm called Compuware. It was started by a couple of incredibly bright guys from MIT, who had developed some very innovative software. I won't bother to explain what the software did, I'm not sure I ever completely understood it myself, but they needed someone to run the business-side of the company for them. I knew it was a high-risk venture when I signed on, but it sounded like a great opportunity and, as it turned out, it was."

"So why, then, did you get fired?" Adam asked.

"I didn't get fired, I got downsized and I was downsized because Compuware was doing so well. Are you following me?"

"To be honest, I'm more than a bit confused," Adam admitted. "Apparently I missed the lecture when they explained that employees tended to be laid off when the companies they worked for were doing well."

"Oh, it was discussed we just never paid that much attention since we knew such a thing could never happen to hot-shots like us. Anyway, Compuware was doing very well, so well in fact, this huge California-based computer company came out of nowhere and offered to buy the company at a price that simply couldn't be refused. The two guys who'd started the firm became instant millionaires, multi-millionaires actually. As for me, well, I was redundant; the new owners had no need for my services so they bought me out; I was downsized in other words. Of course, I came out of it pretty well since I had acquired quite a bit of stock in the company and on top of that they gave me a very generous severance package. But, the whole thing is still pretty weird."

"I guess, but now you're retired at what 28? 29 years old? I must say I envy you," Adam laughed.

"It's not anything like that, but I do have the luxury of taking my time deciding what I want to do next."

Adam got up and took my glass; he poured another shot of Maker's Mark and put it in my hand.

"So, what about you, Adam, has your father forgiven you yet for not attending Harvard B-school and following him into the wonderful world of corporate banking, as you used to sarcastically refer to it?"

"My dear father," Adam chuckled. "Oh, he's forgiven me, he just doesn't understand how I could ever do such a thing. You see, making money is all that's ever mattered to my father; it took precedence over being a good father or a good husband. I've always suspected it had something to do with the fact that his father had lost everything in the stock market crash of '29 and in so doing dishonored the sacred Winthrop name. So, anyway, he dedicated his entire life to making money for himself and for his clients. He literally worked seven days a week, never ever taking a real vacation. In fact, when he came down here to visit with my mother last month, it was the first time he had been out of the country in fifteen years. But, please, I don't want to say another word about him, in fact, there's nobody I'd less rather talk about. I want to hear about Rachel; she was one foxy broad as I remember.

"You never thought that, but anyway there's not really much I can say, other than she dumped me for some Yale law school type," I explained. "But, it did make my mother happy. She never did like Rachel, I suspect because she was Jewish, though I really don't know why that fact bothered her so much; it's not like we were a particularly religious family; we were Congregationalists for God's sake. It was probably pure old-fashion prejudice. On the other hand, I do have to admit that Rachel was the quintessential Jewish-American princess. So, do you really want to hear all this? I don't want to bore you."

"I want to hear every detail. After all, I live a very sheltered life down here; I never get any honest-to-goodness gossip from back home," he responded with a laugh.

"All right, so anyway Rachel was raised on Long Island, her father was an incredibly successful heart surgeon, she attended Brandeis undergrad, as I said, she was your classic JAP. So I know, I know, you're wondering how we ever got together in the first place? All I can say in hindsight is that we had a great time together and at least for us religion never became an issue although I suspect Rachel picked up on my mother's disapproval, how could she not. Subtlety has never been one of my mother's great qualities. And the fact she threw me over for a Jewish guy would seem to confirm it. I think she simply decided it would never work and as much as it pains me to say it, Rachel was probably right."

At some point we decided not to go out to dinner. Adam suggested that given the number of drinks we'd had it might be wiser to stay home and eat some of the soup that Consuelo had left in the refrigerator. I didn't argue.

"Look, I wonder if you'd mind for just a moment if we could completely change the topic of conversation," I said as we sat down at the kitchen table. "I'm curious to hear what you know about Atahualpa's gold?"

"Atahualpa's gold," he exclaimed. "When you say you want to change the conversation you're not kidding."

I told him about Carlos and explained how he'd said one of his customers, an impoverished-looking peasant, had promised to pay him because he knew where to find Atahualpa's gold. Carlos, I reported, had been a little surprised that I had never heard of Atahualpa. I was even more surprised, I said, that he seemed willing to take the peasant at his word.

"I don't think many people would know of Atahualpa or about the gold; I certainly had never heard of him until I got down here and saw his name everywhere. Still, I would seriously doubt this peasant, as you call him, would have the kind of information needed to locate the gold. Believe it, or not, there are people who have spent their entire lives searching for it."

"OK," I replied, "you've got my attention. So, tell me, who exactly was Atahualpa and why did he have so much gold that he had to hide it?"

"I'll tell you the little bit I know, but if you're really interested in the topic you'll have to do your own research."

Adam proceeded to explain that when the Spanish invaded the Inca Empire in the Sixteenth Century they captured the head Inca who subsequently promised to pay a huge ransom in gold and silver if only they would spare his life. True to his word, huge quantities of gold and silver began pouring in from all over the empire, but for some unknown reason the Spanish decided to kill him even before all the ransom arrived. When word of his death reached Rumiñahui, one of Atahualpa's generals here in Ecuador, who had been charged with gathering gold and silver for delivery to the Spanish, he decided to hide the treasure he'd amassed in a place where the Spanish could never find it. Apparently, he did a god job of hiding it since no one has ever found it unless, of course, your peasant friend is telling the truth

"It's certainly a great story," I exclaimed. "But, is it true or is it just an intriguing legend?"

"Well, this much I know. There really was a Rumiñahui since his is one of the other names you see everywhere in Ecuador. Beyond that, I don't really know anything for a fact."

"So, do you think it's possible that this guy may have stumbled onto the gold?"

"I suppose anything's possible, though if I were a betting man I'd probably bet against it. But, look, if you're interested, why don't you get on the internet and see what you can find; I'll bet there's tons of information on the topic. If you want I can show you how to access the internet on my computer. I almost never use that computer now that I have my Blackberry. In fact, I wonder how I survived before I got one. "

"I intentionally left my Blackberry back in New York. Frankly, I don't want to hear from anyone right now, and I decided if I brought my Blackberry with me I'd constantly be checking it to see if anyone cared to contact me. That said, I just might use your computer to do a little research on Atahualpa, if you don't mind."

"Hey, it's not like you have anything more important to do, and oh, speaking of that how would you like to go with me to a reception at the ambassador's house on Friday afternoon. She's a former Congresswoman from Texas and a genuinely nice person. So, are you up to going?"

"Sure, why not; so, what's the occasion?"

"It's nothing special," Adam replied. "She has one every couple of months. It's just a chance to get together with the various government officials we have to do business with in a more relaxed setting. She usually makes sure any American businessmen in town are invited; that's you."

"All right, but what if someone asks me what I'm doing in Quito? What do I tell people I do?"

"Well, let's see," Adam mused. "Hey, you can always say you're here to conduct research on Atahualpa."

"Yeah, right," I replied sarcastically. "Other than what you just told me I don't know a thing about him, and if I learned anything from my two years at business school it's don't ever bring up a subject about which you know nothing. That reminds me, you've never told me what you do down here. Are you allowed to talk about it or is it all kind of top-secret stuff?"

"I work for the Foreign Service, remember, not the CIA, so yes, of course, I can tell you what I do. One reason I don't say a lot about it is because most people don't find it that interesting; you can see their eyes glaze over as I'm talking."

"No, seriously," I replied quickly, "I am curious about what you do, and though I clearly haven't seen very much of Quito I've been fascinated by the little bit I've seen."

"Well, right now all of us at the embassy are focused almost exclusively on the efforts of Ecuador's president, Roberto Acosta, to carry out, what I'd guess you call, a populist revolution; it's a peaceful revolution, but a revolution nonetheless. What he's calling for is an end to the exploitation of Ecuador's energy resources by foreign oil companies while radically expanding the social and economic programs directed at the poor, who tend mostly to be indigenous. The whole thing is very similar to Hugo Chavez's so-called "Bolivarian revolution" in Venezuela, which, by the way, draws far more of its inspiration from Fidel Castro than Simon Bolivar. And, I might add this radical shift to the Left has occurred in several other Latin American countries as well: Bolivia, Nicaragua, Brazil and even Paraguay. Amazingly, it wasn't that long ago these countries all had Right-wing dictatorships. Down here they're calling this political swing to the Left *la marea rosada*, 'the pink tide.'"

"I don't know what planet I've been inhabiting, but I haven't even been aware of most of what you've just said. I mean, yes, I've heard of Chavez and his efforts to nationalize the foreign oil companies working in his country but I'm embarrassed to admit I don't know much about these populist revolutions and I'm certain I've never heard the name Roberto Acosta," I responded.

"Believe me," Adam explained gravely, "even in Washington there aren't many people who understand completely what's going on down here. That's why we're paying such close attention to the situation. Roberto Acosta, by the way, is not the most engaging personality in the world; in fact, I personally find him a downright nasty individual. He can be especially vindictive towards critics of his policies and it doesn't matter whether they're members of the business community, the media or other politicians. People are becoming afraid to cross him. As for the US he seems to have an almost pathological dislike of us; he opposes literally all of Washington's major initiatives down here from NAFTA to the war of drugs."

Adam stopped for a second and took a sip of his drink.

"The only thing I can say on Acosta's behalf," he continued, "is that he's been careful what he says publicly about the US. He hasn't made anti-Americanism as integral a part of his populist program as Chavez has done in Venezuela. Of course, he can't really afford to; he doesn't have the political leverage Chavez has. There's a big difference between exporting oil and exporting bananas. Ironically, Acosta lived in the United States for several years; he even earned a Master's in Public Administration from Florida State University. Now, I have no idea what he experienced living in Florida but whatever it was, judging from his attitude towards Americans, it couldn't have been very good."

"Here I go showing my ignorance of Ecuador again but was President Acosta elected or did he overthrow the previous president. I vaguely remember a couple of Ecuador's presidents have fairly recently been removed from office."

"In fact, several recent presidents have been victims of coups but Acosta was democratically elected. There are many political parties here in Ecuador, too many in fact since most of them are very small, only a few hundred members. President Acosta is a member of one of the larger ones, The Party of the Democratic Left. This party draws much of its support from the indigenous population, which is predominantly rural and poor."

"Is he himself indigenous?" I interrupted.

"Yes and no; he's what they call a *mestizo* here in Ecuador but he comes from a middle-class family, some money though not what you'd call wealthy. However, his call to halt the exploitation of Ecuador's energy resources by foreign oil companies and to dramatically expand social and economic rights for the poor has struck a very responsive chord. Ironically, one of the reasons people like Chavez, Acosta and Moreno in Bolivia were able to espouse such a radical change in their governments' policies was because energy prices were so high and those petro-dollars were pouring in faster than they could spend them. That, of course, has all changed so these presidents are now desperately trying to rewrite their constitutions so they can remain in power indefinitely. That's one of the things we're most closely monitoring."

"I gather, then, that Washington is really concerned about all this, but why? I know everyone thought the Cold War was over and that communism had been buried once and for all, on the other hand, it seems these governments are only responding to the most immediate needs of their people."

"Setting aside Washington's habitual dislike of socialist governments in general, there are substantive differences between the two governments. As I mentioned before, President Acosta vigorously opposes both the North American Free Trade Agreement, which the White House considers critical to the future of the hemisphere. In addition, he wants no part in America's war on the FARC and Colombia's drug cartels. The Colombians even claim they've uncovered evidence that the Acosta government has well-established links with the FARC rebels and he's turned a blind-eye to their actually setting up camps on Ecuadorian territory. President Acosta naturally believes that Washington is behind this claim, which only serves

24

to reinforce his dislike of the US. And, by the way, NAFTA and war on drugs are not the only contentious issues between the two sides; there are several more that have the potential to develop into major crises. Believe me, working here is a real challenge these days. Anyway, enough of this for now, it's been a long day and I need to get some sleep."

"Could you just quickly show me how to use your computer," I asked. "Just for the heck of it I'd like to learn a little more about Atahualpa's gold. The whole thing may only be a myth but it's fascinating nevertheless."

Five

The maid's room where Adam kept his computer was tiny; it didn't even have a window so it felt more than just a bit claustrophobic. It was easy to understand why Adam preferred using his computer at work. The room contained only a table, upon which sat Adam's computer, and a chair. The computer, however, was new, a Mac with a very large screen. Sitting down in front of it I couldn't help admiring the style in which Adam did things.

I had intended to spend the entire morning conducting research on Atahualpa but once I became connected to the internet, I couldn't resist the temptation to check my e-mail. I don't know what I was thinking only that I hoped there would be some kind of a message from Rachel, perhaps one where she apologized for breaking up with me the way she did. Needless to say there wasn't one. Alas, my only messages were the usual ads that for some reason did not get filtered out—did I wish to purchase Viagra or perhaps have my penis enlarged or better yet refinance the mortgage on my non-existent house. Disappointed, and feeling like an idiot for even thinking she might write, I turned to the news which on this day at least was dominated by reports from Iraq and Afghanistan—the surge appeared to be working but the number of suicide attacks being carried out by women had increased dramatically; two marines were reportedly injured in Mosul by a roadside bomb; nine American troops were killed in Afghanistan in a firefight with Taliban rebels; several thousand more troops were going to be withdrawn from Iraq to bolster American and NATO forces fighting in Afghanistan. There was concern being expressed that the Taliban were not only becoming stronger in Afghanistan but that they were now posing a threat to our main ally in the region, Pakistan.

I had almost forgotten about the fighting in the Middle East and while it would have been comforting to believe it was because I was in Ecuador that wasn't the case. I had been opposed to the war from the beginning, never truly believing Iraq possessed weapons of mass destruction. But, the main reason I didn't dwell on the fighting there was because it was having so little impact upon me; in fact, it was having none. Unfairly or not, the heaviest burden of the fighting had fallen to a small group of Americans, less than one percent I had read somewhere, none of whom I knew personally. Furthermore, there was no universal military draft as there had been during the Vietnam War as if I were going to be called to serve. The fact remained, I wasn't being asked to make any sacrifice; I didn't even have one of those Support Our Troops stickers on my car. To be honest, though, there was nothing for me to do even if I felt guilty about it. So, like most Americans, after quickly reading about recent events in the Middle East I checked the sports news and then the stock market report, which was especially good; we were finally coming out of the recession.

It was surprising how starved I was for news even though I had only been in Ecuador for a few days. Of course, on a typical day back home I would have already read the New York *Times*, maybe the *Daily News*, and I'd never go to bed without watching ESPN Sports. I loved watching sports on TV; I watched just about everything. That made me wonder about Adam; even with access to the internet, to the cable and with his American colleagues at the embassy, didn't he miss being away from home? Of course, as soon as I thought about his beautiful apartment, his housekeeper, the delightful Ecuadorian climate, I concluded even I could get used to living outside the United States.

When finally I pushed my chair back to take a momentary break from the computer, I was amazed to see it was nearly noon; I had been trolling the internet for nearly three hours and had yet to search the web for any references to Atahualpa. Fortunately, it was Thursday, which meant Consuelo was around; I had heard her come in and had closed the door to the study where I was working. Stretching my arms and back I got up, opened the door to the kitchen and went out to greet her. I hoped she might be able to find something for me to eat since my breakfast had consisted of a single cup of coffee.

"*Buenas tardes*, Mister Michael," she said, smiling.

"*Buenas tardes*, Consuelo," I replied, pleased to see she had already prepared a place for me at the table. No sooner did I sit down than she brought me a steaming plate of fish, rice, a kind of potato pancake and vegetables, which she served with a delicious fruit drink she called *jugo de mora*. As I was eating, all I could think about was finding an excuse that would enable me to stay in Ecuador forever. And what a delight Consuelo was even though we could barely communicate. When finally I could eat no more, I thanked her profusely and wandered back into the study.

It was nearly two o'clock before I finally called up Google, typed in the name Atahualpa and hit the search button. As Adam had predicted, there were scores of references, over a million to be exact. I tried to be selective, reading only those appearing somewhat authoritative, but even so it soon became obvious there was a tremendous amount of repetition, many of them, in fact, seemed to be copied verbatim from the same source. Nevertheless it did seem that the story Adam had given me was essentially correct.

Atahualpa was the Inca of Peru at the time of the Spanish invasion in 1532. He had not been Inca for very long, however, as he had only recently overthrown his half-brother, Huascar, who had been the legitimate heir to the throne. While both Huascar and Atahualpa were sons of the Inca, Huayna Capac, Atahualpa's mother had been a princess of Quito and not a blood relative of Huayna Capac. Under Peruvian law the principal wives of the Inca had to be blood relatives or their children would be illegitimate and could not be heirs to the throne. This was the unfortunate position in which Atahualpa had found himself.

A number of references seemed to imply that Atahualpa was Huayna Capac's favorite son and that as he lay dying, Huayna Capac had asked Huascar, the legitimate heir to the throne, to divide his empire; Atahualpa would rule the recently conquered kingdom of Quito, while Huascar would govern the southern half of the empire from Cuzco. Huascar apparently agreed to his father's request but no sooner had Atahualpa ascended to the throne of Quito than he set about raising a huge army, which he sent south to attack Huascar. The ensuing civil war lasted for five years before Huascar was finally defeated. In 1532 Atahualpa became chief Inca of the now unified empire.

No sooner had he disposed of Huascar than Atahualpa suddenly found himself confronting an entirely new threat. Two years before he had become the chief Inca, a detachment of about two hundred Spanish soldiers under the command of Juan Pizarro had landed almost unnoticed on the southern Ecuadorian coast. After months of bloody fighting the Spaniards had finally arrived at Cajamarca, in present day Peru, where in spite of being vastly outnumbered by the Incas, they were able to capture Atahualpa while slaughtering hundreds of his followers. Atahualpa now promised Pizarro that if he would spare his life he would deliver to the Spaniard a ransom of gold and silver sufficient to fill the cell in which he was being held. Pizarro agreed and within weeks over twenty-four tons of gold and silver were delivered, melted down and sent off to Spain. But, apparently fearful that Atahualpa's followers might attempt a rescue, the Spanish suddenly decided it would be in their best interest to execute him. When word of his death reached Rumiñahui, one of Atahualpa's generals in Quito, who was at that very moment gathering even more gold and silver to send to Cajamarca, he quickly hid what he had amassed in an inaccessible location where the Spanish would have no hope of ever finding it.

"So," Adam asked later that evening after I had explained to him what I had learned about Atahualpa, "were you able to discover what actually happened to the gold? Is it still out there somewhere?"

We were sitting in the living room once again listening to a CD by Yo-Yo Ma and enjoying some of Adam's favorite Maker's Mark of which, I had promised myself, on this evening I would have no more than one drink

"I honestly don't know," I replied. "For one thing there's so much information on the Incas it's very easy to get sidetracked into reading about things totally unrelated to Atahualpa; the Incas were an amazing people. All together I was on the computer for nearly five hours. Even, then, I quit only because my eyes were so tired. But, I'll do some more research on the topic tomorrow. I did read that the Celtics beat the Atlanta Hawks in the first round of the NBA playoffs. Now, please don't tell me you're not a Celtics fan growing up right there on Beacon Hill."

"I'm not," Adam answered quite seriously. "The only reason I became a Red Sox fan was because of my uncle, my father's brother. He loved the Red Sox and often took me to games at Fenway Park."

"Your uncle sounds like he was a pretty good guy."

"He was a great guy," he replied. "I think he realized early on that my father would never do those kinds of things with me; it really bothered him and I know he spoke to my father about it on more than one occasion. You know what's funny, my uncle never got married and he would have been a great father. It's ironic when you think of it, or maybe I should say sad; my father is the one who should never have gotten married."

"So, your father never did much of anything with you," I asked, aware I was probably pushing it.

"He was never around. No matter what you tell me, your parents had to have been so much better than mine, or at least better than my father.

My mother tried but she was so intimidated by him she didn't dare to say anything," Adam replied.

"In hindsight my parents were probably all right, though growing up I always envied my friends whose parents always seemed so much more normal, whatever that means. For example, I would have loved it if my father had taken me to Fenway Park or Yankee Stadium, but he couldn't have cared less for sports and, of course, when you're a young kid sports can be the most important thing in your life, at least until girls come along. Probably, the only time my father ever spoke to me directly was at the dinner table and it was almost always to ask how I was doing in school. He'd want to know how was I doing in this class and that class. Since he was the principal of the school he probably already knew all that from having talked to my teachers during the day. I suspect he just wanted to see how honest I'd be about it."

"Did it ever occur to you that just maybe you're being a little hard on your parents," Adam proposed. "Look at it this way, you ate dinner together, your parents asked you about school, and you even went to church together occasionally, or at least I remember you telling me that once. And, they made sure you received a good education, Wesleyan, Tuck. I'd say you were pretty lucky."

"Yeah, I guess you're probably right," I continued, "but still as I've gotten older and had a chance to think about my childhood, I've decided my parents were rather strange, or I guess I should say are rather strange since they're still alive. Do you know I was never allowed to have friends over to my house? My mother always said it would be awkward for them since my father was the school principal, but the fact is, they simply didn't want them around. That's one reason I threw myself into sports; I wanted to be sure I fit in. I played soccer in the fall, basketball in the winter and baseball in the spring. I didn't especially excel at any of them but I wasn't a bad athlete. I made varsity in all three sports my senior year and I do have to say it helped my social life. Still, I think my teenage years would have been a lot more enjoyable if there had been brothers or sisters around. Being an only child can be a drag sometimes. But, what am I saying, you're an only child, right?"

For just a second Adam gave me the strangest look; I couldn't even interpret it. And, for what at least seemed a long time, he said nothing. When finally he did speak, I was dumbfounded at what he said.

"No," he murmured quietly, and with some reluctance, "I was not an only child. I had a brother, Stephen, who was three years older than I; he was eight when he died. I know, I've never said anything to you about this; in fact, in the years since his death I've spoken to very few people about it and I'm not even sure why. I guess it was probably because neither my father nor my mother ever talked about it."

"So, what happened to your brother, that is, if you don't mind my asking?"

I tried to sound nonchalant though my curiosity could not have been more aroused. He had never even intimated to me about having a brother.

"He drowned on Nantucket," he replied sadly.

Adam then proceeded to explain how his family would rent a cottage on Nantucket each summer. Typically his father would only come over on weekends. With little else to do he, his mother and brother would spend most days at the beach. On this one particular day there was a storm out to sea and the surf was pretty rough. His mother had made the two boys promise not to go in the water, which hadn't seem like such a big deal since it was a cool, overcast day. But his brother, who seemed to take great pleasure in disobeying their parents, ran suddenly into the surf, not very far, but there was a strong undertow and it pulled his legs out from under him; his brother simply disappeared from view. Unfortunately, the beach didn't have lifeguards on duty that day and there was no one near enough to do anything. His mother had raced screaming down to the water's edge, but it was to no avail. The Coast Guard found Stephen's body the next day.

"My father never forgave my mother for losing Stephen," Adam added angrily. "For that matter he never forgave me either. The fact he's never forgiven me I can handle but for my mother it's made her life a living hell."

"I guess I can understand why you never mentioned your brother; it must have been incredibly painful. But, I don't understand your father's reaction; it doesn't sound like it was your mother's fault and it certainly wasn't yours. What is it about fathers? There are times when I think I don't ever want to be a father, like right now for instance."

"Let's just drop the subject," Adam responded, wearily. "There's nothing to be gained by talking any more about it. I must admit I have no idea how we got from Atahualpa to my father. Anyway, let's go into the kitchen and see what Consuelo has left for us to eat. And, by the way, don't forget tomorrow afternoon—the reception at the American ambassador's house. I'll meet you at the front gate at four o'clock. And, remember to bring your passport, you'll need it to get through security."

Six

Adam was long gone by the time I hauled myself out of bed and wandered barefoot out to the kitchen. He had made coffee so I poured a cup, then, helped myself to a couple of breakfast rolls. Having several hours to kill before the reception at the American Embassy, I took a long hot shower after which I slipped into a pair of jeans and a polo shirt. Since at least for the moment I had no interest in getting back on the internet, I decided instead to hike down and see Carlos. I took neither my iPod, nor my wallet though I did stuff a few dollars into my pant's packet. I did this because of what Adam said had happened to a friend of one of his colleagues at the embassy.

Apparently, this guy had gone to the Banco del Pacifico just down the street on Gonzalez Suarez to withdraw some money. It was a sizable amount, twelve thousand dollars or something like that. He went in the middle of the afternoon when he knew the bank would not be too busy. After receiving his money, which he placed in a leather pouch, he returned to his car parked just outside. Barely had he opened the car door when a motorcycle pulled up with two guys on it one of whom shoved a pistol into his stomach and demanded the money. Having little choice, he turned over the leather pouch and the two roared off. Later, when he reported the robbery to the police they speculated that a bank employee, possibly even the young woman who had waited on him, had alerted the two guys through some pre-arranged signal, but the police were never able to prove anything. Clearly, then, if something like that could happen on busy, upscale Gonzalez Suarez in broad daylight, it could happen anywhere in the city.

As I stepped out of Adam's building I was instantly made aware of something else about Ecuador—how beautiful the weather could be. The day was exquisite again—sunny, temperature in the sixties with absolutely no humidity. It was the kind of day one prayed for in New England though here it was probably taken for granted. My route was entirely downhill and in less than twenty minutes I was standing in front of *El Café de Los Toreros*; I wasn't even breathing heavily. As usual, the door was wide open so I strode in expecting to find Carlos. Instead I found a rugged-looking guy sitting at the bar with a half-empty bottle of beer in front of him; I couldn't help but notice his massive hands, the knuckles of which were knobby and misshapen. However, when finally he glanced over at me his nose made me instantly forget about his hands since it appeared as if it had been broken so many times it no longer even looked like a nose. He probably guessed I was staring at it so he turned back to his beer, then shouted, "Carlito, *un cliente*." A few seconds later Carlos came out of the storage room in the back.

"*Buenos días*, Michael." His greeting was as enthusiastic as his handshake. "You've met my brother here, Miguel? He doesn't speak much English; to be honest, he doesn't speak a word."

"*Buenos días*," I said, nodding at him since that appeared to be all he was prepared to do. If he nodded in return he had to have done it without moving his massive head. I had the distinct feeling he didn't like me, or maybe he just didn't like Americans. I remembered what Adam had said about President Acosta and wondered if Miguel was the type of guy from whom he drew his support. It was not a comforting thought.

Noticing my reaction Carlos added, "Miguel is my older brother. He doesn't say much but he's a good guy. As you can probably tell from his nose he did a little boxing when he was younger; Miguel was a real brawler. He didn't always win but none of the guys he fought ever left the ring without looking like they'd been run over by a truck. And, of course, because of that I never had to worry about anyone picking on me, everyone was afraid of Miguel; for that matter, they still are."

Carlos smiled at his brother, slapping him good-naturedly on the shoulder; his brother only scowled in return. I could see why people were afraid of him; I'd certainly be if I met him anywhere outside of this bar.

"So, Michael, what have you been doing, enjoying our beautiful city, I hope?"

"What do you mean, I've been doing research on Atahualpa like you suggested,' I replied, trying to make a joke of it.

"You have, really? That's great," Carlos exclaimed, clearly pleased I had actually taken his advice. "So now you know all about one of Ecuador's most famous historical figures. Just about everything in this city that's not named for that Spaniard, Orellana, is named for Atahualpa.

"Well, I don't know if I'd say I know all about him, but I do know a heck of a lot more than I did the last time I was here," I admitted. "I must have spent three hours on the internet doing research on him. If nothing else I now know he was a real person; I didn't even know that before."

"But what about the gold? Do you think there really is gold hidden out there and if so, where do you think it's hidden?"

Before I could answer, Miguel said something to his brother I couldn't make out.

"Miguel says I talk too much and don't pay enough attention to business," Carlos explained with mock seriousness. "In other words, he's reminding me that I haven't asked you what you'd like to drink. So, what can I get you?"

"Oh, I really just stopped in to say hello, but I'll have a coke. I have to go to a reception at the American ambassador's house later."

"Well, excuse me, you do get around," Carlos laughed, repeating what I had said to his brother, whose glance suggested he liked me even less now.

"My social life needs all the help it can get. But, anyway, you were asking about whether I thought the gold really existed," I continued, trying my best to ignore Miguel's presence. "I haven't done enough research on the gold to decide whether it ever existed or not, though many people seem to believe it does and think it's hidden in some inaccessible mountainous area to the south of Quito."

"Yes, in the Llanganates," Carlos offered, clearly impressed that I had actually done some research on the topic.

"Yes, that's the area," I replied quickly. "And I gather many people over the years have gone in there looking for it? Do you think the old man who was here the last time I was in has been in there? Didn't you say he claimed to know where the gold was hidden?"

"Francisco?" Carlos laughed loudly and again said something to his brother, who this time glanced over at me with a smirk. "He doesn't have the vaguest idea where the gold is hidden and he certainly never went looking for it in the Llanganates. By the way, you just missed him."

"I thought he only came in here at lunchtime?"

"He usually does but lately he's been coming in at odd times and he's also been acting very strange; well, I should say, even stranger than usual. He seems to think someone broke into his place, though he claims nothing was stolen. Just the same he brought in something he wanted me to look after for him, an antique box of some kind."

"Is the box supposed to be valuable," I asked, wondering why such a poor-looking old man would have something of value that he hadn't tried to sell.

"I think there's something inside the box he seems to feel is important but I haven't any idea what it might be; the box is locked, though it certainly wouldn't take much effort to open it," Carlos explained.

Our conversation was interrupted as Carlos' brother got up to leave. He whispered something to Carlos, then, walked straight out the door without as much as a glance in my direction.

"He said I should listen more and talk less," Carlos hurriedly translated.

Judging from the look on his face I was willing to bet my last dime that wasn't what Miguel had whispered to his brother. And, for the first time since arriving in Quito, I began feeling a little nervous.

As much as attending the ambassador's reception had seemed like fun when Adam had first suggested the idea, it quickly turned into a nightmare once I began to get ready; I hadn't brought any decent clothes with me. I remembered thinking when I was packing for the trip that I should probably include at least one suit, but then I couldn't imagine why I'd ever need it. Now, of course, I wished I had because the only thing I had to wear was a slightly wrinkled blue blazer and a pair of chinos, the latter, at least, clean and pressed. I did borrow one of Adam's neckties but everything else like his shirts and jackets were all too big for me. When finally I stepped before the full-length mirror in my bedroom, I was singularly unimpressed by the person I saw staring back at me. All I could think of was what Adam was probably going to say: "I said we were going to a reception at the ambassador's house, not to a fraternity party." Oh, well, there wasn't much I could do about it now; I just wished I hadn't wasted the morning visiting Carlos when I could have gone to the mall and bought some new clothes.

It was already nearly four o'clock when I exited the apartment building so I took off down the sidewalk on the run; fortunately, the ambassador's house was only a few minutes away, less if I could keep up my present pace. It was only as I was approaching the oddly art deco-ish Quito Hotel that I heard the first rumbling of thunder. Glancing up I could see the sky readying itself for battle; huge clouds, black and ominous, were racing menacingly in my direction. As I turned the corner onto Avenida Orellana a drop of rain struck my face, then several more and all at once great sheets of rain came pouring down. Up ahead I spotted Adam waiting just outside the entrance to the ambassador's compound with an umbrella. When he saw I didn't have one he started towards me though by this time I was already drenched, a fact that for some reason the security officers found rather amusing.

Entering the ambassador's residence, I was quickly reminded how out of place I must look; the men were dressed in business suits, while the women, though few in number, wore very fashionable outfits. A few had obviously been caught in the downpour though none appeared to be as wet as me. My immediate thought was to slip back out the door before anyone noticed the condition of my clothes. Unfortunately, I was too slow in reacting and suddenly found myself standing before the American ambassador, an elegant, very attractive fiftyish something woman. She greeted Adam warmly and they exchanged small talk for a moment before he introduced me to her.

"It's a delight to have you here with us, Michael," she said with a smile that made me believe her completely. And, then, as if sensing my embarrassment over my wet clothes, she added, "I'm sorry about the weather; most of those who attend these things have their drivers deliver them. Next time I'll make certain we do that for you." And with that she turned to greet the person behind me.

"Now you know why she's an ambassador," Adam whispered, as we quickly greeted her bored-looking husband.

The cocktail party was to be held under a large tent on the back lawn though because of the rain people appeared in no great hurry to go out there. But, it did give me the opportunity for a brief look into the ambassador's living room. Assuming the furniture was hers, it was obvious the ambassador's favorite color was white; everything I could see was white—the thick, plush rugs, the couches, the drapes—everything. And, then, as if on signal the crowd ahead of us moved outside and I had no choice but to follow along. We entered a tent so huge it could have comfortably held twice the number of people that were presently there. It was also perfectly dry inside, which I found amazing considering the almost monsoon-like weather. Suddenly, the sound of the rain drumming on the tent became louder and more incessant; the downpour had changed to a violent hailstorm. In but a matter of seconds the lawn outside the tent turned white with a layer of madly bouncing hailstones. The speed with which the weather changed down here reminded me of that old New England proverb: If you don't like the weather just wait a minute, except down here it literally was true.

Adam seemed to know just about everyone at the reception, and after making certain we were well armed with good American bourbon, he wandered around introducing me to a number of them. The majority seemed to be from various government ministries but there were also quite a few Americans, from the embassy as well as from international organizations like the World Bank, the IMF, and the Inter-American Development Bank. One of the Americans he introduced me to was Jennifer Albright, a stunning brunette with the most engaging smile; she apparently worked with Adam at the embassy but the way the two of them looked at one another made me suspect they had more than just work in common. I had to laugh because it appeared they were trying to be discreet about their relationship but, if that were the case, they clearly weren't doing a very good job of it.

As the three of us were talking I suddenly noticed everyone's attention drawn to a tall, handsome man with wavy gray hair and a politician's smile who entered the tent accompanied by a very attractive young woman. So quickly was he surrounded by admirers that I decided he must be one of Ecuador's more popular actors or musicians.

"Who is that," I asked Adam out of curiosity.

"That is Eduard Mayer, the man Washington hopes will be the next president of Ecuador," Adam replied. "Oh, and by the way, that's Eduard with a 'u', not Edward with a 'w'; for some strange reason he gets very upset when he's called Edward. Maybe he thinks it's too American; I don't know."

"You said hopefully, but do you think he will be the next president?"

"There's a better than even chance of it though he's never actually held elective office before. Still, he seems to have the backing of the Christian Socialist party, which ironically, given its name, represents the business community here in Ecuador. The party is closely identified with the city of Guayaquil, which is interesting only because Mayer is not from there. On the other hand, he's been smart in that he's never allowed himself to be closely identified with any particular region of the country, not the coast, not the Sierra, not the Oriente. Mayer is a very savvy individual."

"But, how," I asked, "did he come to be such a strong candidate for the presidency if he's never even run for political office before and especially given what you've said about President Acosta."

"Money," Adam replied, matter-of-factly. "Mayer's one of the wealthiest men in Ecuador; he has his hand in everything—bananas, shrimp, cattle, though the single greatest source of his income these days comes from growing flowers, roses mainly, which he exports to the US. He has operations in every part of the country and, thus, he's able to draw support from a wide range of interest groups, including even some segments of the indigenous community. The one thing about him that seems to trouble some people is the question of where his family's money originally came from. In a country where everyone knows everybody else's business, he remains a bit of a mystery."

"Maybe he's found Atahualpa's gold," I suggested facetiously.

"Well, if he has at least it would explain a lot of things, and probably also strengthen his candidacy," Adam laughed.

"So, he's here today because the US supports him?"

"Oh, believe me," Adam responded in all seriousness, "Washington is desperate to have him elected; politically he is the complete antithesis of President Acosta. At the same time, the US has to be very careful not to embrace him too openly; that could easily backfire. In other words, President Acosta could use it against him in his bid for reelection. So, yes, we have invited President Acosta here this afternoon but he won't show, though I suspect someone will attend from his office if only to see who else comes."

"Now, not to change the subject," I suddenly interrupted, "but, who is that woman with Mayer, she looks kind of young. Is she his trophy wife, as we'd say back in New York?"

"Oh no, that's not his wife, it's his daughter; I think her name is Carolina. Would you like to meet her, well, would you like to meet both of them? Come on, I'll introduce you."

"Are you sure you want to do that, I mean, right now? It looks like everybody is trying to get a piece of him," I observed, worried more actually about the wrinkled condition of my clothes.

"Come on," Adam insisted, "And forget about your clothes will you. You're an American; everyone will expect you to be a little eccentric."

We walked over to where the candidate was talking to several of the ambassador's guests. And, Adam being Adam, he simply walked up and introduced himself. I could never have done that.

"Mr. Mayer, I'm Adam Winthrop from the American Embassy, and this is a colleague of mine, Michael Henrick."

"A pleasure to meet you, Mr. Winthrop," he replied with a smile that could only have come from hours of practice. "Ahh, and, Mr. Henrick, is that possibly a German name?"

"Swedish, actually," I answered.

"Oh, Swedish. Do you speak the language?" He was probably the first person in my life I could ever remember asking me that.

"Not a word; my father doesn't either. His parents came over in the 1880s and they, like so many immigrants at that time, wanted their children to become Americans, which to them meant speaking exclusively English. Of course, what makes it all so ironical is the fact that today Americans spend millions of dollars to have their children speak a second language and most end up like me, still speaking only English."

"Well, Mr. Henrick, if you're going to speak only one language, English is definitely it. You can get by just about anywhere in this world if you speak English. It's just unfortunate that one has to give up his native language and culture to become American. You should always be proud of your Swedish heritage and not dismiss it too casually. I wish we could discuss this at greater length but unfortunately I see there are some people waiting to talk to me. Goodbye Mr. Henrick, it's been a pleasure."

"Excuse me, father, but aren't you going to introduce me before you move along," asked the young woman who had been standing quietly next to him throughout the conversation. "Oh, never mind, I've had plenty of practice learning how to introduce myself. I'm Carolina Mayer," she said, extending her hand first to me, then to Adam.

"Forgive me, Carolina, it's just I always enjoy meeting Americans; they're so Germanic. Ironically, not at all like the British I met while studying in London; they were so...stuffy, or maybe arrogant is the better word. But, you're right, my dear, it was quite rude of me not to introduce you immediately. Gentlemen, this is my daughter, Carolina, and as you've probably already concluded she is as impetuous as she is beautiful." On this occasion his smile was clearly genuine.

And, he had every reason to smile; Carolina was a stunning-looking woman. She was tall, almost as tall as me and I was only an inch or so removed from six feet, and though she was not slim by Hollywood standards, her expensively tailored pantsuit looked great on her. Her face was oval with high cheekbones and the largest coffee bean-colored eyes I had ever seen. As for her hair, which she wore nearly to her shoulders, it was the same dark color with a lustrous sheen to it. However, it was her smile that most captured my attention for not only was it warm and friendly, but in addition it seemed to suggest a fascinating hint of both humor and flirtatiousness

"So, Mr. Henrick, do you work at the American Embassy, too," she asked, studying me intently.

"No, I don't," I responded, a little flustered. "I, ah, am just down here for a couple of weeks or so. I'm staying with Adam; we went to business school together."

"So, what do you do when you're not down here visiting Mr. Winthrop," she continued in what seemed to be an almost playful tone.

As I hesitated, thinking about how I should answer her, Adam spoke up. "Michael is probably too embarrassed to reveal that he's down here to conduct research on Atahualpa and, in particular, what may have happened to the gold that was hidden by Rumiñahui."

I knew Adam was joking but at that moment I could have killed him. How could he have said something so ridiculous? But, then, what can only be described as a miracle happened.

"Is that so," she replied, clearly interested. "Then, you must come down to San Francisco University where I teach and meet one of my departmental colleagues, Dr. Moreno. The Incas are a specialty of his and he's done a great deal of research on the topic of Rumiñahui and the gold."

I glanced over at Adam with the intention of giving him a smirk but found he had already wandered off with her father to meet some other guests.

"So, you're a professor at the university," I asked. I had actually meant it rhetorically but she seemed to detect a hint of surprise in my voice.

"Yes, I am. Now, why should you, an American, be so taken aback by that," she responded, though I suspected she knew that was not what I meant.

"No, it's just you seem so young for a university professor. What do you teach," I asked, desperately trying to get the conversation back on track.

"Anthropology; my specialty is the peoples of the Amazon, the Oriente, as we call it down here. I'm one of a number of anthropologists from America, Europe, and the various South American countries that share the Amazon, who has been trying to study the cultures of the Amazon before they entirely disappear. As you may know, in recent years, the drilling for oil in the Amazonian rain forests has had a devastating effect on these peoples. It's fascinating work but heartbreaking, too."

"I'd love to hear more about your work," I declared, suddenly aware how badly I wanted to see her again.

"Why don't we just begin with my colleague, the one who specializes in the Incas. Could you come down to the university on Monday, that's my easiest day, and I could introduce you to him then?"

"That would be great; I'd love to," I replied, barely able to contain my excitement.

"Then meet me at the front gate of the university at ten," she explained with a smile. And with that she walked away in the direction of her father.

I, on the other hand, was too stunned to do anything but just stand there. Did what I think just happened really happen? One minute I was unexpectedly being introduced to this attractive, charming, intelligent woman and the next she was actually inviting me down to the university where she taught. I knew I shouldn't read too much into it, but at least I was going to have an opportunity to see her again. All I could think at this moment was "thank you, thank you, Adam, for mentioning Atahualpa to her." That's what had started this whole thing. And, while I knew I'd have to tell her the truth at some point, for the moment that was not my major concern. Right now simply getting through the weekend was my most immediate worry; Monday just couldn't come quickly enough.

Seven

I awoke the next morning to find Adam already up and packing a small suitcase.

"So, where are you off to this time? No, no, let me guess, you wouldn't be slipping away for a romantic weekend with Jennifer Albright would you," I chided, honestly expecting him to reply that he was, though had he informed me he was going with some other woman, that wouldn't have surprised me either. I was not prepared for him to explain he was heading to Washington.

"Yes, I received a phone call early this morning telling me to pack and get up there; I'll be flying from Guayaquil later this afternoon," he explained.

"What's happened that requires your presence in DC, and so quickly. I mean it has to be something important, can you tell me?"

"I can tell you what I know about the events leading to my being called back to Washington, but I can only guess about the nature of the meeting. I suspect you remember reading a few weeks ago of an incident in which Colombian military forces crossed into Ecuador to attack a camp established by the FARC. You know about the FARC, right?"

"I've heard of it though I have to confess I don't really know much about it," I responded.

"Well, the FARC controls a large portion of southern Colombia from which it engages in drug trafficking and kidnapping; FARC leaders claim their goal is to overthrow the government of Colombia and to this end they've been fighting a guerilla-type war against government forces for over forty years. Well, anyway, the attack generated a tremendous uproar with protests being lodged by the Organization of American States as well as by a number of governments down here; Bolivia, Brazil, Nicaragua, Cuba. The loudest protest came, of course, from our boy Hugo Chavez, who even went so far as to mobilize several thousand troops and send them to the Venezuela's border with Colombia. But, in the passed month or so the crisis has generally faded from public consciousness, though beneath the surface there is still tremendous resentment at Colombia's actions."

"But wait, there's something here I don't understand," I responded. "I can see why people were initially upset with the Colombian government for undertaking what was clearly a violation of Ecuador's sovereignty, but these countries can't approve of the FARC. And, there's no way Ecuador must like having the FARC as neighbors. Shouldn't these governments be in favor of anything that weakens that organization?"

"Well, now, this is where the whole story begins to get much more interesting," Adam explained with a wry smile. "It's also the reason I'm flying up to Washington. And, by the way, the reason I'm going is because the ambassador is in Madrid attending a conference on the Americas. Anyway, during the course of the attack on the camp two computers were seized belonging to a high-level FARC leader who was killed during the fighting. It has taken awhile but apparently the contents of those computers have now been completely analyzed and it appears substantial evidence has been found linking, not only Hugo Chavez to the FARC, that's been suspected for some time, but a number of emails were found that demonstrate a link between the FARC and the Acosta government. As you might expect, this is only going to worsen relations between the US and Ecuador, especially since Chavez has been proclaiming loudly and often that the US planned and helped carry out the attack; he's also claiming the evidence linking him to the FARC was manufactured by the CIA. I suspect the Acosta government is far more concerned about all this than Chavez; after all, he's used to it."

"So, what do you think the purpose of this meeting is," I asked, fascinated by the whole issue.

"I suspect we'll be briefed on the White House's position in this dispute and we'll probably be instructed how we are to respond to whatever provocations that may ensue from the Acosta government, if there are any."

"So, what can the Acosta government do to the US it's not already doing? I thought you said only Chavez had real leverage with us because of the oil."

"One thing it's already done is to halt American surveillance aircraft from using Ecuadorian airbases to over-fly FARC-controlled territory in Colombia. This is in spite of the fact most Ecuadorians have no use for the FARC, whom they blame for much of the violence that takes place here."

"Do you think it's possible that Colombia and Ecuador might go to war," I asked, beginning to wonder what I might be in for.

"Not a chance. The Colombian army is much larger than the Ecuadorian army, not to mention better trained and better equipped so believe me Ecuador won't go to war. And, anyway, Ecuador only recently lost a war to Peru, in which it had to give up significant territory, so it would be suicidal to get involved with Colombia. No, not even if Venezuela promised to fight with them would they do it. I suspect Venezuela would lose as well."

"Well, it sure sounds like an interesting trip; I envy you."

"I shouldn't be gone more than a couple days. I'll leave the names of a couple friends at the embassy just in case, well, just in case. I'll also leave you my card to the health club over at the Swissotel. There's a swimming pool, all kinds of equipment; it's great. All you have to do is show my card and you'll be given a guest pass for the day."

"Thanks, I might just do that; I could really afford to get some serious exercise," I replied.

"OK, I've got to finish packing; the embassy is sending a car for me in an hour. You know where the keys to the Montero are if you need it."

An hour later Adam was gone, and I was suddenly left to fend for myself. Of course, it was hardly any great hardship since Consuelo had left tons of food for us, Adam's liquor cabinet was well stocked and he owned scores of DVDs. I decided it would be wise to get on the computer and begin preparing for my meeting with Dr. Moreno. But, before I typed in Atahualpa's name, I "googled" to see if there was any mention of the incident that sent Adam racing off to Washington. In fact, there were several, all of which seemed to describe the incident pretty much as Adam had described it to me: Colombia had launched a strike against a FARC camp located within Ecuador killing twenty-four rebels including a top FARC commander. What proved most interesting, and something Adam hadn't mentioned, was that the Colombians found evidence not only that Chavez had been funding the FARC but that the Ecuadorian president may have removed from his own army, officers who had objected to the presence of FARC camps on Ecuadorian soil. Intrigued, I suddenly found myself wishing I were the one attending the briefings in Washington.

In time I did get back to my research on Atahualpa. I didn't want to appear completely stupid in front of Dr. Moreno, even though, in all fairness to myself, I had never heard of Atahualpa until a few days ago. But, of course, it wasn't Dr. Moreno I was really worried about; it was Carolina. I didn't want to embarrass her, not after she had been so nice as to set up this appointment for me. After all, it was Carolina I wanted to see again, Dr. Moreno was only an excuse. I could only hope the meeting with Dr. Moreno was an excuse for her as well.

The weekend mercifully ended and Monday morning arrived. I rolled quickly out of bed, showered, dressed, grabbed a quick cup of coffee, and took the elevator down to the front door. I had done it all in under twenty-five minutes, amazing! As I walked out to the curb to hail a taxi, it suddenly struck me, I hadn't thought about Rachel once in the past twenty-four hours. For just a second I felt a little guilty about it before coming to my senses. She had dumped me, I reminded myself; she had dumped me for another guy. Therefore, if anyone should be feeling guilty it was she, though I was fairly certain she wasn't.

The route the taxi-driver took to the university was down through Guapulo, passed the church I could see from Adam's window and continuing down a narrow two-lane road that snaked along the edge of a steep ravine. There weren't even any guardrails, just a strip of bushes that would have done nothing to slow us if we had gone off the road. At one point we came upon a spot where a landslide had actually taken out a small section of the road. Although there was evidence that efforts had been made to repair the damage, one did not have to be an engineer to realize it was only a matter of time before a landslide made the road entirely impassable.

Passing now a line of small one- or two-room stucco houses on the ravine side of the road we suddenly came out onto the main thoroughfare of the town of Cumbaya with its supermarkets, auto dealerships, and, of course, the ever-present McDonalds and Kentucky Fried Chicken. Turning and looking back in the direction from which we had just come, I could just make out the apartment buildings in Quito looming up through the haze. The difference in elevation between those buildings and where I was now had to be at least 1500 feet, maybe more; it was an amazing drop.

The driver pulled up directly in front of the entrance to the university. When I stepped out of the taxi I found myself unexpectedly blinded by the bright sun; as for the heat, it must have been at least ten degrees warmer than Quito and considerably more humid. The first thing I noticed were the security guards who were systematically checking the identification of everyone entering the grounds of the university which were enclosed by a formidable looking eight-foot concrete-stucco wall. It was easy to understand now why Carolina had suggested meeting me here. As I walked towards the gate I caught sight of her just inside talking with a thin, balding middle-age man in a poorly fitting brown suit that from where I stood could easily have been a double for my high school guidance counselor. I could well imagine how pleased the university had to be to have the daughter of the country's next president on its staff.

Carolina still hadn't noticed me and I hesitated calling to her for it gave me the opportunity to observe her without her being aware of it. It suddenly struck me how young she looked. Had I not known otherwise, there was no way in the world I would have guessed she was a professor; she honestly looked like just another student asking one of her teachers about the next day's assignment. She was dressed casually as everyone seemed to be--dark slacks, a white blouse open in front to display some kind of necklace with dark stones and long dangling earrings. And with her hair pulled back from her face she really did look like the other women students, though if pushed I might have to admit she didn't look much older than twenty-one, though she clearly had a more sophisticated and self-confident manner about her.

As I watched her all I could think about was how my male colleagues back at Wesleyan would have reacted to having a professor like Carolina. Many of them were clearly animals. The comments and the way they would have mentally undressed her would have undoubtedly driven her out of the classroom. I could remember an instance when a couple of the more obnoxious members of the football team had driven a young, newly hired woman to tears. I remembered it because I had been too intimidated to come to her aid in any way. Carolina had no idea how lucky she was to be teaching down here.

Just as I was thinking all this Carolina looked over and spotted me. She quickly excused herself and came rushing over to where I was standing.

"Michael," she called with that delightful smile of hers. She took my hand and offered me her cheek. "I'm so glad you were able to make it and right on time. Now I know you're an American and not just an Ecuadorian in disguise."

"Listen, I'm the one who's delighted to be here. It's my first little excursion out of Quito. And, the weather down here in the valley is so different; it's so much warmer," I replied, trying with little success to hide my obvious excitement at seeing her again.

"Well, let me show you around a little before I take you in to meet Dr. Moreno," she said, her arm brushing mine as we walked next to each other. "As you can see it's a small school, only about three thousand students, most of whom come from Ecuador. But, surprisingly, we also have quite a few Americans; they come down here as participants in off-campus programs from their own universities. I think we have over two hundred this year; I have two in my class this semester. However, unlike American universities, we don't have dormitories so our students tend to live at home or, in the case of the American students, with host families."

We were walking across a parking lot towards the main administrative building. The university appeared to consist of about a half dozen two or three-story buildings, and with numerous palm trees scattered about, there was something of a California feel to the place. The buildings, however, did not possess any kind of architectural uniformity so typical of American campuses; eclectic was the only descriptive term that seemed to fit. One structure seemed to have taken its influence from Japan with its profusion of gardens, small wooden bridges and ponds. Another building, only the top of which could be seen, had Moorish overtones. Still, the campus had a relaxed atmosphere to it.

"Did you go here," I asked as we entered the administrative center.

"Oh, no, I graduated from the University of Buenos Aires in Argentina. Have you heard of it?" she replied, directing me to a doorway that led out to a small plaza filled with students killing time between classes.

"I've obviously heard of Buenos Aires though I'm not familiar with the university. Is that where you became interested in anthropology?"

"I had an interest in the subject long before then," she replied. "My grandfather had a large farm in the Oriente and as a young girl I used to spend a lot of time there. My grandfather would tell these wonderful stories about the various indigenous peoples that lived in the surrounding jungle."

"He sounds like a wonderful grandfather," I replied.

"Oh, he was. I can remember so clearly sitting spellbound as he told me about the Huaorani, a very warlike tribe that raided my grandfather's farm on a couple of occasions and had to be driven off with guns. You may have heard of them if only because they tend to behead their enemies and shrink their skulls; they sell these plastic shrunken heads in all the souvenir shops down here. I know it sounds gruesome but this practice was one of their most important tribal rituals. Unfortunately, most of these incredibly unique cultures are disappearing as oil and other mining industries invade their territories. It's really quite depressing."

"I must admit, your work sounds incredibly interesting. So, you've been teaching here since you graduated from the University of Buenos Aires," I asked, becoming more impressed with her by the moment.

"Oh no; I then went to the University of Texas where I received my Masters Degree. I'm sure you've heard of the University of Texas," she said with mock sarcasm.

"I have and though I've never actually been there I understand Austin, Texas, is a beautiful place."

"Oh, it is. I wanted to stay there longer and get my Ph.D. but my father insisted I come back. My mother's been ill and in addition to helping look after her, he often asks me to attend various political events with him. That's why I was at the reception last Friday."

I would have preferred just spending the morning talking to Carolina but I couldn't very well blow off Dr. Moreno, not after she had set up an appointment for me.

"His office is in this building, on the second floor," she said, indicating a yellow-stucco building with two large white columns in front. As we entered the building, she directed me to the right. The interior was dominated by a massive sunlit atrium from which classrooms and faculty offices extended on three sides. We climbed a marble staircase and proceeded only a short distance down the corridor before she stopped at a heavy wooden door.

"This is it, 213," she announced. For all her poise, I couldn't help but notice she seemed a little nervous. I couldn't tell whether it was because Dr. Moreno intimidated her or because she was just a little nervous about what kind of an impression I was going to make on him. I hoped for her sake it wasn't the latter since there was simply no chance I could come across as anything other than your typical uninformed gringo.

As she was about to knock, she stopped and looked at me. "My office is right over there, 221. When you're finished stop by, if you'd like. Maybe we could get a cup of coffee or some lunch?"

"Count on it," I replied. But as I turned to enter Dr. Moreno's office I realized I was now the nervous one.

Sitting before Dr. Moreno I felt I was back in grammar school where teachers seemed to know everything worth knowing; I felt the same discomfort as then, probably because I had no real business being there. Dr. Moreno was a distinguished scholar and authority on the Incas, a subject about which I knew next to nothing, and I was there to ask him about what, the possible whereabouts of the gold? On the other hand, if I had been concerned that Carolina may have had a crush on Dr. Moreno, I need not have worried. He was short, overweight and totally disheveled. Even worse, for him at least, his face was covered with terrible acne scars that he did his best to hide behind a wiry gray beard. His clothes as well as his office reeked of cigarette smoke. Fortunately, he was not smoking at that moment but judging from the pile of cigarette butts that overflowed the single ashtray on his desk, it was only a matter of time before he'd light up again.

"So, Carolina tells me you are doing research on Atahualpa, Mr. Henrick, though she's said little of your scholarly background. Are you by chance a university professor in the States," Dr. Moreno asked in heavily accented English.

"Right then I knew this interview was a mistake but I had no choice, I had to press forward with it. The question was how; I couldn't just say I had met some peasant in a bar who claimed to know where the gold was hidden. In fact, it suddenly occurred to me just how stupid this whole thing about Atahualpa had become.

"I'm a businessman, Dr. Moreno," I lied, though there was probably more truth to the statement than anything else I was about to say. "I had read about the gold in a magazine article back in the States and became fascinated with the whole subject. Since I have a little money I decided to put it to use by coming down here to Ecuador to learn more about it."

"And, Carolina? How do you know her? You do understand her father will probably be Ecuador's next president."

I found his tone annoyingly impertinent, but then I decided he was probably just being protective of her because I was an American. In the brief time I had been in Ecuador I hadn't experienced anything even resembling anti-Americanism but Adam had warned me to be prepared for it, especially among intellectuals for whom it was always in fashion, even in the US.

"I've met her father, a very charming man; I met the two of them actually at a reception hosted by the American ambassador." I decided I'd leave it up to his imagination to come up with a reason why I was at the reception. And, he must have come up with a good one for his tone immediately softened.

"Ah, I see Mr. Henrick, so how may I be of help to you?"

"Well," I replied, feeling a bit more confident, "let's begin with the most obvious question: Do you believe the gold is actually out there?"

"The gold, ah yes, you foreigners are always interested in the gold but for we Ecuadorians the issue is really quite different. Let me try to explain. The story that most people have heard is that Rumiñahui was in the process of transporting an enormous load of gold and silver from Quito to Cajamarca when he was informed of Atahualpa's death at the hands of the Spanish. Not wanting the Spanish to gain possession of this treasure, he hid the gold in an almost inaccessible location somewhere in the Llanganate Mountains and then had all those soldiers who helped him bury it put to death."

"So, Rumiñahui himself was the only person left who knew the location of the gold."

"Yes, as it turned out, and though he was later captured and tortured by the Spanish he never revealed its location."

"But, why was it so important to Rumiñahui to keep the Spanish from finding the gold," I asked, wondering if the answer wasn't self-evident.

"Well, first of all, gold and silver were sacred to the Incas, though not as a source of wealth as they are to us. Gold was considered to be the tears of the sun, silver the tears of the moon. But, there's more to the story than that," he explained, gently stroking his beard. "You see, the Spanish told Atahualpa that if he would convert to Christianity they would not burn him at the stake; they would hang him instead. Having no other real option, Atahualpa agreed."

"He agreed to be hanged rather than burned at the stake," I interrupted, not understanding why that should be so important.

"Oh, it was very important to Atahualpa but unfortunately the Spanish remained fearful that his followers might rise up against them so they garroted him and then burned his body. However, with the help of some of Atahualpa's subjects his body was spirited away during the night and mummified. Rumiñahui, who was by the way a half-brother of Atahualpa, now took possession of Atahualpa's body and along with some twelve to sixteen thousand warriors, as well as the largest quantity of gold assembled for the ransom, raced northwards in the direction of Quito. What he hid in the Llanganates, then, was not simply an enormous treasure but Atahualpa's mummified body. So, the spot where the gold is hidden is actually Atahualpa's crypt which from our viewpoint is far more significant."

"But why? I read somewhere that the gold and silver buried there was probably worth at least two or three billion dollars. How can Atahualpa's remains be more significant than that," I asked, fully aware the question must have sounded incredibly naïve to Dr. Moreno.

"If Atahualpa's body were to be found," he responded, "the consequences would be cataclysmic and not just for Ecuador but for the entire Andean region. The indigenous peoples of Peru, Bolivia, Ecuador would in all probability rise up and unite into a massive political force that could easily overcome the present governments in these countries."

"Why would they do that? What is so important to them about Atahualpa's body?" I was becoming more confused yet more fascinated by the minute. And, for the first time I was beginning to see the possibility of a story here.

"There is a legend in Quechua," Dr. Moreno continued, "that claims when Atahualpa was killed by the Spanish the sky suddenly darkened; 'the children of the sun' had lost the source of their power. But, the legend goes on to say that at some point in the future the Sun God will call for the Inca's return. When this happens the sky will once more brighten and the power of the Incan people will be restored. The indigenous peoples, I should point out, have only recently begun to exert any kind of political clout but they waste too much of it bickering among themselves. However, if Atahualpa's body were to be found, those differences might very well disappear and if they did, the indigenous would become a force to be reckoned with."

"If what you suggest is true, and I have no reason to doubt it isn't, why after all these years hasn't someone been able to find Atahualpa's burial site?"

"You clearly don't know much about the Llanganates, do you? It is an almost inaccessible range of mountains whose highest peaks exceed 15,000 feet in elevation though they are seldom seen beneath the thick blanket of clouds that perpetually cover them. The slopes of these mountains are carpeted with an almost impenetrable tangle of stunted vegetation that makes walking almost impossible; in many places the only means of getting through is literally to crawl on hands and knees along trails made by animals. As for the valley floors, they are even more difficult to negotiate because the jungle is even thicker there and covered with an eerie, cold fog. No, Rumiñahui knew what he was doing when he hid Atahualpa's body here. Personally, I suspect he placed Atahualpa's mummy along with the gold in one of the many abandoned gold mines that were scattered throughout the region. At some later time the mine was probably buried under tons of rock by an earthquake-triggered landslide; earthquakes are a common occurrence in the Llaganates. Of course, if that's the case Atahualpa's burial place will never be found."

"So, may I conclude the gold, and Atahualpa's body, are still probably out there," I asked, eager to conclude our discussion so I could meet Carolina.

"Oh, I'm certain the gold is out there," he replied wearily, as if that were the only thing people ever asked him about. "But, you do realize, Mr. Henrick, that Atahualpa's is not the only gold buried out there? Are you familiar at all with the term *waka*?"

"*Waka*? No, I've never even heard the word, what is it," I asked.

"A *waka* is an ancient burial site, typically for wealthy Incas. The body was often buried with gold and silver jewelry and masks, again worth millions at today's prices. There are probably hundreds of them scattered throughout the Andes, some of which have been discovered but many of which haven't. Again, there is an entire industry devoted to finding them."

"So, if you find one of these *wakas* you're allowed to keep what's in them?"

"Not anymore. In the past people smuggled the gold artifacts out of the country; they probably still do, though officially the government now claims anything found in these *wakas* is the property of the state. I think the finder gets something like fifteen percent of the value. Still, the search for them goes on and your chances of finding one of them are much greater than finding Atahualpa's gold."

At this point, as interesting as it all was, I realized there was little more to be gained by continuing our conversation. I had the information I needed, especially about the fact there were maps and documents out there claiming to describe the location of Atahualpa's gold. But, now I also knew about the existence of these *wakas*. It was entirely possible, then, that the peasant who ate in Carlos' bar everyday might actually have information about the location of one of these *wakas*, though where he got the information was clearly a mystery. Anyway, all I wanted now was to make as gracious an exit as possible from Dr. Moreno's office so I could do what I had been hoping to do since Friday—spend some quality time with Carolina.

Eight

The door to Carolina's office was open so I rapped lightly and walked in. She appeared to be correcting papers but quickly came out from behind her desk when I entered. She seemed delighted to see me and suggested we go to lunch at a place called the Cactus Café, located just across the street from the entrance to the university; she had to be back in an hour for her next class, she explained. From the outside the Cactus Café didn't look like much although the interior turned out to be very attractive with an exceptionally homey ambience. It was small, less than a dozen tables. The walls were painted a burnt orange and covered with replicas of paintings by Guayasamin, Ecuador's most famous artist. And, of course, faithful to the name there were cactus plants of every size and shape generously scattered about. Only a large flat-screen television attached to the back wall marred the otherwise traditional appearance of the restaurant. Since the television was not on, we chose a small wooden table directly beneath it, which allowed us to simply ignore its existence.

A quick glance around the room only confirmed what one might have expected, the place was a hangout for students from the university. Judging from the books and backpacks strewn about, we may have been the only ones who weren't students. We also appeared to be the only customers not smoking, a fact that wouldn't have appeared strange had there not been several signs prohibiting smoking in the restaurant; on the other hand there were ashtrays on every table suggesting the owner was not serious about enforcing the ban. Unquestionably he'd have far fewer customers if he did, especially women customers, who appeared to represent a disproportionate share of the college's young smokers. As for Carolina, I was pleased to note that she had not acquired the habit or, at the very least, that she had the good manners not to light up in my presence.

"So, tell me, did you find Dr. Moreno to be helpful," Carolina asked, with her usual disarming smile.

I was about to answer when our waiter arrived to hand us menus. "Let's order first," I said. "I had no breakfast to speak of this morning and I'm really starved. So, what would you recommend? Actually, I have a better idea, why don't I just have whatever you do."

"Are you sure? What if I'm one of those women who eats nothing but a tiny salad for lunch?" she teased.

I was about to say she didn't seem the type but fortunately caught myself before I opened my mouth. While Carolina was definitely not overweight, in fact she had an incredible figure, I wasn't about to say anything she might take exception to.

"I'll take my chances," I quickly answered.

Carolina ordered a *jugo de mora* and a breakfast wrap, which according to her contained baked potato, egg and pieces of ham. I was so hungry anything would have sounded good to me at this point.

"All right, so was Dr. Moreno helpful," I began. "He was incredibly informative and very passionate about his field. I should also point out he was also very impressed with you and I can only assume that's the reason he was willing to spend as much time with me as he did. So, for that I sincerely thank you."

"You're more than welcome," she replied, "but to be honest, I haven't the slightest idea exactly what kind of information you were looking for. All I know is what Adam said, that you were doing research on Atahualpa; that's why Dr. Moreno immediately came to mind. I was just trying to be helpful. But, I suspect we both know that Altahualpa is not the real reason you've come down here to Ecuador, is it?"

Again we were interrupted before I could answer, this time by the waiter bringing our food. When he left she pointed to the wrap, "Put that white creamy sauce on the potato, it's really good that way. And, don't worry, trust me, it's nothing mysterious. It's only yogurt."

There was something so guileless about Carolina that I decided I might as well tell her the truth about my reasons for being in Quito; the weird part about my sudden interest in Atahualpa I'd just have to play by ear. I began by explaining how Adam and I had become friends at business school and how after graduation we had continued to stay in touch even though our careers had gone in radically different directions. I joked about his inviting me to come to Ecuador never dreaming that I'd take him up on the offer. But, I added, I probably never would have had I not lost my job just as my girlfriend was exchanging me for another guy, and that it was largely out of desperation that I had decided to take Adam up on his offer.

"I had to get out of New York," I admitted plaintively, feeling like a weight had been lifted from my shoulders just from admitting it.

"That's quite a story," she remarked with a smile. "I especially like the part about being exchanged for another guy, I don't think I've ever heard it put quite that way. Still, you seem to be handling it well. Did you really love this woman, Rachel?"

"I must have since I was intending to give her an engagement ring. And, I was certainly hurt, OK that's an understatement, I was crushed when she told me she was leaving me for someone else; she was the only woman I'd ever been serious enough about to contemplate marriage. That's the main reason I had to get away from New York; just the thought of bumping into her with her new boyfriend was more than I was prepared to handle. But recently I've begun to wonder how much of that hurt was a product of my bruised pride. Whatever, the whole experience was a humiliating one. But, please, may we leave this depressing topic and talk about something else?"

"Of course, though I still don't understand what any of this have to do with your interest in Atahualpa."

This was the part of the story I was reluctant to talk about since I realized it was going to sound ridiculous. But there was no way around it so once again I decided to just plough ahead with the truth.

"This whole thing about Atahualpa came about entirely by accident," I confessed. "To be perfectly honest, I had never even heard of him before I arrived here in Quito last week. The fact is I've become friendly with the owner of a bar down on Amazonas. Carlos, that's the owner's name, spent a number of years in the U.S. so his English is pretty good. I'd stopped by his place originally just to use his bathroom. Anyway, there's this peasant who frequently has lunch there and he claims to have information on the location of Atahualpa's gold. All right, it all sounds crazy, doesn't it?"

"Yes, Michael, I'm afraid it does sound crazy but please continue. I do find Americans fascinating," she laughed.

"OK, so I told the owner I'd do a little research on the topic, though even as I agreed to it I wasn't sure I'd really do it. But, then, after thinking about it I got curious about whether there really was information out there that might point to where the gold was hidden. I'm not sure what I intended to do with any information I found, I mean, I couldn't exactly see myself mounting an expedition to find the gold. Still, when Dr. Moreno reported there were even maps showing the approximate location of the hidden gold I realized this guy might quite possibly be on to something. But, now, if I might be brutally honest, I have to admit that the real reason I'm here is because I wanted to see you again."

"Oh, so now we're getting to the real story. I can't believe you're so devious? Are all Americans like this? I really should be upset at you for using me in this way, having me set up an appointment for you with Dr. Moreno just so you'd have an excuse to see me again. How could you be so impertinent"! She delivered this little soliloquy with the most delightful expression on her face. Right then I realized I had become completely infatuated with this woman, and I'd been with her for all of an hour. I knew it was insane, but I couldn't help it; I found her incredible.

"But, you also wanted to see me again, isn't that true," I replied, trying my best to make it sound like I was just joking when my heart had stopped beating as I waited for her answer.

She quickly glanced at her watch; it was not exactly the reaction I was looking for.

"I have to rush, I'm sorry. I have a class at one o'clock and I need a few minutes to prepare for it." She stood up, then, leaning over, gave me a light peck on the cheek. "Thank you for lunch; I really enjoyed it in spite of your coming down here on false pretenses. But, since you did, may I ask you what you're doing on Saturday; I thought perhaps you and I might go to Otavalo for the day?"

"Otavalo," I asked, doing a poor job of hiding my excitement. "What or where is Otavalo?"

"Otavalo is a small town north of Quito and every Saturday there is a huge market there; it's a big tourist attraction. Would you like to go?"

There was a hint of a smile in her voice, if not on her face.

"Yes, of course," I blurted out. "But, how do I get in touch with you?"

She handed me her business card. "I know this is inappropriate, though probably not by American standards, but my email address is on it; I hope you'll write me."

As she hurried off I suddenly realized I had barely touched my lunch; her plate, I noticed, didn't have a crumb left on it.

"*La cuenta*," I called to the waiter. As hungry as I had been when we had first sat down, I was now too excited to eat just thinking about Saturday.

"So tell me," I asked Adam later that evening on his return from Washington, "how did your meetings go? Did you find them worthwhile, or at least, interesting?"

Typical of Adam, he had breezed through the door of the apartment, dropped his luggage on the floor, slipped off his jacket and had immediately gone over and made us a drink

"It's always worthwhile to return to Washington," he replied, dropping onto the couch, "if for no other reason than to discover what the White House is actually thinking about the country you're working in. Ecuador is so small it easily becomes lost amidst all the crises emanating from Mexico, Argentina, Venezuela, Cuba. But, I have to admit it was fun being back in DC for a couple of days. I saw some old friends, had a couple of excellent dinners, but you know what, at the end of the day I was more than happy to come back here."

"Over and above your enjoying Washington, did you learn anything new about the situation here in Ecuador? After all, you're the guys working here, so don't you know a lot more about what's going on than the White House?"

"It's not so much about learning something new as trying to determine how best to respond to President Acosta's policies. Much of our discussion focused on his efforts to rewrite Ecuador's present constitution and get it approved by his congress. One of his main goals is to eliminate term limits so he can run again for president; at the moment he can't succeed himself. But, he has to move quickly since there isn't that much time before the next election and there's plenty of opposition to what he's trying to do."

"So, what do you think, is he going to get his new constitution," I asked.

"It's almost too close to call, though he probably has enough votes in congress to get it through. One of the things really beginning to hurt him is the economic situation. I remember telling you before I left for Washington that these populist revolutions were being made possible only because of the windfall in revenues from oil exports. A barrel of oil was then selling on the futures market for nearly $150; now it's less than half that. So, all those dollars that were to fund these expansive social and political programs have largely dried up. In Venezuela ironically Chavez has had to ask the oil companies he previously nationalized to increase their investment in his country."

"So, Ecuador is an oil exporting country? I never knew that; I didn't even realize Ecuador had oil."

This, of course, was just one more example of how little I knew about this country. For an educated young man the extent of my ignorance about the world was breathtaking.

"Not only does Ecuador produce oil, though it's only a tiny fraction of Venezuela's production, it exports that oil primarily to the United States which, of course, only further complicates political relations between the two countries. And, now, with this latest flap over the Acosta government's ties to the FARC, well, we'll just have to wait and see what happens."

"What options does President Acosta have? I doesn't seem like he has many."

"He can always expel someone from the embassy although he's already done that just recently. He can also take a page from Chavez' book and become more overtly anti-American. In fact, there's a good chance that's something he'll do blaming not only the Colombian attack on the Americans, as Chavez has done, but claiming the Americans manufactured the intelligence linking his administration to the FARC. In fact, he might very well do both. Those things will certainly play very well with his supporters. On the other hand, there is this little issue of budget deficits now that the price of oil has dropped. He'll probably end up borrowing money from the IMF or the World Bank even as he's threatening to default on the country's previous loans."

"I guess I can understand then why Washington has such an interest in Carolina's father. So, was there much talk about him up there?"

"Plenty, believe me," Adam replied emphatically. "Eduard Mayer has become the toast of Washington; he's actually going to be meeting with a number of administration officials in Washington next month. That's almost unheard of for a man who's only a candidate for the presidency of Ecuador."

"Tell me again, now, why Washington is so taken with him?" Like Atahualpa, I had never even heard this guy's name mentioned before I came down here.

"There's a number of reasons among them he's made it clear he won't allow any FARC camps on Ecuadorian territory. In addition he's pledged to be a strong supporter of Colombia's efforts to destroy the FARC. And, if that weren't enough for Washington he claims he will cease Ecuador's attempt to nationalize foreign-owned companies and will repay the government's loans to international banks on schedule. I had to remind my colleagues not to get overly excited about him on the grounds 'if he seems too good to be true he's probably too good to be true.' After all, it's not the first time we've heard such promises from a candidate."

"But, that's enough talk about politics for now, I'd rather ask you about Carolina," Adam added. "And, don't leave anything out."

"Just one more question I'd like to know your impression of Carolina's father. I only met him that once, though I suspect I'll be meeting him again."

Adam did not answer immediately; he was clearly thinking how to word his response.

"Personally, I think Carolina's father is a bit of a fascist and Washington does, too, for that matter. They just hope he'll be our fascist!"

"Why is that?"

"Well, over and above what I've already explained about him, he wants to vastly improve and modernize the Ecuadorian army, which he claims is necessary to gain the support of the military since he himself has no military background. The US has informally agreed to do this for him, though only on the condition that he renew the agreement allowing US surveillance aircraft to fly from bases in Ecuador. But, now, will you please stop avoiding my question and tell me how your lunch with Carolina went."

"OK. OK, lunch with Carolina was great; she's a really delightful person."

"That's it," he responded. "You had a great time and she was delightful; that's all you can say about her? I really am disappointed in you."

"What else do you want me to say for crying out loud?"

For some reason I was feeling just a little embarrassed talking about her.

"Oh, yes, there was one thing," I added, trying my best to act nonchalant. "Carolina has invited me to go with her to Otavalo on Saturday."

"All right, now that's more like it, though I have to say this clearly must be a new you. The guy I knew at business school would never have moved so fast. This really is amazing; I'm impressed," he said with a huge smile. "Think of it, you've been invited to Otavalo by the most eligible woman in Ecuador, a woman who is well educated, wealthy, and, may I add, so much more attractive than Rachel."

"Whoa, wait a minute, while I'm not saying I disagree with you, I don't think you even remember what Rachel looks like. You met her once," I exclaimed. "And, I'm not even certain you were sober at the time."

"I may have had a couple of drinks but I remember her perfectly, in large part because I could never picture the two of you together. Come on, now, you were so different from one another. Rachel was just so, well, I guess the best way to put it is, she was the quintessential Jewish American Princess. You'd never have been happy married to her."

"And you never said anything?"

"Give me a break; it wasn't my place to tell you. And, as you just pointed out, we didn't see each other much in those days. So, are you going to tell me more about Carolina or what?

I could tell he was becoming a little annoyed at my unwillingness to confide in him. I just didn't want him to know how strongly I was already beginning to feel about her; I was worried what he might say if he ever bumped into her at one of the many cocktail parties he was invited to.

"Really, there isn't that much to say; I've only spent a couple hours with her."

"Well, at the very least you should be sounding a little more excited about going to Otavalo with her. This is the daughter of the next president of Ecuador! And, how long have you even been here in this country? Like I said, Michael, this is amazing. Now, how are you getting up there, by the way?"

"Good question though I know she has a car of her own. I'll have to email her to get the details. Now that I think of it, I have been leaving everything up to her."

"All right, then, why don't you take the Montero," Adam suggested. "It's about the safest car around, though I'm sure she has a security detail that follows here everywhere, right?"

"I don't honestly know," I responded. I hadn't even thought about it. "Anyway, if she does those guys must be pretty good because I didn't notice anyone following her,"

"I'm sure she'll have one for the trip to Otavalo," Adam explained. "I have a feeling her father would insist upon it. And you should immediately ask which car the security guys are in so you won't panic when you realize someone is following you. You have to understand that in general this is a very safe country but car-jackings and kidnappings do occur and you have to take some precautions. That's why you'd better get accustomed to being followed when you're out with Carolina. In fact, now that I think of it, does her father even know the two of you are going to Otavalo?"

"I have no idea, why," I asked, wondering why that would matter.

"Just don't be too surprised if she suddenly can't make it, that's all. Ecuador is a lot more restrictive socially than the States, and no doubt that's probably even more true for someone in Carolina's situation."

"Thanks a lot, Adam, that's precisely what I didn't need to hear right now."

Nine

No sooner had Adam left for work the next morning than I turned on his computer and sent Carolina an email. Adam's comment last night about Carolina's father not letting her go with me to Otavalo had me worried. What made it so worrisome was that I could understand perfectly well why he might not want her to. He knew absolutely nothing about me, and for that matter, neither did Carolina. Adding to this was the fact I was an American, who was completely ignorant of Ecuador and Ecuadorian culture. Taken together these things didn't exactly make me the perfect suitor for Carolina. On the other hand, what we were doing was no big deal; it was simply a day trip to Otavalo. What could be the harm in that? It was not like I was proposing to her.

As I sat at the computer, becoming more desperate by the minute, a notice flashed on the screen that I had mail; it was from Carolina. It would have been great to think she had been just waiting for me to contact her but I realized it was probably just a coincidence that she had been sitting at her computer at the moment I wrote her. Nonetheless, I was relieved she had answered so promptly. I quickly read her note and when she said that she was delighted I'd be coming to pick her up, my only thought was how would I get through the next three days. Wisely she included directions to her house, which appeared to be located not too far from the university. I didn't ask about whether we would have a security escort though I secretly hoped we wouldn't.

I was now too anxious to idly sit around the apartment so I decided to wander down to see Carlos and pass along what Dr. Moreno had said about Atahualpa and the gold. I took a quick shower, got dressed and grabbed a cup of coffee before heading for the elevator. It was an extremely bright morning so I put on my sunglasses. I never wore sunglasses back in the States even on sunniest days but down here I found I needed them. At 9,000 feet the atmosphere is so thin and clear it does little to screen out ultraviolet radiation. But, here again, I found one of those contradictions that made Ecuador so fascinating. While there was no shortage of people on the street selling sunglasses, I noticed very few actually wearing them and this was especially true for the indigenous peoples.

As I walked down Avenida Orellana in the direction of Carlos's place the usual assortment of individuals were busily out on the streets selling candy, fruit and flowers. But, on this day my attention was drawn to a young boy of no more than six or seven, who each time the traffic lights turned red, would step in front of the idling cars and begin doing cartwheels. He was not very talented and, at least, while I watched, not a soul offered him any money. But oddly, I didn't feel especially bad for the boy; in fact, I felt a sort of grudging admiration for him. He was out there trying desperately to make money the only way he knew how. I couldn't help myself; I called him over and gave him a five-dollar bill. For a moment he just stared at me blankly, as if I had made a terrible mistake, but then, realizing I had meant to give it to him he gave me a smile that would brighten the dreariest day, and took off running. I gathered he had decided he'd made enough money on this particular day.

One of the other things that always intrigued me about Quito was the intermingling of traditional indigenous cultures with the modern. I was confronted by yet another example as I neared Carlos' place. A young woman was walking towards me dressed in what I now recognized as traditional clothing—a black ankle-length skirt, black sandals, a white blouse and an intricately designed red sweater. I had already passed a number of young women dressed the same way, but she definitely stood out from the rest because covering her long dark braids was of all things a New York Yankees baseball cap!

I was still smiling at the thought of the woman as I walked into the bar where almost immediately I sensed something was wrong. That's when I noticed the bull's head that ordinarily hung from the wall behind the bar was now lying incongruously on the floor in front of me, a portion of one of its massive horns lying next to it. Glancing around, it became clear very quickly that the place had been trashed. Only then did I notice several very tough-looking individuals, Carlos' brother among them, standing around at the end of the bar where customers tended to watch soccer games on television. But, now, all that was left of the TV was the metal supports that had once attached it to the wall.

"Carlos, what happened here," I asked incredulously, my feet crunching on tiny pieces of glass as I walked towards the bar.

"I had visitors last night," he replied with no attempt to veil his sarcasm. "Obviously they were looking for something and when they didn't find it, I guess they wrecked the place, probably out of frustration, since I can't imagine why else they'd smash the TV and rip down the bull's head."

As he was speaking I could sense the men staring at me as if I might have had something to do with this. It was not a comfortable feeling, so right then I made up my mind to get out of there as quickly as possible; my presence was only making a bad situation even worse. But before I could make my escape Carlos called out, "Wait, I want you to look at something." He handed me a copy of the previous Monday's *Extra*, a newspaper that seemed to specialize in reporting on the country's most sordid crimes. It was already open to page five where in the upper corner was a photo that should have been on page one.

"That guy in the picture there," said Carlos. "It's our old friend Francisco; somebody killed him and, as you can see, they did quite a messy job of it."

"My God," I stammered. I had to take Carlos at his word that the person pictured there was Francisco since it wasn't obvious from what was left of the face. "How did they ever identify him? It's horrible. What happened?"

"Whoever did this clearly wanted him to be found," Carlos explained.

But why," I asked, genuinely uncertain what he was talking about.

"So as to intimidate the person holding Francisco's box," he explained.

If it hadn't been clear to me before it certainly was now I had no business frequenting a place like this; it was far too dangerous, especially for an American. And the looks thrown my way by the men at the end of the bar seemed to be growing less friendly by the minute.

"Do the police have any idea who might have done this?" I inquired, trying to be nice to Carlos when all I really wanted to do was get out of there as quickly as possible.

"Not according to the newspaper. The only thing the police have reported is that they have reason to believe that Francisco was killed somewhere else, and that his body was dumped in the alley where it was found."

"Does he have any family," I asked.

Carlos thought for a moment. "I don't think he had any close family; at least, he never mentioned any. The only person I ever remember him saying anything about was an uncle; he was the one who had apparently given him the box. And, if I'm not mistaken, he too was killed, though I don't recall any details about his death. All I remember is Francisco telling me something about it."

The men at the end of the bar were still staring at me and by this time I was becoming so obviously uneasy that Carlos was forced to say something just to calm me.

"Look, these guys are friends of my brother's," he explained, nodding at the men without introducing us. "They're here because I called them, or at least, my brother called them. I suspect poor Francisco must have talked before he died because this place was broken into last night. As I said, they were clearly looking for something and I suspect you and I both know what it was. I seriously doubt whoever did this will come back again soon, though just in case these guys are going to look after the place when I'm not here."

"Are you going to report the break-in to the police?"

"Not on your life," Carlos responded quickly. "The last thing I need is for the police to go searching through this place. Now that's when I'd find things are missing. The national police here in Ecuador are badly paid, badly trained and incredibly corrupt."

The last sentence he must have repeated in Spanish to the men at the bar for they nodded grimly.

"So, you don't think it's just a coincidence, between the break-in and Francisco's murder, I mean?"

"I don't believe in coincidences, not when they involve murder," he scoffed.

"Well, if it was Francisco's box they were after, you'd better be careful too; clearly they suspect you have it so they'll keep looking for you. You do still have it, don't you?"

Carlos nodded but didn't say anything. I realized I shouldn't be speaking quite so loudly even though the brother's friends probably understood little English. Still, one couldn't be too careful when the people looking for the box were clearly prepared to do whatever was necessary to get their hands on it. I was even beginning to wonder now if they might come after me.

"So, what are you going to do with it? You said yourself he has no immediate family. Aren't you even the slightest bit curious what's inside? It has to be incredibly important to these people, whomever they may be, to kill someone for it. Have you ever thought maybe it does have something to do with Inca gold?" I remembered what Dr. Moreno had explained about the *wakas*, though I decided for the moment there was no point in saying anything about them to Carlos.

"All I can say is, I'm glad I didn't leave the box here or it would be gone, that's for sure," Carlos remarked. "Francisco seemed so worried that I decided to take it home. Of course, after last night I suspect it's not safe there either. So, the answer is yes, I'm going to find out what's in it, you can be sure of that. And, I'd better do it sooner rather than later, before I end up dead."

There was an obvious edge to his voice I had never heard before. I concluded that in spite of his easy-going manner Carlos, in his own way, was probably just as tough as his brother.

"You know, we've been operating on the assumption that whomever these people are, they want to find the location of Atahualpa's gold, but it's entirely possible that what they really want is for that gold never to be found."

Carlos looked at me quizzically.

"Look, I know it may sound crazy but, please, hear me out. On Monday I went down to San Francisco University where I spoke with a Dr. Moreno, who's a specialist on the Incas. We talked for nearly an hour and just as I was about to leave he recounted to me a very interesting story about Rumiñahui, or maybe it would be more accurate to call it a theory. According to him, anyway, Rumiñahui actually buried Atahualpa's body with the gold. He claims the gold was entirely incidental to the Incas, it was hiding Atahualpa's body from the Spanish that was so important. And, not only that, but there is a prophecy among those who speak Quechua that the power of the Incas will be restored upon receipt of a sign from Heaven or wherever it is that Incas go after death. Dr. Moreno feels that the discovery of Atahualpa's body would represent such a sign and it would cause the indigenous peoples of this country as well as of the other Andean countries to rise up and unite against the present power structure. Maybe, that's the reason someone doesn't want Francisco's information to get out. I know it sounds far-fetched but maybe there is something to it and these individuals don't want to give the indigenous peoples any excuse to unite and become a political force. On the other hand maybe it's the indigenous peoples who are behind all this; maybe they don't want Atahualpa's body to be found. Anyway, it's something to think about."

By the expression on his face I couldn't tell whether Carlos thought I was crazy or not but I could tell he was intrigued by what I had just told him.

"I've never heard anything like that," he mumbled. "And, anyway, who is this Dr. Moreno and how come he knows so much about this?"

"All I know is what I've just told you, that he's a professor in the Anthropology Department at San Francisco University and supposedly an expert on the Incas. He's apparently written a number of books about them but beyond that I know nothing about him."

"Well, even if this Dr. Moreno is right about Rumiñahui burying Atahualpa with the gold, I don't think much of this prophecy idea. Let's wait now until we find out what's in this box Francisco apparently died for. It may be nothing," Carlos added.

"I should be off," I said, slipping off the bar stool where I had been sitting. "I'll check back with you once you find out what's in the box. *Hasta luego* and be careful."

"*Hasta luego,* my friend," Carlos responded. "And, you'd better be careful too."

None of the others even acknowledged my leaving. Once outside I quickly hailed a taxi. I was not about to walk back to the apartment alone, not after what had happened to Francisco. All I could think of was that they might have the bar under surveillance, whomever "they" were. My anxiety level was now so elevated I spent the entire trip looking out the back window of the taxi to make sure we weren't being followed.

"You've got to be kidding, tell me you are," exclaimed Adam, slowly placing his fork down on the plate in front of him. Consuelo had stayed later than usual to prepare our dinner, though she had now left for home, a good hour away by bus. As we were eating I had casually mentioned Francisco's death, which had led to Adam's sudden outburst

" You have the incredible good fortune to meet Carolina and have her invite you out to Otavalo and then you get yourself mixed up in something like this. You're not thinking clearly, Michael. You had never even heard of Atahualpa before you came down here yet all at once you believe some old guy, who frequents a bar you accidentally entered looking for a bathroom, might know where his gold is hidden. Or at least you believe him enough to begin doing research on the topic. Now, suddenly, this old guy turns up dead, the victim apparently of a brutal murder and, to top it off, the owner of the bar, what was the name of it?"

"*El Café de Los Toreros,*" I reply quickly.

"OK, so the owner of *El Café de Los Toreros,* the bar where this guy apparently hangs out, claims the place was broken into though he can't figure out if anything was taken. For God's sake, Michael, stay away from that place. Life can be tough enough around here for an American without getting into the middle of something like this. Believe me, Quito can be a violent, dangerous place. And, please, don't tell me New York can be a dangerous place too. This is a very different situation, one you know absolutely nothing about."

"I know the way I've described it probably makes the situation seem more serious than it is; the break-in after all could very well be a coincidence. Apparently these things happen all the time in that part of town. But, whether it's a coincidence or not, Adam, I'm not involved in it," I replied, wondering whether if I just repeated it often enough it would become true. "I just happened to stop by this bar when all these things began to occur; now, that is a coincidence. Really, I'm not involved and I have no intention of going back there."

"I sincerely hope you're right," Adam replied, in all seriousness. "But, tell me, what is it that somebody wants so badly they're willing to kill this old man for, do you have any idea?"

"All I know is that the guy who was killed left a wooden box of some kind with Carlos, he's the owner of the bar, for safe keeping. Obviously the guy knew someone was after him, or at the least, after the box. But, I've never seen the box and according to Carlos he has it hidden in a place where the person or persons who broke into his bar apparently will never find it. That's it, that's all I know, honestly."

I suddenly felt as if I were nine years old and having to explain to my father what I had done to have Mrs. Lancaster keep me after school. I could actually remember saying to him, "That's all I did, honestly." I suspected my father never believed me, as I doubted Adam believed me now.

"Let me give you some advice, Michael."

I could see he was deadly serious.

"You don't want to get in trouble with the police down here. The laws are vague and judicial procedures can be arcane. As for the police themselves, they aren't much better than the criminals. In addition to all this, you don't have any idea who's behind this murder. There's a good chance it could be someone with connections to the government or the military or the police. So, be very careful. Even the embassy occasionally finds itself unable to help Americans who get in trouble with the law down here."

"I'll stay out of it," I promised, and at that moment I honestly meant it. "Carlos warned me about them, too. Anyway, I've got more important things on my mind, like going to Otavalo with Carolina this weekend,"

"And, that's another reason to be careful. Don't get her mixed up in this or her father will make certain the two of you never see each other again. And, his security guys are more than capable of making sure of that; they're very tough characters. I know from talking with some of our own security people at the embassy who've had to coordinate with them on a couple of occasions. On the other hand, I have to admit that any guy running for the presidency of this country has no shortage of enemies so he probably does need protection, his family, too. You, however, do not have any protection and while you may honestly believe you're not involved in anything, there may be people out there who think otherwise."

"Don't worry," I assured Adam, "the last thing I want to do is get Carolina involved in anything. And believe me, I have no intention of going back to Carlos' place."

Ten

I had made up my mind that on Thursday morning I would take Adam's Montero out for a test run in order to familiarize myself with it before driving to Otavalo. It was a dream to drive, although I was initially intimidated by the complexity of the dashboard; there were so many more indicators and gauges than on my modest little Honda Civic. There was even one that continuously displayed the Montero's elevation above sea level. And, while I knew Quito was located at 9,000 feet from the sign at the airport, to actually see the gauge read 2,848 meters, over 9,300 feet, was unbelievable.

All I could think of was how baseball fans back in the States were always talking about the advantage the Colorado Rockies enjoyed playing in mile-high Coors Field because baseballs traveled so far in the thin air of Denver. I could only imagine how much further Alex Rodriquez or Albert Pujols would be able to hit a baseball here in Quito.

Driving about the city the only problem I faced was making certain I didn't get lost so I didn't initially go too far from Gonzalez Suarez. I drove up the street, around the traffic circle and then back. I did this several times before finally becoming more brave and exploring new routes. My concern was not so much getting lost but the fact if I did I might not be able to ask anyone how to get back to the apartment building. Life here would be ever so much simpler if only I could only speak a few more words of Spanish.

After driving for about an hour I had had enough and started back along Avenida Gonzalez Suarez; driving, I decided, would present no problem on Saturday as long as Carolina provided the directions. It was then I noticed a large black SUV behind me. I wasn't sure of the make though it looked similar to the Montero I was driving. The windows were tinted making it difficult to see who was in the front seat, but it appeared there were two men. I began to feel a little nervous and had to force myself to keep my eyes on the traffic ahead of me rather than staring into the rearview mirror. Nearing the entrance to Adam's garage I slowed, then, turned down the ramp. The driver of the SUV had also slowed before suddenly hitting the gas pedal and roaring up the street. I could have sworn before he did so he took a good look at the building.

As I pulled into Adam's parking spot, my hands were trembling. Had the SUV sped up because the driver now knew where I lived or had he just become impatient because I had been driving so slowly as I approached the apartment building? And, had the SUV's occupants really been watching me as I had descended the ramp? But, even if they had how could they have recognized me driving Adam's car? Why would they even know what it looked like? Of course, they could have been on the lookout for me and it was just coincidence they noticed me driving his car. Whatever the case, it was making me paranoid. After all, it was almost certain they had Carlos' place under surveillance and they might easily have noticed me entering and leaving

It was disconcerting enough that I decided to stick around the apartment for the rest of the day. I even found some comfort in the fact Consuelo was there, especially after Adam called to say he wouldn't be home until eleven or eleven-thirty. But, the day passed slowly; I read, watched a little television, and even on occasion looked out the front window to see if I spotted any black SUV's on the street. In spite of Carolina there was something about Ecuador that was beginning to unnerve me.

By the next day, however, I was beginning to experience a touch of cabin fever; I needed to get out of the apartment if only for a few minutes. I thought about going to one of the nearby malls to buy a new shirt or pair of pants for my trip to Otavalo, but I quickly talked myself out of it; I had plenty of casual clothes I had yet to even wear and, to be honest, I really didn't feel like shopping. But, what did I feel like doing? As much as I hated to admit it, what I found myself most wanting to do was pay a quick visit to Carlos; I was dying to find out what was in Francisco's box. All right, poor choice of words because I was already worried someone was following me, and that alone should have been reason enough not to set foot in *El Café de Los Toreros* again. Unfortunately, I could not suppress the urge to go in spite of my promise to Adam that I wouldn't do so. Even the thought that I might jeopardize my relationship with Carolina was not enough to stop me. And, of course, if whatever was in the box turned out to be nothing of importance, then all the worrying had been unnecessary. Clearly, I was going to check in with Carlos, the only question now was whether I'd walk or take a cab.

I opted for the cab though as it turned out it was the weather that made the decision for me. The morning, that had dawned so warm and sunny, had suddenly turned overcast and cool; rain was almost certainly on the way and probably very soon. Ironically, I had forgotten to grab an umbrella as I left the apartment though luck was with me as I quickly found a taxi. The trip took only about ten minutes, which didn't keep me from continually turning around to confirm there was no black SUV following us. By waiting until noon to visit Carlos I hoped it would appear to anyone watching the café I was there for something to eat; I even decided I would actually order something, the soup, at least. The crucial factor would be how many other customers were present. It would be far too conspicuous if I were the only person having lunch there.

To my relief there were several men at the bar watching the usual soccer game on a new TV. As best I could tell I'd never seen any of them before. The fact that Carlos' brother was not present, nor any of the men who had been with him the last time, I took to be an encouraging sign. Carlos was behind the bar with his back turned towards me so for a second he didn't notice me. I didn't speak until he turned.

"*Buenos días*, Carlos," I said in my very best Spanish. In fact, I was pleased the way I had pronounced it; I made it sound almost native. Unfortunately, those were about the only words I had learned so far and one reason was that most of the people I had met, other than Consuelo, spoke English extremely well. In fact, one of my hesitations about coming down to Ecuador was my nearly total lack of Spanish; I honestly wondered how I would ever be able to move about the city if Adam weren't with me. I had now come to realize I could survive down here speaking only English, at least until I had begun to learn a few words of Spanish.

"Ahhh, Michael, I'll be right with you; I have something I want you to look at."

He finished poring a couple of beers before disappearing into the back room. I felt a slight rush of anticipation since I assumed whatever it was it had to do with the contents of Francisco's box. On the other hand, there was a noticeable absence of excitement in his voice, which disturbed me. When he returned he was holding a sheaf of papers; they looked like copies of something.

"Over here," he said, beckoning to an empty table. "Sit for a moment; no one can hear us, the television's making too much noise."

Disappointed at the sight of the papers, I asked, "Is that all there was in the box?"

"Oh, no," he replied. "The box contained what appears to be a diary. It's old, battered and hand-written. But, what do you make of this?"

He slid the papers over, which I quickly spread in front of me. It took only a second to understand what he meant; they were written in a style and language I couldn't begin to decipher. And, yet, it looked familiar.

"This is strange," I mused. "I think it's written in German script. Unfortunately, I can't read it or translate it myself, though I've seen things written in this style. But, where would Francisco get something like this, and more importantly, why would he think it has anything to do with gold, much less with Atahualpa's gold?"

"I have no idea, my friend, but he was convinced it did," Carlos responded. "Possibly it mentioned gold, perhaps an old Inca gold mine, and Francisco or whomever he got the diary from, just assumed the gold referred to Atahualpa's gold. There aren't many indigenous people who haven't heard something about it; they think of it as a national treasure of theirs."

"On the other hand, maybe it refers to the location of a *waka*," I suggested. "Dr. Moreno down at the university mentioned them to me. He said they were burial sites of wealthy Incas whose graves often contained gold and silver objects worth millions. Apparently, there are hundreds of them scattered throughout the Andes and many Europeans and Americans have come here in search of them."

"You've done your homework," Carlos exclaimed, seemingly pleased I knew so much about the subject.

"But, the only way we'll ever truly know is to have the diary translated and for that we need to find someone who reads German script. By the way, is the entire diary written in this script?"

"Yes, it appears to be. I've got it well hidden though; I had these eight pages reproduced in the hope that you might be able to find someone able to translate them," Carlos explained. "I thought eight would probably be enough to figure out what the diary was about. I also decided it would be better if you found the translator. I don't know if I can trust anyone around here, and if I start asking about for someone who might know German, the guys who killed Francisco will almost certainly learn of it. Right now, they're only guessing who has the diary; they can't be sure I have it. But, you'd better be careful as well. Having these papers in your possession is only going to increase the danger you could be in."

As he handed them over to me something caught my eye. "You see that," I said to Carlos, pointing to the top page. "Right there. That must be the date this was written: 1945. I suspect this is going to prove to be a very important clue though at the moment I'm not certain to what. If the guy who kept this journal discovered the location of Atahualpa's gold way back then, why hasn't someone heard about it before now? I can't imagine in a small country like this you could keep such a thing a secret, and writing your diary in German script wouldn't do much."

"Unless," Carlos added, "he did what Rumiñahui is said to have done: kill all the soldiers who helped him hide the gold. He knew if any survived and were captured by the Spanish they'd be tortured until they revealed the gold's location. So, maybe this guy killed whoever helped him and he just quietly took gold as he needed it."

"Yah, maybe," I agreed without much enthusiasm for his theory. "Still, I find this whole thing strange. You know, it's very possible it has nothing to do with Atahualpa's gold; on the other hand, why would Francisco have been so certain it did? Well, anyway, I'd better be getting out of here. The less I'm seen around here right now the better for all of us. And to think I was actually going to order lunch; I'll just have to wait for another time."

Carlos burst out laughing, which came as welcome relief after our conversation.

"You were going to eat here? Michael, look around at my customers? When it comes to the food here, this place is one step above a soup kitchen. So, if I were you I'd stick to the beer."

He had a point.

Sliding the pages of the diary off the table, I stuffed them in my pocket thinking, I can't believe I'm really doing this. And worse, I hadn't tried to talk Carlos out of my doing it, even with Adam's warning to stay out of this thing echoing through my mind. For the first time in my life I was beginning to question my sanity.

"Be sure to put those papers in a safe place," he murmured, though it was the last thing I need to be reminded of. "I doubt anyone suspects you're involved but that alone is a good enough reason not to be seen around here. Let me know what you find out; I'll keep the diary safe."

"I'll be in touch," I replied, sliding my chair back and trying my best to act casual as I made my way towards the door. But, even before I got there, I could see it was pouring rain outside. Why hadn't I gone back for an umbrella when I was leaving the apartment; I had suspected then it was going to rain. And, now, there wasn't an empty taxi in sight. Not wanting to hang around the front of the bar, I began trotting along the sidewalk. It was only then I remembered that one got wetter running rather than walking slowly; of course, by this time it didn't really matter since once again I had gotten completely soaked. Still, fortune hadn't deserted me entirely for a taxi that had just raced past me, stopped ahead to let off a passenger. I caught up to it before the driver could pull away from the curb. As I climbed in dripping water all over the seat, I checked to be certain the papers had not gotten ruined; fortunately, they hadn't. Barely had I sat back and closed my eyes to relax, than we were pulling up in front of Adam's building.

Once safely back in the apartment, I pulled the reproduced pages of the diary from my pocket, glancing at them one more time. There was no question they were written in German script but I decided to check anyway. Without even first getting out of my wet clothes, I went over to the computer and typed the term German Script into Google; I was rewarded with over a million sites to choose from. Settling on the first two or three I quickly ascertained that the diary was, in fact, written in German script but what caught my attention was a note on the Sutterlin script. This script, created by the graphic artist L. Sutterlin in the early twentieth century, was used in German schools from 1917 to 1941. After 1941 the Latin alphabet was taught instead. But, as the site pointed out, members of the older generation continued to use the Sutterlin script. Presumably, then, the author of the diary was someone who had been educated in German schools between the wars. So now we had two possible clues, at least, the date, 1945, and the use of the Sutterlin script. It was a start.

Feeling just a little pleased with myself over these discoveries, I decided to put the papers away for the weekend. I had no intention of doing anything further until Monday at the earliest; I was determined to enjoy my trip to Otavalo with Carolina. I had long since concluded I'd say nothing about the diary to Adam; I could only imagine how he'd react if he knew I had several pages of it in my possession to be translated. That also meant I would have to find a translator on my own. There had to be someone at the university and logically Carolina would be the one to ask about it. But there was no way I was going to get her involved in this; it was potentially too dangerous.

That, of course, raised the even larger question what was I doing getting involved. Clearly, if it were dangerous for Carolina, it was almost certainly dangerous for me, probably even more so. After all, Carolina at least had a wealthy, influential family to protect her; what did I have? I couldn't even figure out what was my motivation for getting involved? Obviously, it had nothing to do with Carolina. I wondered if it could be the same misguided sense of adventure that had driven others to spend their lives searching for this hidden treasure? It certainly didn't sound like the Michael Henrick I knew, but for the moment I couldn't come up with a better explanation.

Eleven

I'd been ready to head out for at least a half hour when Adam shuffled into the kitchen wearing a pair of light tan shorts, a faded maroon Harvard T-shirt and flip-flops. For once I was the better dressed even in my jeans, yellow polo shirt and New Balance sneakers.

"My, my, someone's eager to get going this morning," he teased. "Now, what do you think, is Carolina also sitting impatiently waiting for her date to show up?"

"It would be nice to think she was," I replied, actually hoping it to be true. "And while we're on the subject, how long will it take me to get to her house? She wants me there at nine."

Adam glanced up at the clock over the sink. "Well, let's see, it's ten after eight now, so you should probably leave here about eight-thirty. Of course, it really depends upon whether you want to be right on time, fashionably late, or like most Ecuadorians, incredibly late, jokingly referred to down here as running on Ecuadorian time, and that reminds me of a funny story. When Gutierrez was president of Ecuador his government launched a nationwide campaign to eliminate the practice of arriving fifteen to twenty minutes late to business meetings and social events. He claimed such tardiness was costing the Ecuadorian economy over seven hundred million dollars a year. So, anyway, the campaign began with a huge ceremony in downtown Quito to which President Gutierrez arrived, yes, you guessed it, forty-five minutes late!"

We both laughed.

"And, I should remind you, that's a true story," Adam added, pouring himself a cup of coffee and sitting down across from me.

"So, tell me Michael, where do you think this thing with Carolina is heading? I have to admit in all honesty she's an incredibly intriguing woman."

"Where can it go?" I answered with a sigh. "I'll be returning to New York sometime in the next week or so; I can't just hang out here indefinitely."

"What do you have to rush back to," Adam asked, surprising me a little by his question. "It's not like you have a job or a girlfriend waiting for you, and Carolina seems anxious enough for you to stay. So, why not stay around for at least a little while longer?"

"Look, you said it yourself, Adam, I'm an American, I don't speak a word of Spanish, I don't have a job and this girl's father may well become Ecuador's next president. And, even if he doesn't become president, he'll still be very careful about the men his daughter is seen with. Ironically, I think he likes me personally, he even likes my Swedish heritage for some reason, it's just all the other stuff he probably won't accept."

"You're probably right, but all I'm suggesting is for you not to be so quick in making assumptions about your future, or hers for that matter. She clearly thinks for herself, which for down here is highly unusual. Anyway, you'd better be off, it's eight thirty. Have a great time and say 'hello' to her for me. After all, Michael, if you return to New York that leaves the way open for me. Hey, hey, I'm kidding, OK?"

I had to wonder if he was. But, either way, his comment really annoyed me.

Though I had ridden down through Guapolo on a couple of occasions, this was the first time I was the one actually doing the driving. The road seemed so much narrower that I remembered and I found myself driving very slowly, too slowly, in fact, for the driver directly behind me who honked repeatedly, tailgated me, then swung past me on a curve and gave me the finger; I got the hint. Part of my problem was that I was unaccustomed to driving such a huge car. And, then, when I met an equally huge car coming towards me the road seemed far too narrow for us to pass without side-swiping one another. But, none of this prepared me for what was to happen next. Rounding a particularly sharp curve I suddenly found myself confronting a cow, a black and white cow standing directly in the middle of the road. Slamming on my brakes I screeched to a halt no more than ten feet from it. While I sat there momentarily shaken from the near collision, the cow simply looked at me as if to ask what on earth I was doing on this road. Its owner obviously let it wander freely foraging for whatever grass it could find, which judging from its gaunt appearance could not have been much. Finally, it must have dawned on the cow that I was not going to move, so it wandered slowly over to the edge of the road. I quickly stepped on the gas to get out of there before another car came racing around the corner and rear-ended me.

To my relief the remainder of the trip down to Cumbaya went without incident. I was even able to follow Carolina's directions without difficulty. As I was nearing the turnoff to her house, I suddenly realized one of the landmarks she had listed was the German School. And, there it was on my right; it was also the answer to my problem. There had to be any number of teachers at the German School who could read German script. All I'd have to do is call the school, I'd do it on Monday, and ask for a name; I could do that on my own without having to ask Adam or Carolina for help. What an unexpected break. This really was going to make things easier, for everyone.

Following her directions I turned left past the school and onto a cobblestone roadway. The stones were surprisingly large and very uneven causing the Montero to bounce wildly. Along both sides of the roadway ran high yellow-stucco walls covered with brightly colored hibiscus blossoms. Where there were breaks in the vegetative cover jagged shards of glass could be seen inserted into the top of the wall to discourage would-be intruders from climbing over. And, if the wall were not security enough, just ahead I saw a metal gate blocking my way along with a couple of uniformed guards.

As I came to a stop and rolled down my window, one of the men came over to ask where I was going. I didn't really understand him, of course, but what else would he be asking me. When I mentioned the Mayers' name, it had an instantaneous effect. Politely, he asked for my name and went back inside the small guardhouse to call for confirmation. In almost no time the gate slid open and I was beckoned to pass through. A few seconds later as I rounded the final corner indicated in Carolina's directions I spotted her house at the end of a cul-de-sac. There was one more gate but this one was already open and the security guard was waving me on obviously having been informed of my approach.

Passing through the gate I spotted a silver-gray Mercedes sedan parked directly in front of the house and pulled up behind it. A short distance in front of the Mercedes was a four-car garage, two bays of which were open to reveal a silver-gray Honda Pilot and a black Isuzu Trooper. The house was built along traditional Spanish lines--single-story, white-stucco, with a veranda that extended the entire length. There were flowers everywhere, as well as black wrought iron; there were wrought-iron railings and wrought-iron gratings over the windows. The front door was made of some thick, dark wood the finish of which blended perfectly with the flooring of the veranda. It was certainly beautiful, the kind of place that back in the States would be featured in some home-and-country magazine, and yet, thinking back on Adam's comments about the father's wealth, I would have expected something far larger, more ostentatious.

As I was about to get out of Adam's car, a huge dark-haired German shepherd bounded around the corner of the house and rushed towards me. It didn't bark but the look it gave me was hardly friendly. I decided to wait for help, which didn't take long in coming as I saw Carolina step out onto the porch and yell to the dog.

"Bismarck, come over here!"

Bismarck minded instantly and trotted over to her with his tail wagging; she scratched his head and ordered him into the house. He went but reluctantly so. I suspected he was disappointed he had not been allowed to have me for breakfast.

At long last, I was able to devote my full attention to Carolina; she looked great! She was wearing a pair of navy blue slacks and a yellow v-neck sweater that did nothing to hide her ample breasts. It would be a few minutes more before I noticed her silver necklace matched her earrings.

"Somehow I knew you'd be right on time," she laughed, extending her hands to me and offering me her cheek.

"I probably shouldn't be telling you this," I whispered, "but I had to drive slowly just so I wouldn't be early; didn't want to appear too eager."

Carolina seemed delighted with my response. I had the feeling people tended not to flirt or joke with her, probably because of her family's position in the society here, yet she obviously enjoyed it.

"Come in, my father would like to say hello again. I really wish you could meet my mother but she's in bed and doesn't feel up to meeting anyone right now. I'll be right back, I'm going to tell my father you're here."

Once inside I quickly realized the outside of the house did not do justice to the interior. In the first place, it was ever so much larger than it initially appeared for the house was in reality u-shaped with two wings extending diagonally outward from the back of the house. Between these wings was a huge swimming pool with an equally large patio area containing wicker chairs, tables, sofas, as well as a very modern-looking gas grille. And, out beyond the swimming pool I could see a tennis court that even included a backboard and rim. While I couldn't quite imagine the father playing basketball, I could at least understand why he had such a good suntan. Carolina, on the other hand, either spent little time by the pool or, if she did, was very careful not to get much sun.

My attention was so focused on the pool that several seconds went by before I even noticed the interior of the house. The floors were a brilliantly polished hardwood and largely devoid of rugs. Of course, I said to myself, I'd never cover my floors with rugs either if I had maids to clean and wax them all day. And, then, the walls, they were adorned with oil paintings of all sizes, many of which looked to be antique. To the right of where I stood was a huge dining room that could probably seat thirty people while to my left was the living room; whoever furnished them, I decided, had exquisite taste.

Carolina suddenly appeared next to me. "He'll be right along," she announced, touching my arm lightly. "Lord knows what he may say; he still treats me at times like I'm a little girl."

"Well, aren't you," her father asked, advancing towards us through the living room.

"See what I mean," she responded, rolling her eyes.

"Michael, good to see you again," her father said, extending his hand. He was dressed casually in gray slacks, an open collared white shirt and black loafers. I had to admit he was a handsome man and though I had never seen her mother, I suspected Carolina took after her father.

"I hope you've been enjoying your stay in Ecuador," Carolina's father continued. "I've traveled to many parts of the world but I've yet to find any place more beautiful."

"I sorry to say I haven't seen much of your country, that's why I've been so looking forward to visiting Otavalo. It'll actually be my first trip outside of Quito, other than coming down here."

"Well, then, I hope the two of you have a good time. There is one thing though."

I could tell by Carolina's expression she was thinking, "Here we go again."

"I'm going to have a couple of my security people follow you. I know Carolina hates it, but I'm afraid it's necessary. The route north to Otavalo goes through some pretty desolate country. I don't know if you're aware of it, Michael, but there are more kidnappings in Latin America every year than any place on this earth. And, at least here in Ecuador, few suspects ever get caught, in large part because the police are often working with the kidnappers. So, I'm sorry but I must insist. I will promise to have them stay well back; you won't even know they're there."

Oddly, I felt reassured by the knowledge we'd have a security detail. In my excitement to spend a day with Carolina I'd almost forgotten about Francisco's murder.

"Just once I'd like to go somewhere without them," Carolina grumbled.

But, I could tell she was resigned to it. She'd probably had to put up with them all her life.

"You won't even see them. Just go about your day as if they're not there," he said soothingly. But then he made a request I thought strange.

"Michael, my security people just informed me you have diplomatic plates on your vehicle. Those plates will draw unnecessary attention to the two of you, especially outside of Quito. Why don't you use Carolina's car instead; it's the Honda Pilot you probably saw in the garage. At least that way you'll end up being a little less conspicuous."

I thought it strange only because of what Adam had told me about the plates, that people are less apt to steal diplomats' cars because they don't want the extra hassle that goes with it. But, after a second, it dawned on me; he had probably installed a device on her car that allowed his security people to know her whereabouts at any moment. It was a good idea; I'd have done the same thing in his situation.

"No problem with me," I replied.

If Carolina were annoyed she said nothing. I, on the other hand, was feeling just a little bit relieved after her father's comments.

Twelve

The first few minutes of our trip to Otavalo was anything but exciting as our route took us through a series of small nondescript villages with such heavily congested streets I had to drive incredibly slowly so as not to hit a pedestrian or animal of some kind. But, soon enough the landscape changed, becoming more rural. The economy here had clearly once been dominated by dairy farming; the evidence was everywhere in the form of abandoned barns and poorly maintained fences and stonewalls. Now, however, the fields were covered with huge plastic-sheeted hothouses, acres of them.

"I assume they grow flowers in those things, or is it vegetables," I asked.

"Flowers, and especially roses, which are sold all over the world. Quito is the rose capital of the world, I bet you didn't know that," Carolina explained, like the teacher she was.

"No, I didn't. And, I was good in geography, too. But, I think I was taught that bananas were Ecuador's major export."

"They are," she replied, "but flowers are really important, too. My father actually owns a farm out here. Anyway, the next time you buy roses for someone when you're back in New York, check to see where they come from; I'll bet they come from Ecuador."

I wasn't exactly sure what she was implying with her comment but I had to admit it stung a little. The last thing I wanted to be reminded of was that very soon I'd be returning to the States. For just this one day I wanted to pretend I would be here forever.

Carolina must have realized she'd struck a raw nerve for she quickly changed the subject.

"The countryside will become more beautiful up ahead, I promise," she said, briefly touching my arm. It was a sweet gesture and I needed it at that point.

"This market or fair we're going to, do Ecuadorians go or is it mostly for tourists," I asked, wanting to keep the conversation away from my return to New York.

"Oh, no, there will be lots of Ecuadorians there," she replied. "But it's also a favorite destination for tour groups; you'll see plenty of busses there. The Otavaleños, as they are called, are a fascinating people. First, of all they are world famous for their textile weaving skills and just about everything sold at this market they will have made themselves from the wool of their own llamas and sheep. They're entrepreneurs unlike any other indigenous group in Ecuador and the most prosperous, too. Yet, what makes them unique is that even with all their success they've managed to maintain their ethnic identity. Many Otavaleños still speak their native Quichua and wear the traditional dress, even those who are well educated. You'll quickly learn to recognize them. The men typically have long, braided hair and wear calf-length white pants. You won't have trouble recognizing the women either since they'll be about the only indigenous woman there. They'll be wearing these beautifully embroidered blouses, which they tend to adorn with numerous beaded necklaces. You're really going to love the place, I guarantee it."

"I'm looking forward to it; it's really my first opportunity to see something of your country. And, there's so little traffic. Now, if we were back in New York, the roads leading out of the city would be packed bumper-to-bumper on a beautiful Saturday morning like this. Not that I'm not complaining, mind you."

What I neglected to mention was why, with so few cars on the road, I couldn't see the security detail that was supposed to be following us. These guys were either really good at their job, or at the last moment the father had decided not to send them; I decided it was probably the former.

We continued to drive north, making small-talk as we went: she asked my opinion of Ecuador, how I spent my time, what Adam's apartment was like; I asked about her teaching at the university and her father's political campaign. We were both careful, staying away from topics that we thought the other might feel too personal. I also had to focus more on my driving as the road had now become a series of steep uphill climbs followed almost immediately by sharp curving descents. The scenery, when I could take my eyes off the road long enough to notice, was really quite spectacular.

The surrounding hillsides had been cleared of all woodland over the years; this was now dairy country and there were herds of cows everywhere one looked. Beyond these hills, at a considerable distance away, could be seen a higher range of mountains whose snow covered peaks seemed to glisten in the light of the morning sun.

"So, why don't you tell me about your research with the indigenous peoples," I asked. "The little bit you've told me sounds fascinating."

"Are you sure you want to hear about it? I warn you, once I get going, I can talk for hours."

I could tell she was delighted I had asked about her work. I suspected once again that in her world people were so into her father and his political campaign that there was little time for her, which was a shame since to me, at least, she appeared to be a far more interesting personality.

"I'll give you a just the briefest synopsis of my research, I promise. As you already know there are several indigenous peoples who inhabit the Ecuadorian Amazon. The principal groups are the Hourani, the Schuar, the Ashuar, the Siona and the Cofan, although there are others. In total these groups number only about ten thousand, their populations having been decimated over the years by contact with the Europeans who brought the usual deadly diseases: malaria, measles, tuberculosis. Today, however, the greatest threat to these peoples is posed by the oil companies, which have invaded their ancestral lands with their network of roads, pumping stations, and pipelines. Not only has the oil industry caused serious environmental damage it has all but destroyed the social cohesion of these communities as well. Are you still with me, or have I lost you completely," she laughed.

"No, go on, please, I'm listening," I replied. "I just have to keep my eyes on the road since I'm not familiar with it. But, I find what you're telling me completely fascinating. It's all so totally different from anything I've ever done, which I'm embarrassed to say is not very much."

"I'm sure that's not true but let me just quickly finish. From the beginning my research has focused on the Cofan peoples who live in northeastern Ecuador along the Colombian border. In fact, I did my Master's thesis at the University of Texas on the Cofan. Unfortunately, there are only about seven hundred living in Ecuador today with perhaps another eight hundred in Colombia so their future is precarious; three centuries ago they probably numbered fifteen thousand. The Cofan peoples have probably been impacted by the oil industry more than any other group. They suffered horribly from oil spills, gas flaring, and the dumping of untreated wastes into their water supplies. In fact, a lawsuit was brought against Texaco, the original developer of the oil field, fifteen years ago asking for damages of twenty-seven billion dollars. Imagine that, twenty-seven billion! You've probably heard about it since it's received so much publicity though today Chevron is the company being sued since they recently bought out Texaco. I often wonder if the Cofan will ever see one cent of that money; the lawyers will probably get most of it. Anyway, to wind up my lecture, the Ecuadorian government has recently set up what they call Zonas Intangibles as a way of trying to protect these people. No human activity that may harm these people is permitted in these zones. The Cofan are presently in control of almost four thousand square kilometers, which may seem like a lot but it's really not for a people who hunt, fish and gather most of their food. The real problem, of course, has been keeping timber and mining companies from trespassing on their lands. My research has focused on how the Cofan society has been adjusting to these traumatic changes to their existence. But, that's it for now; we're almost at Otavalo."

"That was fascinating, Carolina, and I mean that honestly. You know, I envy you your work and I'm not saying that simply to flatter you. It's just I've never met anyone who possesses so much passion for her work."

"Oh, thank you, Michael, that's probably the most beautiful compliment I've ever received for my work."

Just then the road abruptly began to descend in a long sweeping curve and a few seconds later we were entering a broad valley across whose floor sprawled the town of Otavalo.

"Now, Otavalo may not be one of Ecuador's most elegant towns but its location is spectacular," Carolina declared. "Look around; this valley is surrounded by a series of volcanoes, though two are particularly important to the region's indigenous peoples, that one which they refer to as Mama Cotacachi, and the one over there they call Tatia Imbabura, or Father Imbabura. In legend Mama Cotacachi was a young white-skinned woman with blonde-blonde hair. Cotacachi, by the way, was snow-capped until a few years ago when the last remnants of the glacier melted away. Anyway, Mama Cotacachi is said to have seduced Imbabura into marrying her, making him give up his adulterous ways; together they now protect the valley's inhabitants. And, on any morning that snow can be seen on Cotacachi, that's taken as a sign that Father Imbabura visited Mama Cotacachi during the night. Isn't that a wonderful story?"

"It certainly is," I replied, thankful to be in the company of such a delightful and attractive storyteller.

For a moment she seemed to be reading my thoughts until suddenly she pointed to a narrow street on our right. "You'll want to take that one and stay right on it for four or five blocks; then we can start looking for a parking place."

The town was mobbed with people; cars were parked along both sides and the sidewalks were so crowded that many pedestrians had little choice but to walk in the street. I inched along doing my best not to hit anyone. Finally, I saw a sign for public parking written in English, a sure indication tourists were welcome. We parked Carolina's car, locked it and set off for the market. I had yet to see any indication we were being followed by a security detail, although at this point there were so many people moving about the streets we wouldn't have noticed it anyway.

"So, what do you think," Carolina asked as we entered the plaza where the market was being held.

"Amazing," I responded, overwhelmed for the moment by the sheer size of the place.

The plaza was absolutely crammed with stalls selling just about every imaginable item: hand-woven sweaters, hats, ponchos, gold and silver jewelry, beaded necklaces and bracelets, stone carvings, wooden musical instruments, leather goods, and indigenous art reflecting local landscapes and animal life. The narrow passageways between the stalls were likewise crowded with tourists and I found myself constantly brushing against Carolina. While she didn't react, neither did she move away.

"Where do all these people come from," I asked, as we squeezed through one more group of people. "They can't all be tourists."

"On Saturdays people come from all over," she explained. "Many of them are from Colombia; the border is only a few miles north of here. And then, there are a great many tourists. If you listen carefully you can hear all kinds of languages being spoken."

When I stopped for a second to look at some exquisite woolen tapestries, Carolina leaned towards me.

"Now, remember," she whispered, "if you ask the price of something you like that doesn't have a tag, it will probably be higher than what the person is expecting to sell it for; they expect, even want you to negotiate with them. Europeans always try to get them to lower their prices, but Americans for some reason feel guilty about doing so, like you'd be taking advantage of them, am I right?

"I don't know. It's probably more that Americans just don't want to be bothered. We tend to be a very impatient people even, for example, when we come down here on vacation. I've already seen Americans impatient that everyone doesn't speak English or that the service in a restaurant isn't fast enough. We can be incredibly inconsiderate and rude; it's why so many people love the idea of America while not always pleased with Americans."

"I think you're being a little hard on your countrymen and I'm not really sure I agree with you but we can talk about it later; right now I want to show you something."

She grabbed my hand and pulled me over to a stall selling Panama hats. She picked one up and carefully placed it on my head.

"This hat is definitely you. You look great in it, may I buy it for you," she asked, with that demure smile of hers.

"I know you haven't really known me for very long but have you ever seen me wear a hat? I don't even wear a baseball hat, which in the US is almost sacrilegious. So, no, please don't buy me one; it will truly be a waste of money, though I thank you for the thought."

As we moved on I hoped she wasn't offended. Fortunately, it seemed that she wasn't as she'd already gone back to explaining how the different items being sold were made or what their significance was. Before long we came upon a group of indigenous women sitting in a circle talking animatedly as they ate their lunch.

"They're definitely Otavaleños," she observed, stopping to watch them. "Notice how dark-skinned they are. And the way they're dressed with all the necklaces and the embroidered blouses and black shawls. Many of the younger women today dress in jeans and sneakers, but I must admit, I much prefer seeing them dress like this. So many of the indigenous cultures of this country are being lost; it's really sad."

"Like that woman over there," I nodded in the direction of a woman in traditional dress. "She's probably speaking with her stockbroker."

Carolina glanced over at her and smiled sadly. The woman was talking animatedly on a bright, red cell-phone.

"For all I realize they must accommodate themselves to life in the twenty-first century," Carolina remarked, "it pains me to see how that accommodation dilutes their culture. On the other hand, I also realize it's presumptuous of me to expect them to retain their way-of-life untouched by modernization just for the sake of anthropologists like me, who by the way, live very affluent and twenty-first century lives."

I couldn't think of an appropriate response so we continued walking silently with only the vendors calling to us or stepping out to show us some particular item. I began to feel just a bit guilty about not buying anything; most of the other tourists appeared to be loading up with hats and sweaters and ponchos. I had just made up my mind to buy something when we approached a young man selling paintings of different kinds of humming birds. I was particularly drawn to one and announced to Carolina I wanted to buy it. Immediately she said something the guy, then explained he wanted eight dollars for it; I had no idea what he was originally asking but I'm sure she had him come down on the price. I wished she hadn't done that but I had to admit the painting was gorgeous.

While I was waiting for the painting to be wrapped I lost track of Carolina; I assumed she was right behind me. But, when the painting was ready, and I had paid the young man, she was not to be seen. Finally, I spotted her a short distance away talking with two men whom she clearly knew. My first reaction was to be annoyed but after a moment I concluded they were probably the two security guys whose job it was to look after her. When she saw me looking she said something to them and headed back in my direction; the two men simply melted back into the crowd. "They just wanted to know what our plans were, whether we intended to go directly back to Quito from here," she reported, though with a mischievous smile that made me wonder what was on her mind.

"We are, right," I asked, as naïve as ever.

"We are what," she asked coyly.

"We are going back to Quito?"

But there was just something about her smile that told me we weren't.

Thirteen

I couldn't believe how excited I felt when she informed me we would not be returning to Quito but instead would be continuing north to the town of Cotacachi.

"It has the most marvelous leather stores there," she explained, as if it were necessary to convince me to go. "In fact, that's about the only thing you can buy in the town. But, there is one other thing there, an incredible restaurant called La Mirage, and that's where we're going to have lunch. I hope you're hungry."

"I'm starved," I replied, frankly happy to be moving on. I loved walking about the market but there was a limit, especially since I had no intention of buying anything else. I had always been a terrible window shopper. I could only assume it was much the same for her since she had probably been to the fair so often.

When finally we got back to the car and began making our way slowly out of Otavalo, Carolina apologized, saying, "This has probably felt like a school fieldtrip. All I've been doing is telling you about my research and explaining to you what we've been seeing as we drive along. It must all be so terribly boring. I promise lunch will be very different."

She had an almost sad expression on her face at the moment. I wanted so badly to kiss her.

"I honestly hope you're kidding," I replied. "You can't possibly imagine how much I love listening to you talk about your country; I actually feel a little embarrassed that I know so little about it. Coming from New England, we've always been so European oriented. In school we typically studied European history, we learned French for a language, and as for my classmates they were typically Irish or Italian or German. It's not like we don't get news about what's going on down here, it's just that we've grown up hearing more about events occurring in Europe or even Asia than Latin America. It's clearly beginning to change, however. I suppose it has to since the number of Hispanics in the US is growing rapidly. I think now they're our largest minority; they even outnumber African-Americans."

"I'm well aware of that," she replied. "I spent a year and a half in Texas remember. I heard so many people speaking Spanish it was hard to believe I was in the United States."

The drive north to the small town of Cotacachi was not as long as the trip to Otavalo, though we still had plenty of time to talk. At one point something must have been said that reminded me I still hadn't done anything about the diary.

"Is there a large German-speaking community in Ecuador," I suddenly found myself asking.

I realized it was a strange question given the nature of our conversation, and she must have thought the same thing.

"Why do you ask that," she responded, giving me a quizzical look.

"I don't know," I replied, desperately trying to come up with a plausible answer. I had absolutely no intention of telling her anything about the diary. "I guess it was something your father said when we met at the American Embassy. He asked if my name was German and then said something about how unfortunate it was that to become an American one had to lose his language or culture or something like that."

"Oh, that; you have to understand my father is very proud of his German ancestry and, by the way, it's a very sensitive issue with him and something you should be conscious of. I think it originates from the fact that here in Ecuador many people just automatically equate being German with being Jewish since most Jews here either came directly from Germany during the Nazi era, or at least, their parents did. It's all very innocent; Ecuadorians are not in the least anti-Semitic. But, in a political campaign rumors abound and one such rumor has it that my father is Jewish and that he's chosen to hide it in order to enhance his chances of being elected president. Well, anyway, this rumor has infuriated him and he's unfortunately made a big issue of it. He's even gone so far as publicly claim that there isn't an ounce of Jewish blood in our family. Now, would you like to know what's so ironic about all of this? And by the way, it's something that I doubt even my father is aware of? According to my mother, some of our Spanish ancestors were Jewish."

Yes, how ironic, I thought to myself. First, it was Rachel, whom my mother never approved of because she was Jewish, and now Carolina; fortunately, Carolina had at least been raised Catholic, though that probably wouldn't mollify my mother very much either.

"And, I gather, none of this bothers you," I inquired, then quickly added, "about your father's reaction, I mean."

"I've become used to it," she replied matter-of-factly. "Though to be honest I don't understand why it bothers him quite so much. I mean we're Ecuadorian, not German, though he doesn't seem to think so, even though he's running for the presidency of this country. And, I've heard him make comments that are clearly anti-Semitic. I don't know why he does it and I've picked him up on it. I guess once again he thinks it will help him politically though I've reminded him that it's not really going to help much since Ecuadorians are not particularly anti-Semitic. As a matter of fact they welcomed Jews fleeing Nazi persecution during the war so all it's really done is make certain he'll never get a vote out of the Jewish community."

"Well, I can't believe that will matter much; there can't be that many Jews in Ecuador," I responded.

"The number of Jews living in this country may be small but politically they're a very influential group," she said. "The funny thing is, if it were not for my father's anti-Semitism, they would probably support him enthusiastically since they share many of his views on the economy. I honestly don't understand my father at times; we can look at the same world yet see it so incredibly differently."

She said these things almost wistfully.

I was touched that she had confided this to me. Still, this intimacy made me feel a little uncomfortable and I had already decided to change the topic, when she announced we were there.

The outskirts of the town had the same dusty, empty feeling I had experienced passing through similar sized places on the way to Otavalo. But when we reached the center of Cotacachi this all changed abruptly. The town's main street was jammed with automobiles and pedestrians; it was very much like Otavalo only there was only a tiny outdoor market here. Instead, there was a network of several streets filled almost entirely with stores selling leather goods, just as Carolina had said. Huge signs, jutting well out into the streets, advertised luggage, handbags, shoes, jackets, furniture, even saddles and riding tack.

"Keep on driving straight ahead," she directed. "We'll have lunch first, then we can stop and visit some of the stores on our way back."

"Sounds like a good plan to me," I replied, still concentrating on my driving. Fortunately, the road was one-way.

"Just up ahead we're going to be taking a left so slow down," she warned. "OK, take this next left."

We turned onto a narrow, bumpy roadway; it hardly looked like the kind of place where you'd find a good restaurant.

"Are you sure this is the way." I asked. "You have been here before?"

"Many times; it's a hotel, restaurant and spa; it has tennis courts, swimming pool, everything. I used to come here often with my parents, though with my mother so ill we don't get out much together anymore."

I was relieved at her response. For some strange reason I did not want to think she had come here with other men, though I knew she would never have said so anyway.

Just then I spotted a sign for Hosteria La Mirage and then the entrance, which was gated and had a security guard. As we pulled up, I lowered the window and Carolina leaned across to speak with the guard. A second later the gate slid open and we drove ahead into the parking area. There were perhaps a dozen cars there, several of which had diplomatic number plates.

"You see, there really is a restaurant here," she teased as I pulled into a parking space. "Come on, let's go in."

The restaurant had the look of a colonial hacienda a low, white-stucco structure with large picture windows that looked out over immaculately manicured lawns and lush colorful gardens. There were fountains, and even peacocks strolling about the grounds.

"It's owned by a French company," Carolina commented, when she noticed me admiring the grounds. "I'm sure that's the reason for the peacocks."

For a restaurant that advertised itself as a country inn, the interior was really quite luxurious. There were lots of yellows and beiges—drapes, tablecloths, the upholstery, all of which contrasted perfectly with the exposed woodwork of the ceilings and floor. It did have a French provincial feel to it, or at least it did to me, even though the waitresses scurrying about where dressed in traditional indigenous clothing.

No sooner had we sat down than a man, who had been sitting at a nearby table with his family, immediately arose and came over to our table. He greeted Carolina warmly and took my hand in a surprisingly firm grip when Carolina introduced us. The two spoke for a few moments in Spanish before he bid a hasty goodbye and returned to his family. As he sat down, his wife looked over at Carolina and gave her a big smile.

"He's a close friend and sort of a political advisor to my father. I've known them all my life; they're very nice," she said, acknowledging the wife with a casual wave.

"You know, one of the things I find interesting about Quito is that for a city of over a million people it seems almost like a small town."

"I suppose it is for the wealthy," Carolina replied, with just the tiniest edge to her voice. "If you have money, you live in the northern part of the city, Avenida Gonzalez Suarez, for example, where Adam has his apartment. The northern part's where all the expensive shopping malls are, the private schools, the country clubs like the Contado. To people like you and me the city of Quito ends at Mount Panecillo, with that ugly Soviet-looking statue, but for the poor that's where the city begins. Quito stretches for miles to the south and that's where most of the poor make their homes. Didn't you tell me that Adam has a maid?"

"Well, yes, he has someone who comes in a couple days a week to cook and clean," I answered, suspecting I knew where this conversation was going.

"Do you know where she lives," Carolina asked.

"No, I only know she has a long bus ride to get to work."

"Of course, because her home is in the south of the city. Anyway, I'm not trying to pick on Adam; I just get so frustrated with my country at times. The poverty here can be appalling. But, please, let's order; you must be famished."

The meal was delicious. We had several courses, each of which the waitresses served in large covered silver plates. And, something I had never seen before, small flags placed on each table reflecting the occupants' nationalities; we, of course, had flags representing Ecuador and the US. It was a nice touch; it also gave me the opportunity to see just how international the clientele was. There must have been a dozen different flags visible from where I was sitting.

When we had at last finished our dessert and the waitress brought out bill, Carolina reached for her handbag.

"No," I insisted, "I'm going to pay. I've been here nearly two weeks and I've spent almost nothing. Even Carlos, who owns the bar I go into now and then, refuses to let me pay. And, I'm the very last person in that place who needs a free beer."

"Well, that's Ecuador for you," Carolina said with a sigh, "the wealthy receive all the favors, and the poor end up having to pay for them, not that it's relevant in my case."

She did let me pick up the check and I assured her my doing so would not put me out on the street. I was hoping she realized I was kidding, though I couldn't be sure.

Before walking back to the car we took a long and leisurely stroll about the grounds. At some point I summoned up my courage and took her hand. She drew herself close to me and smiled. I suspected she had been waiting for me to do something like that. But ultimately the time came for us to head back to Quito. We decided not to stop in Cotacachi; it had been a long day and it was beginning to get dark. She scrunched herself over as close to me as possible but the gearshift between the seats didn't allow for much romance or comfort.

"Everyone talks about how great these big SUVs are, but I much prefer the old American cars with their huge front seats. The gearshift was on the steering post in those days, " I explained, "so there was nothing to prevent a girl from draping herself all over her boyfriend driving the car."

"So, those are what you refer to as the good old days?" she joked.

"Well, actually they were my parent's good old days, though to be honest, if you met them you'd probably find it difficult imagining what they must have been like as teenagers."

"Now why would you say such a thing; we all change as we get older," she replied in her delightfully scolding manner.

"Yah, you're probably right. I guess it's hard for anyone to picture their parents making out in a car, but really, my parents are such humorless people. They're so different from your father, for example; your father is such a charming, interesting guy. It's so easy to see why people might vote for him."

"Well, to you maybe, but there's a real question as to how well he'll do in the upcoming primary; he's going to need a lot of support from the indigenous population, which he may not get," she responded matter-of-factly.

"Adam tells me the American government certainly wants him to win," I replied, thinking I'd be cheering her up a little.

"Oh, I'm sure; he's the perfect candidate from the American viewpoint. He will make the country a better place in which to do business and thus encourage foreign investment; he will stop the process of nationalizing industries like the current president and, he won't default on legitimate debts the country owes. So, yes, the Americans will love him."

"But, I'm a little mystified; you don't exactly seem enthusiastic about all this," I remarked.

"Let me answer your question, but, then, let's not talk about it anymore tonight, is that all right," she asked.

"I promise."

"The reason so many left-wing candidates have been voted into office in Latin America of late is because they have promised to help the poor, especially the indigenous, who have been largely left out of their country's growing prosperity. They've probably gone too far but they've begun to make some progress. Unfortunately, their policies have alienated the foreign business community and international loan agencies, the groups who can help the most. Even worse, these same governments, in many cases, are not promoting education the way they should. I mean, making Quichua the national language of Bolivia, for example; that's what I mean about going too far. I worry about what will happen to the indigenous in this country under someone like my father; we look at the world so differently. I guess that's what comes from being an anthropologist; you understand better that most what it's like for people who have to straddle two totally dissimilar worlds. Sometimes, I think, I'd be happier if I were actually doing something for the indigenous peoples rather than just studying them."

"But, you are doing more than just studying them," I replied in all honestly. "Aren't you introducing these people to your students, who thanks to you, will grow up with a better appreciation of the indigenous peoples and with far less prejudice than their parents."

"Oh, I hope so, Michael, I really hope so. But, I also want you to know how much I appreciate what you've been saying about my work. I just can't thank you enough," she whispered, almost in tears.

By the time we had ended our discussion we were close to Quito. I assumed the security guys were behind us somewhere, but I had to admit, they had certainly been discreet. It was only after we had pulled up in front of her house that I finally noticed them as they drove in behind us.

"I had a really great time today, Carolina, thank you for everything. I'd love to be able to repay you somehow, perhaps with lunch? Unfortunately, we'll have to do it soon since I'm not sure how much longer I'll be staying here in Ecuador. For all Adam insists he doesn't mind having me around, I realize there's a limit."

"I had a wonderful time, too, Michael. I really enjoy being with you. You're the first person I've ever met with whom I feel totally comfortable. And, yes, let's have lunch," she responded eagerly. "How about Tuesday?"

"How about Monday," I shot back instantly. I tried to think if I'd ever felt so excited at the prospect of spending time with someone. I certainly couldn't remember experiencing anything like this with Rachel, though I supposed I must have. After all, I had been planning to marry her. But, Carolina, she was so much more fascinating than Rachel. Now, there's a word, I thought to myself; I never used the word fascinating to describe Rachel.

"Yes, Monday." She was looking at me strangely. It dawned on me I hadn't heard her the first time because of all things I had been thinking of Rachel.

"Terrific," I replied, feeling a little embarrassed. "So, can we go to lunch somewhere in Quito? Do you have a favorite restaurant?"

"As a matter of fact, I do and you'll love it too," she explained excitedly. "It's in the old part of Quito near the Presidential Palace. And, I'll tell you what I'll do; I'll drive up from Cumbaya and park in the Hotel Quito's lot; it's just down the street from your apartment. Then, we can take a taxi from there since there's not a lot of parking in the old city."

Reluctantly, we got out of her Honda and walked over to where Adam's car was parked. Opening the door I turned uncertain what more to say. Fortunately, she knew exactly what to do; she kissed me. And, it was no quick peck on the cheek but rather a long, delicious kiss on the mouth. Her lips were so warm and eager. Then, just as suddenly, she gave me one last kiss and hurried off in the direction of her house.

As she reached her front door she turned. "I'll meet you Monday at eleven," she mouthed. And with that she opened the door and disappeared.

Fourteen

When I shuffled into the kitchen on Sunday morning, Adam was sitting at the table reading the Miami *Herald*. Quickly putting it down, he nodded at the counter and said, "Grab yourself a cup of coffee and sit down; I want to hear all about your date with Carolina yesterday. The two of you amaze me; you meet once for no more than five minutes and wham, you're dating. Talk about chemistry. Thinking about it now, I can see that Carolina appears to have this chemical reaction on some people, of course, it's probably just plain sex appeal. And, it doesn't hurt that she also happens to be intelligent, attractive, charming and very, very wealthy. Naturally, that doesn't explain what she sees in you, but obviously she sees something. So, whatever it is you'd better take advantage of it and not let this woman get away. Let's be honest, Michael, what are the chances you'll ever meet another woman like her in this lifetime?"

"Were you just complimenting me or insulting me?" I laughed. But, while I suspected he might be right I also decided I should be very careful what I said about Carolina in front of him. I simply couldn't be certain he wouldn't repeat something I might say to him assuming it was only between the two of us. He wouldn't do it intentionally and it would probably be said in a joking manner, but nevertheless, it would come out. A perfect example was the whole thing with Atahualpa where he kept telling people I was down here to do research on him, though admittedly if he hadn't said that to Carolina I would never have had lunch with her at the university. Nevertheless, I decided I'd only tell him what we did, not what we talked about. That way there was little chance anything would get back that might embarrass her or me, especially since the chances of Adam running into her at some reception or dinner were fairly high.

"Well, let's see, I picked her up at her house, which by the way, was really nice as I guess you'd expect—swimming pool, tennis courts, riding stable. Now, I could get accustomed to living like that."

"Play your cards right," Adam replied with that ironic smile of his, "and you might very well just do that. I have a feeling Carolina is probably too sophisticated and, well, cerebral for most Ecuadorian men. As difficult as it is for me to say this, Michael, I think you'd be perfect for her."

"Thanks for the vote of confidence," I replied, "but I'm not sure Carolina's father feels that way about it. I've concluded he's very controlling individual. Do you know he insisted on having two of his security people follow us, though admittedly they weren't really visible most of the time? And, he also wouldn't let us go in your car; the diplomatic plates were too conspicuous, was what he said. So, we went in Carolina's Honda Pilot, a really nice car, by the way. I decided he probably had some kind of a homing device on the car so it would be easier for his security guards to keep track of us."

"I wouldn't have thought of that, but you're probably right. A man with his money has to be careful. There have been several well-publicized kidnappings of children, not necessarily young children, from wealthy families in the past few years and the families have ended up paying very substantial ransoms for their return. It's all very murky but it does seem that if you pay and don't go to the police, you get your family member back unharmed."

"Well, as funny as this sounds," I said, "I actually felt more relaxed knowing the security guards were in back of us somewhere. Of course, Carolina was not especially happy about them being there but I guess it's different when you have to put up with that kind of thing all the time."

"For the average American woman it would almost certainly cramp her style having two of her father's heavies always following her though show business personalities certainly have to do it. Down here it's a very different matter; young women don't have the same freedom American women have. Women here live at home until they marry; far different than in the States where they go away to college at seventeen and take an apartment on their own after they graduate. But, it's slowly beginning to change."

"So, anyway," I said, steering the conversation back to where we had started, "we drove to Otavalo and then walked around the market for, I don't know, maybe two or three hours. I really enjoyed it; there were so many beautiful things for sale. I suspect you've been there often enough you don't experience a feeling of guilt for not buying more. I did purchase two paintings of hummingbirds. And, by the way, that was the only time I actually saw our two babysitters; I guess they were just checking on our plans so they could keep out of the way. After Otavalo we drove north to Cotacachi, the leather place, where we had lunch at this incredible restaurant."

"Oh, sure, La Mirage; delightful place, isn't it?"

"Yes, it is, so I gather you've been there too," I replied, just a little annoyed. I would have preferred it, had he never been there, in which case it would have seemed just a little more special. That was one of the great drawbacks to having Adam for a friend; there were few things one could do that he hadn't already tried.

"In fact, I spent an entire weekend there once with a woman I began dating seriously when I first arrived here. Unfortunately, she got transferred to Honduras; that's kind of a long commute. We had a great time while it lasted, especially that weekend at La Mirage. The bedrooms are incredibly plush. You should think about going again and staying overnight."

Now, I felt even less like telling him about the day before. How could I hope to compete with his special weekend? Fortunately, the telephone rang and Adam went into the other room to get it. When he came back into the kitchen he mentioned casually he had a dinner date that night; that was her calling to confirm the time.

"So, this date tonight, is it with Jennifer Albright," I asked, anxious to see his reaction.

"Why on earth would you think that?" he responded, clearly surprised and now maybe he was a bit annoyed.

"Well, let's put it this way," I explained, happy to have gotten away from the topic of Carolina, "I believe you now, that you're not working down here for the CIA."

Adam looked at me strangely, having no idea at that moment to what I was referring.

"I saw you and Jennifer talking together at the reception where I first met Carolina, and if the two of you were trying to appear discreet, you failed miserably. Even the ambassador must realize the two of you are seeing each other," I joked, certain he wasn't concerned regardless of any rules forbidding such relationships.

"Yah, the American community is a small place and the next secret will be the first one. But, listen, I haven't been much of a host since you've been down here so what I'd like to do this afternoon is take you to a rather unusual museum. It's called the *Capilla del Hombre*, or The Chapel of Man. It was designed by Ecuador's most famous painter, Oswaldo Guayasamin, and includes many of his most controversial murals and paintings. Do you remember the Orozco murals in the basement of Baker Library back at Dartmouth? Well, his style is very similar; in fact, I think I read somewhere that he studied under Orozco in Mexico. So, what do you think, would you like to go?"

"Absolutely," I replied standing up. "Let me go take a quick shower and throw on some clothes."

Returning to my bedroom I was reminded of the papers I had hidden away. For some reason I checked just to be certain they were still there. Tomorrow I'd have to call the German School. But, no, there probably wouldn't be time; I was having lunch with Carolina. It would have to be Tuesday, but I couldn't put it off any longer than that. I had to find someone who could translate those pages; I should have done it already.

Walking towards the *Padilla del Hombre* I understood why Adam referred to the museum as unusual, that is, if he had been referring to the museum's exterior. The building was shaped like a truncated pyramid and made mostly of stone. On the roof was a cone, also truncated, that I would learn once inside was intended as a monument to the American man.

"Guayasamin designed the museum himself, if you were wondering who the architect was," Adam explained. "It's supposed to be one of the most unique designs in the world with its blend of modern and pre-Colombian architecture. Carolina can probably tell you a lot more about it than I can."

"It certainly is unusual; I've never seen anything quite like it even in New York which has more than its share of modern architecture."

"Up there," Adam explained, pointing to a large white-stucco house, "is where Guayasamin lived for at least some period of time. He's supposed to be buried there in one of the gardens or something. You know it was Dartmouth's own Nelson Rockefeller who helped introduce Guayasamin to the outside world. On one of his trips down here in the early 1940s he saw some of his work and was so impressed that he purchased a number of paintings and took them back to New York with him. He then not only arranged for Guayasamin to visit the United States but used his influence to have Guayasamin's work included in an exhibition of Latin American art at the Museum of Modern Art."

"Well, let's go in," I said excitedly. "I'm really looking forward to seeing his work, not to mention the interior of the museum."

"Let me warn you though, he has always been highly controversial. He was commissioned to do an enormous mural for the auditorium where the Ecuadorian Congress meets; you really have to see it. Guayasamin meant it to portray the various periods of this country's history. In one of the panels he painted a skeleton wearing a Nazi helmet with the letters "CIA" written across it. I think this all happened during the Reagan Administration so you can just imagine the reaction from Washington. They put incredible pressure on the government here to have the "CIA" removed from the helmet, but it's still there. On the other hand, he was never again allowed to visit the US."

We entered a vast room with gleaming hardwood floors and cream-colored walls covered with large murals. In the center of the museum was a circular polished railing that surrounded an opening in the floor. On the lower level directly below was an eternal flame burning, which according to Adam was in honor of human rights. I was already impressed and I hadn't even begun to examine Guayasamin's paintings or his sculptures.

Adam was right when he had said there was a Picasso quality to his paintings. They were brightly colored, portraying twisted arms and faces that were meant to reflect the pain and misery suffered by the Andean peoples over the centuries. Looking at them I certainly wouldn't call them beautiful; in fact, if I had to come up with one word to describe them, I decided, it would be "disturbing." But, then, that was probably what Guayasamin was trying to do through his work—disturb, provoke, cause one to remember, to think. Staring at some of his larger murals I couldn't help wondering what had been going through his mind as he painted them.

Since Adam had visited the museum before, he let me roam about on my own only occasionally coming over to exchange impressions on some painting or sculpture. Though the museum was not that extensive Adam and I spent nearly three hours there.

One thing about Guayasamin's work, it was not easy to forget. I continued to think about several of his murals on the ride back to the apartment and it wasn't until we were entering the garage that it dawned on me I hadn't said a word to Adam. I liked that about him; he never felt it necessary to constantly carry on a conversation when we were around the apartment. If we had something to say we talked, if not we did our own thing, which in Adam's case was often work he brought home from the embassy.

"That was great! I really want to thank you for suggesting we go to the museum," I said to Adam as we were riding up the elevator. "I honestly can't remember enjoying an art gallery more, and I've been to most of the galleries in New York. In fact, I definitely want to buy something of his to take back with me."

"What you should do then is visit the Guayasamin Museum," Adam suggested. "It isn't far from here. I think they have a much better selection of his work, including some of his still life pieces; they'd be more appropriate to display in a living room or study than the tortured looking paintings displayed at the Capilla del Hombre."

"Good idea," I replied. "I should probably begin doing some of these things before it gets too late. I can't stay here much longer; I do have to resume my life sometime."

We entered the apartment and closed the door behind us.

"If you ask me, Carolina would be the perfect way to resume your new life," Adam laughed. "I'm even a bit envious. I know I've said it before, but she really is an incredible woman."

Coming from Adam that was quite a compliment, but it also made me a little nervous. I honestly wouldn't put it past Adam to make a move on Carolina if I were back in New York.

"Well, I've got to go change. It's an early dinner night; we're going to a movie afterwards. Are you going to be all right? I'm sure Consuelo has left plenty of food in the refrigerator."

"No problem, I'll find something," I replied. "I'm not that hungry anyway, or at least not right now."

When Adam left to get ready for his date, I checked my email. No message from Carolina. I don't know why I thought she'd write; I guess I was just hoping she'd been as excited to have seen me again as I had been to see her. For some reason my mind drifted to her security guards, and I concluded I didn't like them; I didn't like the fact they were always following her. How did she put up with it? Of course, plenty of people in the States had them. And, then, there were the paparazzi, whose only job appeared to be to make life nearly impossible for media stars; no wonder they occasionally took a swing at one of them. Carolina's guards at least looked after her, but for some reason there was something about them that made me uncomfortable. I suspected they wouldn't hesitate to play rough if it became necessary.

Fifteen

Promptly at eleven I spotted Carolina's silver Honda Pilot rounding the corner adjacent to the American ambassador's residence and come racing down Avenida Orellana. It took only a few seconds more before she was pulling up to the entrance of the Hotel Quito's parking lot where I stood waiting for her in the bright sunshine.

"Hop in," she laughed. "I'll drive you to my parking spot."

I climbed into the passenger seat leaning over as I did so to give her a quick kiss. I couldn't tell if it was her perfume or her shampoo but whatever it was it smelled delicious.

She drove forward about twenty feet and pulled into an empty parking space.

"So what do you think of my driving," she asked jokingly.

"It's like everything you do, perfect," I replied, realizing instantly how corny I must have sounded, but fortunately, even if it did, she accepted it graciously and with that beautiful smile of hers.

When she slipped out from behind the steering wheel, I had my first chance to take a good look at her. She was stunning, appearing both casual and elegant at the same time. Thankfully, I had chosen to wear my trusty blue blazer and a necktie though it was still inadequate. Carolina had on a chic wrap-around dress with a tiny collar; it was beige in color and contrasted beautifully with her dark hair. To this she had added a wide brown belt and stylish sandals along with a simple silver necklace from which hung a teardrop-shaped black stone of some kind, and dark glasses. As we walked towards the line of yellow taxis drawn up in front of the hotel, I couldn't help but notice several men turn to admire her as she passed, though they were very careful not to make comments like many

Ecuadorian men when attractive women strolled by. I wondered if they recognized who she was; if nothing else they could obviously tell she came from money.

Opening the back door of the taxi I stepped back to let Carolina climb in, then, followed her. The backseat turned out to be so cramped there was barely enough room for my feet. As we settled in, Carolina leaned forward and asked the driver to take us to Independence Plaza. The driver, an older man with a dark leathery face, didn't immediately pull away from the curb but proceeded to explain something to her that I couldn't understand. When finally he pulled the taxi into the street and headed in the direction of the Old City, I asked Carolina what he had said.

"He was telling me he won't be able to drive us all the way to the Plaza. Apparently there's supposed to be a demonstration in front of the Presidential Palace today so the police have closed the streets leading directly to the Plaza. He'll drop us a couple of blocks away and we'll have to walk from there."

"So, do you think it's safe to go there," I asked, wondering if it might be just a little dangerous. The demonstrations shown on television had inevitably been violent though I realized that was exactly the reason they were being showed.

"Michael," she replied, taking my hand in hers, "we have demonstrations somewhere in this country literally every week; after a while you just get used to them. You certainly don't change your plans for them; you just have to be careful."

"OK, so what is the demonstration about," I asked, resigned to our going ahead to the Plaza.

Carolina leaned forward again and said something to the driver. He did not answer immediately possibly trying to decide who we were. Again, I wondered if he might recognize Carolina. But, just then he began to talk and he quickly got into it. Clearly, it was an issue that he felt quite strongly about.

"The government has decided to increase bus fares; it's something that's been talked about for months. However, it's mostly the poorer people who depend upon busses for getting to work, so they're the ones primarily impacted by any increase. No one in this country who could afford otherwise would ever be caught riding a bus. Anyway, the demonstration today is meant to convince the president either to cancel the proposed increase outright or at a minimum to postpone implementing it to some later date."

As the taxi made its way through the now narrow, congested streets of the Old City, Carolina and I held hands; at one point she even leaned her head on my shoulder. Gradually, the traffic became heavier and slower, to the point where both of us realized it would be quicker to walk. It was just that neither of us wanted to leave the intimacy of the taxi. Finally, the driver turned and spoke to Carolina.

"He said the traffic was from the roadblocks put up by the police and it was only going to get worse from here on so we should probably get out and walk."

"Fine with me," I replied, looking into Carolina's beautiful eyes. I was feeling so excited, so energized—being in Quito, driving to the Old City, the prospect of lunch at Carolina's favorite restaurant, and most of all, just being with Carolina.

"How much do we owe him," I asked, digging my wallet out of my back pocket.

"The meter says two seventy-five so three dollars will be fine."

I handed him three ones wondering why these guys weren't going up on their fares. When I mentioned it to Carolina she simply said people wouldn't pay more. I didn't argue but it certainly seemed to me they would. On the other hand, if people were prepared to demonstrate against increases in bus fares, they'd probably do the same for any proposed increases in taxi fares.

We walked hurriedly along the crowded sidewalks still holding hands. We passed dozens of small stores, their wares spilling out onto the sidewalks making for even more congestion. The atmosphere was almost carnival-like with vendors hawking their wares while shoppers haggled loudly over the prices of things; clearly the demonstration had not started yet. While we were still two or three blocks from the Plaza we came upon our first barricade manned by half a dozen police dressed in black-and-gray camouflage outfits and heavily armed. They were redirecting all busses and cars away from the Plaza though they were allowing pedestrians to pass unimpeded, which made me wonder why they were bothering. Wouldn't the demonstrators be coming by foot anyway?

We kept walking, weaving our way through the ever-growing throng. Suddenly, we rounded a corner and there was the Plaza.

"So, what do you think," Carolina asked with that curious smile of hers.

"I'm impressed," I replied, admiring the large palm-studded square.

Independence Plaza must have been at least an acre in size and was crisscrossed with a series of walkways that wound past statues, water fountains, raised flower gardens and benches, which even at this hour were filled with Ecuadorians apparently unconcerned about the upcoming protest. But, what impressed me the most was how clean and well maintained everything appeared. It was only now, however, I became aware of a large number of heavily armed police scattered about in groups of eight or ten.

Carolina, observing my obvious concern at the presence of so many riot police, gripped my hand more tightly and said, "Just ignore them, Michael; they won't bother us. And, look at it this way, you don't have to worry about having your pocket picked."

"No, your right," I responded. "So tell me about the place."

"Well, the Plaza is the center of government for the country and as its name Independence implies it is dedicated to our liberation from the Spanish. That's what the winged statue of victory in the center commemorates. Come on, I want to show something."

Carolina led me over to the base of the statue that towered over us.

"Now, see that up there," she instructed, pointing to a lion with an arrow embedded in its side and a large bird holding what appeared to be chains. "That bird is a condor, the symbol of Ecuador; it's like your American eagle. The chains represent our break from Spain, which is symbolized by the lion. Since I was child I've always loved this statue, probably because it does such an effective job in describing our fight for independence."

"You're right, it is an impressive statue."

"And, that building straight ahead is the Presidential Palace. It's the equivalent of your White House. The president actually lives there, too. His office, by the way, is on the second floor all the way over to the left."

"Ahh, so that's the office your father will be occupying before long," I added half joking.

"Nothing is ever certain in this country. Let's just say he'd very much like to occupy that office," she responded in a serious tone.

"But, wouldn't you like him to be president?" I asked, detecting just the faintest hint of doubt in her voice.

"Believe me, if you knew how this country treats its presidents, you'd understand. Presidents here must constantly face the threat of impeachment or a military coup. At this very moment two of our former presidents have no choice but to live abroad, one in Panama, the other in the England or the US, I'm not sure which. As for our two most recent presidents, they had to flee the country at least for a period of time. Ironically, they will now be running for president against my father though they have little popular support. I probably should point out that a couple of those presidents had been incredibly corrupt individuals and almost certainly deserved what they got. But let's not spoil our day by talking politics."

"OK, I promise, no more talk about politics." What I had intended to add was the fact that several presidents had been overthrown by the CIA in the early 1960s, but it was probably just as well I didn't. I was coming to understand such comments were not taken humorously outside the US. As it was, there were already a few people who were wondering what I was doing down here; no need to add to that number.

"So what is this church," I inquired, returning to our original discussion.

"This is known as the Metropolitan Cathedral; it dates back to the middle of the sixteenth century. Notice the Moorish influence in the architecture. The church is filled with paintings and other artwork from some of Ecuador's earliest artists. I'd love to have you see the interior but it's closed today."

"And, what about that building over to our right?" We were walking slowly about the Plaza. Now I could see many of the benches were occupied by older men, filling their time gossiping or feeding the pigeons.

"That's the Archbishops Palace, where we're going to have lunch," she explained in a tone of mock seriousness.

"We're eating in the Archbishop's Palace? I'm not even Catholic," I answered, assuming she was somehow joking.

"Not to worry, I'll show you when we get there but in the meantime you probably should look at that absolutely ugly set of buildings behind us. They were built about thirty years ago to replace several old colonial structures that the government declared beyond repair. It's a shame, too, since the rest of the buildings surrounding the Plaza are so beautiful."

We continued to walk about the Old City for another hour visiting the Plaza San Francisco with its monastery that was once the site of Atahualpa's palace. We also visited the Church of La Compañia, which I had to admit I found absolutely amazing with its intricately carved woodwork, altars of gold leaf, and its vaulted ceilings covered with the most awe-inspiring paintings. By the time we headed towards the Archbishop's Palace for lunch, I had exhausted myself of superlatives. I couldn't remember ever having a more wonderful morning.

When we reached the Palace, Carolina explained that the Archbishop still lived there; he had leased about half the structure now occupied by various shops and restaurants, including the Mea Culpa where we'd be eating. She directed me to a doorway that opened into a cobbled courtyard with whitewashed walls and a wooden balcony encircling the courtyard from which various types of flowering plants were hung. To the left was a staircase at the top of which we were met by the maitre d' of the Mea Culpa, dressed in a nicely tailored tan suit. It appeared he had been waiting for us. He greeted Carolina warmly like an old friend, but with the appropriate deference one would expect to be shown to the daughter of the country's next president; I was impressed. I couldn't tell how Carolina felt but I suspected she was just a little embarrassed by it, the deference that is. Carolina was a truly compassionate person, who went out of her way not to act important.

The maitre d' graciously led us through the first dining area, where I noticed a very comfortable-looking bar at one end. We then entered the main dining room, which I found surprisingly small. The room contained only eight tables, four of which were located along the near wall, the other four each set next to a large window that overlooked Independence Plaza. We were escorted to one of the window tables, one that provided us with a perfect view of the Metropolitan Cathedral across the Plaza as well as a view of the huge statue of the Virgin of the Americas perched on one of the high hills that once protected the Old City.

After we had been seated, I had my first real opportunity to take a closer look at the restaurant. The dining room was magnificent. Its walls were covered with an ochre-colored fabric of some kind over which decorative rugs had been hung; the trim over doorways and along the ceiling was made of a dark wood, hand-carved and rich in detail. Dark velvet drapes graced each window and a series of attractive chandeliers overhead provided for a warm, intimate atmosphere. Our carved wooden chairs were upholstered in material that matched the restaurant's décor while our table with its cream colored cloth was set with heavy ornate silver plates and dinnerware. I couldn't remember ever having eaten in a restaurant quite so grand.

"So, when I mentioned we were going to have lunch in the Archbishop's Palace, is this what you imagined?" Carolina was looking at me questioningly.

Before I could answer, the waiter came to take our drink order; we settled on a Chilean red wine.

"To answer your question, I can see why this is your favorite restaurant; it's lovely. I can't wait to taste the food."

"I thought you'd like it and I'm confident the food will meet your expectations. The chef is unquestionably the best in Quito."

And, she wasn't exaggerating; the food was delicious. I started with a seafood-filled crepe, moved to pork tenderloin with a kind of raspberry sauce and ended with ice cream smothered in fruit and a liqueur that was a specialty of the house. Our waiters were attentive yet unobtrusive, not like some American waiters who were forever interrupting to ask if everything was all right.

I kept my promise not to talk politics instead focusing on her family and her childhood. I found it fascinating, so fascinating that I did my best to stay away from my own past. In comparison to hers mine seemed so mundane, so....boring. While Carolina spent her summers at her grandfather's farm on the edge of the Amazon, I spent mine with my grandfather in Albany; while she swam in the caiman-infested Rio Napo, I swam in the local swimming pool reeking of chlorine; and while she went to college in Buenos Aires, I went to Wesleyan in Middletown, Connecticut. Worse still, I decided, had I married Rachel, that's exactly the kind of life she would have wanted, though maybe without the chlorine. No wonder Carolina seemed so exciting to me.

Whatever the topic of conversation we never allowed it to keep us from laughing, and joking, reaching across the table to take the other's hand and on one occasion I swear I felt Carolina's foot rubbing my leg. The only sobering moment for me came when I suddenly thought about what it would be like having Carolina meet my parents; God would it be depressing. My mother wouldn't have any idea what to say to her. In fact, she'd probably ask Carolina some stupid question like what was her religion, as if she couldn't have figured it out for herself. Carolina would naturally answer Catholic and my mother would make a face of such obvious disapproval I would cringe. The fact my mother had all the prejudices common to her generation I had reluctantly come to accept, that she didn't even try to hide them, however, made me furious.

All at once I became aware that Carolina was speaking to me.

"Michael, where did you go? One minute I was asking you about your family and the next you went silent on me; I guess, you were thinking about something."

"What? I'm sorry, I guess I kind of spaced out there for a moment. What did you ask me?"

Just then, the sound of shouting could be heard coming from somewhere below our window. Looking out I could see the riot police moving in our general direction. A few had raised their shields and were walking forward with long menacing-looking clubs in their hands. One of the waiters hastened over to close the window, which had been left open a crack for ventilation. I couldn't understand what he said but I concluded he was worried about the possibility of tear gas fumes coming in. Clearly, this wasn't the first time the staff had experienced such things.

Now it was the maitre d' who came over and speaking in almost fluent English he suggested it would be much safer if we both remained where we were for a while. I had no argument with that. I still couldn't see much because whatever was happening was taking place out-of-view beneath our window, but the noise level was definitely increasing. The riot police appeared to be doing a good job of keeping demonstrators away from the front of the Presidential Palace though I could well imagine what it was like on those narrow streets leading into the Plaza. How we were going to get out of here, I had no idea though I decided for the moment not to worry about it. There were worse things than being trapped in this restaurant with Carolina. In fact, it was like a dream come true.

Suddenly there was a thunderous crash that from within the restaurant sounded like a cannon. Even the maitre d' rushed over to one of the windows and looked out anxiously, worrying perhaps that the rioting in the streets had taken a new and more violent turn. One look at the sky, however, thick with dark, roiling clouds instantly made clear the cause of the crash. An instant later the clouds unburdened themselves of the moisture they were carrying and the rain began pelting down. If we anticipated having a problem finding a free taxi because of the demonstration, with the added factor of the storm it was now going to be impossible.

Sixteen

As we sat, enjoying our coffee and talking, a sudden outburst of shouting caused me to turn and look down at the Plaza. Until now the riot police had apparently been able to keep it free of demonstrators, but one of their lines must have broken for I could now see a number of people racing towards the Presidential Palace, many of them waving banners and yelling loudly. How, I wondered, were we ever going to get out of there without becoming caught up in what was quickly developing into a full-fledged riot. It was hard to believe that only an hour or two before everything had been so peaceful and serene.

I hadn't even heard the maitre d' approach our table but when I turned back from the window he was whispering something to Carolina. She thanked him and began reaching for her purse, which she had placed on the chair next to her.

"We should go, Michael," she softly. "Robert and Eric, the two men my father hires to look after me, are waiting just outside the door. For once I'm thankful there around; they'll get us out of here."

So, they have names after all, I thought to myself, feeling relieved to know they were outside but at the same time annoyed we needed their help getting away. If the scene hadn't become quite so violent I would have suggested we try to slip away on our own. By this time the maitre d' had brought the bill and I handed him a credit card; I didn't even bother to look at the total. I had already learned that dinners at the most expensive restaurants here in Ecuador seldom exceeded what you'd pay at the most average restaurant in New York. When the maitre d' returned I signed my credit card receipt, adding a very generous gratuity for the superb service, and followed Carolina towards the door as literally the entire restaurant staff came out to bid us good luck.

Robert and Eric were indeed waiting for us, though I was never given the opportunity to discover which name went with which face before they hustled us out of the restaurant. They rushed us down the stairs at the bottom of which we turned to the left, away from Independence Plaza. A set of steps led down to another interior courtyard, this one apparently used as an eating area for several nearby fast-food restaurants. I held onto Carolina's hand as we followed the security guards through a short, dark tunnel that came out into a beautifully maintained courtyard; I guessed it was a part of the palace where the Archbishop had his residence. There was no time to take it in because we were being herded towards a heavy wooden door; it was unlocked and once through it we found ourselves in a narrow alleyway that had only a single exit onto a main street. But, even in the alleyway we couldn't ignore the chanting and shouting of the demonstrators.

Carolina's security guards pushed us along at a rapid pace. I felt sorry for her having to end such a beautiful day in this manner. I did have to admit, however, she was a real trooper; never once did I hear her utter a word of complaint. I had to smile thinking back to earlier in the day when, sitting next to Carolina in the taxi, I had felt so excited just being with her, of course, that was before we had gotten to the Plaza where the word "exciting" would take on a whole new meaning.

The main street we came out onto was jammed with people, some trying to make their way to the Plaza, others trying to get away. Initially, I was relieved when I saw we intended to go in the opposite direction, but as it turned out we found ourselves heading directly into a massive wave of demonstrators. We literally had to physically fight our way forward. Eric and Robert led the way with Carolina close behind them as they pushed people aside; they were not always gentle but they were effective. I, on the other hand, was left to basically fend for myself; I wasn't sure if I had gotten lost whether they'd come back for me or not. Carolina, to her credit, never let me out of her sight even though at times it was impossible for me to stay next to her.

I don't know how many blocks we covered before I realized the crowds were thinning out and it was becoming easier to move. Carolina and I were back to holding hands, though we were both too out of breath to carry on much of a conversation. Glancing up the narrow street I spotted a black

Range Rover parked on the sidewalk, two members of the National Police wearing rain ponchos and smoking cigarettes, casually leaning against it.

"Is that your Range Rover up ahead," I asked, wondering what the police were there for before realizing it had to be parked illegally. It meant almost surely they were expecting some kind of payoff for not ticketing or towing it, in other words, no different than the traffic police in New York. But, then, to my surprise, Robert and Eric went over to the two men and greeted them like old friends, shaking hands, patting shoulders.

"They probably convinced the two policemen to look after the car, making it clear, of course, they worked for my father. Needless to say it wasn't even necessary to remind them that my father was about to become the next president of Ecuador so it would be in their best interest to take good care of the car. I hate it when they do that kind of thing and I've spoken to my father about it, but obviously to no effect. Now you know why most people in Ecuador resent the wealthy; it's precisely because of things like this, their sense of privilege and entitlement, and it's so unnecessary."

I could see she was genuinely annoyed, but it was too late to do anything about it now. It was time we got away from here. There was no way of knowing when the crowds might be pushed back this way by the riot police who by this time had probably received reinforcements.

I opened the backdoor of the Range Rover and Carolina climbed in; I clambered in after her. She quickly surprised me by taking my hand, and lacing her fingers through mine as she snuggled up against me. I thought she'd be careful about such things with the two security guards in front and knowing whatever we did would get back to her father, but I shouldn't have been concerned. It was Carolina's own father who had said she was a very independent woman, too independent for him, I suspected.

"I'm really sorry for our having to leave the restaurant like that; I hope it didn't spoil our visit to the Old City," she inquired with a rather sad face.

"Not at all," I exclaimed. "I loved every minute of it including our escape. It made me feel like a rock star trying to get away from the paparazzi." I didn't think it was necessary to add how nervous I'd been before Robert and Eric had arrived on the scene.

"Well, I'm glad I could oblige you," she replied, clearly feeling better for my answer. "It's not that I have to do this kind of thing very often, really, but if I want to be independent and have some kind of a life of my own I have to put up with them. Of course, on days like today, as you can see, they actually come in handy."

Carolina had spoken loudly enough for the two men in front to hear; she had probably done it intentionally. The one on the passenger side half turned and glanced at her but he didn't say anything. There was something about the two men that made me feel uneasy and I wasn't even certain why. I had the impression they resented Carolina in some way, or maybe it was me they resented. I had to admit I couldn't blame them if at times like this they felt more like glorified babysitters than trained security guards. Whatever their problem was, I felt relieved when the Hotel Quito came into view. It was becoming almost suffocating being in the car with them.

When we pulled up to the curb next to the parking lot entrance, I jumped out and held the door for Carolina. She stepped out gracefully, then turned and ducked her head back into the car. I could see she was explaining something to the two men though I couldn't hear what it was. Stepping back onto the sidewalk she shut the car door. The two drove off in the direction of Guapulo.

"Have you ever been up to the top floor of the Hotel Quito," she asked. "There's a restaurant up there, which has the most beautiful view of Quito. I'd like to invite you there for a drink since I realize the ride back from the Old City was anything but romantic with those two guys around. So, what do you think, shall we go?"

The smile she gave me was sweet, romantic, naughty, the kind of smile that would have induced me to say yes to just about anything she asked.

"Let's go," I answered enthusiastically, taking her by the arm and literally pulling her into the hotel lobby. I felt as if I had just been given a reprieve, having this unexpected opportunity to spend another hour or so with her.

The restaurant was on the seventh floor. Stepping out of the elevator Carolina whispered, "If you'll excuse me for a minute I'm going to visit the ladies room. You go ahead over to the window, I'll be right with you."

I turned and walked towards the large windows that extended the entire length of the restaurant. Looking out, I saw spread before me the most breathtaking panoramic view of Quito. And since the city was contained within a narrow valley squeezed between two ranges of mountains, I could observe nearly all of it from my vantage point.

As I was admiring it Carolina walked up next to me putting her arm around my waist.

"It's incredible isn't it? I never tire of looking at Quito from up here. I don't come here very often these days but I'm so delighted to be here with you right now."

"The view is amazing," I responded. "And if you're delighted to be here with me, you can only imagine what it's like for me to be here with you."

We stood there for several seconds without saying a word. It was Carolina who finally broke the silence.

"Do you see that peak up there, a little beyond the main range of mountains? That's Guagua Pichincha; *guagua* is an indigenous word for baby. Anyway, it's an active volcano and erupted a few years ago, nothing serious but it dumped a layer of ash all over the city. I wasn't here at the time; I was in Buenos Aires luckily. My father said it was a real mess to clean up. Everybody had to wear masks over their noses so as not to breathe the stuff; it didn't do much for people's automobile engines either. Even now you can see traces of the dust along roadways leading out of the city."

She pointed out several other features—the funicular that ran up the eastern slopes of the Pichincha, the Marriott that loomed directly down the hill, and the airport to our right. The sky had become almost clear of clouds and the bright sunlight, combined with the thin layer of atmosphere at this elevation, bestowed on the city a well-defined, almost vivid, mien. I'm certain I could have stood there indefinitely, but Carolina had other ideas.

"Let's go over into the bar and sit down; we can still enjoy the view even from there," she suggested.

The bar area was separated from the restaurant by a baby grand piano. It was small and simply designed but attractive. The floor was carpeted in deep blue while several small light blue couches were arranged around the windows each with its own small coffee table; the walls and trim were white. The bar itself, constructed from different types and shades of wood had a distinctly modern look to it; a half dozen chrome stools with black vinyl seats only added to the touch. Over the bar hung a matching wooden rack for holding wine glasses.

Carolina and I took a seat on one of the couches that faced towards the southern part of the city. When I casually mentioned I had not been down there she explained there was little reason to do so. It was the poorer part of the city as well as the area where the majority of the city's residents lived.

"This part of the city around here is where the wealthier families live; it's where the malls and the hotels and good stores are all located.

However, more and more of those with money are moving out of the city and down into the valley. And, now, many of the good stores are following their customers down. I suspect a lot of people who live in the valley and don't have to go to work here, probably visit Quito as little as once a week. They're even building the new airport out in the valley. That will really change things."

"So, what about you," I asked. "How often do you come up to Quito?"

She laughed. "I think I'm slowly becoming one of those people who comes here about once or twice a week. To be perfectly honest I really don't have much reason to come up."

A waiter, dressed smartly in black trousers, a crisp white shirt, gray vest and striped tie, came over to take our drink order. We both ordered a house red wine and when he served them he placed a bowl of popcorn and another of plantain chips on the table in front of us.

"*Skoal*," I proposed, lightly touching her glass with mine.

"*Skoal*," she replied, smiling. "That's a new one for me."

"It's an old Scandinavian toast," I replied. "Means the same thing as *salud*."

It was so relaxing sitting there talking with Carolina. I felt as if I'd known her all my life when in reality it had been less than two weeks; I was even beginning to feel at home here though I barely spoke a word of Spanish. It was when I thought about the future that I began to feel anxious because I simply couldn't conjure up a scenario in which Carolina and I could remain together. I couldn't very well stay in Ecuador; my job prospects here would be next to zero. And, besides, I was here in the country as a tourist and before long I would have to obtain a visa that might not be easy to come by, though obviously I did have connections. For the moment, I told myself I should just push the whole thing from my mind and concentrate on the beautiful woman sitting next to me.

The afternoon moved on in spite of our efforts to prolong it. We had a second glass of wine, which neither of us really wanted, we talked nonsense to each other so as not to become aware of the time, we held hands, stared lovingly into each others eyes, and once or twice even snuck in a quick kiss. Unfortunately, no matter how hard we tried we couldn't stop the afternoon from gradually coming to an end.

"You know, I honestly don't want to but I really must be going home," Carolina announced sadly. "I've been away from the house for hours and my father will be getting annoyed if I'm not there to look in on my mother.

And it's not that I care what my father thinks, my mother will survive nicely, it's just that I don't want him getting upset with you. After all, it's not as if you were forcing me to stay here; I'm the one who doesn't want to go, but we'll see each other again this week, right?"

"Oh, God, yes, yes, I need to see you," I replied, probably more enthusiastically than is prudent for a guy.

"I have an idea," she tendered with a suggestive smile on her face. "Can you meet me on Wednesday? I don't have any afternoon classes. But, it's important you have a car. Do you think you'd be able to borrow Adam's car?"

"No problem; Adam has said I could use his car any time I wanted."

"Great. Then why don't you meet me on Wednesday at the entrance of the Ambrosia Gourmet Shop, it's just around the corner from the main gate of the university. You can't miss the place; it has a green metallic roof and green grille-work. I'll wait just inside and will step out only when I see you pull up in front. I want to leave without Robert and Eric knowing. You think we can do it?"

"Just tell me what time you want me to be there and I'll time it to the second," I replied, excited at just the thought.

She squeezed my hand. "I promise I'll make it worth your while. Why don't you pick me up at eleven; that'll give us the entire afternoon together?"

"I'll be there at eleven on the dot," I replied enthusiastically.

I paid the bill and we took the elevator down to the lobby. I walked Carolina to her car even though, I suspected, her security guards were probably watching us.

"Hop in, I'll drive you to your apartment. It'll give us a few minutes more minutes to be together."

"What a great idea," I said jumping into the passenger side. "I really love the way your mind works, like mine!"

She drove up to the gate, paid the attendant, and headed down the street in the direction of the apartment. It didn't take more than a minute to get there but it was still worth every second, worth it because she pulled over to the curb and gave me an unexpectedly long, passionate kiss.

"So, Wednesday?"

"Yes, Wednesday," I reached for the handle of the door with one hand while squeezing her hand with the other. I climbed out, reluctantly closing the door as I did. She smiled and gave me a little wave before pulling out into the traffic. Watching her drive away I couldn't believe how empty and alone I suddenly felt.

Seventeen

The first thing I did when I awoke, even before pouring my first cup of coffee, was to look up the number of the German School in the phone book. I hadn't really given it much thought but I just assumed whomever answered the phone would speak English. Why I had assumed that at a German school in a Spanish-speaking country a person would necessarily be an English-speaker as well, I wasn't sure. I guess, though I had only been in Ecuador for a few days, I had already become impressed that so many of the people I had met spoke two or three languages fluently. And, so it was with the woman who answered the phone. She actually answered in Spanish but switched immediately to English when she heard my voice. Just as quickly she gave me the name of the chairperson of the German Language Department and proceeded to try his number for me. It rang several times, then, when no one answered, switched to his voice mail system. Since he didn't know me I decided it would be best not to leave a message but to call back later.

As it turned out, it was not until nearly noon that someone finally picked up the extension.

"Erich Kessler, here," said a voice so accented that for a moment I found it impossible to tell whether he was speaking German or English.

"Mr. Kessler, my name is Michael Henrick, may I assume you speak English?"

"You may assume that, Mr. Michael Henrick, so what may I do for you?"

"As you can probably tell from my accent I'm an American and I came down here to Quito a couple of weeks ago to visit a colleague. To make a long story short, I've been given a document relevant to some research I'm doing that is unfortunately handwritten in German script. It's just a few pages but I need someone to translate it for me. Naturally, I'm willing to pay for it. I called you because I assumed there would probably be someone down there at your school willing to do it for me. Or, at the very least, you might know of someone who could."

"Any number of us could do that for you, but where are you calling from at this moment, up in Quito," he asked.

"Yes, I am; I'm staying with a friend who lives close to the Hotel Quito on Avenida Gonzalez Suarez, is there a problem?"

"On no, not at all, it's just that if you didn't want to bother coming all the way down here to the school you could simply walk over to the Lutheran Church and see Reverend Hoffmann; he's an old friend. He could definitely translate it for you and he's a delightful character. You'd enjoy meeting him. That said, you could also bring it down here to me if you'd prefer; I'd be happy to look at it."

"Well, it sounds like the easiest thing would be for me to take the pages over to Reverend Hoffmann. Now, you're pretty certain he wouldn't mind doing something like this?"

"I can't imagine he would. As I said, he's an absolutely delightful individual."

"Then, I guess, I thank you for your help in this matter."

"Not at all; happy to do it. And when you see Reverend Hoffmann please say 'hello' for me; tell him he'll be seeing me at Sunday service soon," he laughed.

"I promise to tell him."

Erich Kessler sounded like a delightful individual himself, I decided after putting down the phone. Maybe I should have taken the papers down to him, but the Lutheran Church was just down the street.

I had no trouble finding the phone number only I wasn't as lucky with the woman who answered; she spoke only the most rudimentary English. I decided what she said was that Reverend Hoffmann was not at the church but that he'd be returning about four o'clock in which case I had a few hours to kill. I checked my email and while there were several messages for me, there was none from Carolina. Why hadn't she written, I wondered? Of course, I was going to see her the next day and she seemed to have something special in mind. What was it she had said to me, "I'll make it worth your while?" It sounded all very mysterious, not to mention just a little bit exciting. For some reason the whole thing suddenly brought her father to mind. I was certain he wasn't pleased that she had begun seeing me. Knowing him, he had probably already planned out her future, and it was doubtful those plans included her marriage to an unemployed American, well an American anyway; I was not intending to remain unemployed forever.

But, marriage, what, in God's name, was I thinking about? I had spent all of two days with her, though admittedly they had been delightful days. And then, of course, there was this little factor of my staying in Quito for at best another week before having to return to New York. While I had to admit that Carolina was unquestionably the most fascinating woman I had ever met, there was still this whole issue of Rachel. It wasn't that I thought we'd ever get back together, that was probably out of the question, it was the worry that just maybe Carolina was simply a rebound affair, that she looked attractive to me only because I needed to fill the void left by Rachel or to repair my damaged ego. But, it couldn't be just that; even Adam questioned how I could be fortunate enough to have met someone like Carolina, and more than once he had called her "an incredible woman." Regardless, all I knew for sure was that I desperately wanted to have lunch with her tomorrow, so please, Carolina, write me before I go crazy!

In the meantime I turned my attention to the papers I had promised Carlos to get translated. There was some urgency here. One person had already been killed because of them and Carlos' place had been broken into. This was serious business; it was a little more than just conducting research on Atahualpa's gold. But, what possibly could be so important about those papers? Could they actually describe the location of Atahualpa's gold or possibly some other wealthy Inca's burial site? I guess if they did that would be enough to make the diary from which those pages came a very important and valuable document. Of course, the real question was what I was doing getting mixed up in all this; I had been here after all just a few days. One thing I had made up my mind about, however, and that was once the pages had been translated and delivered to Carlos, my part in this little drama was over. I was never going to set foot in Carlos' bar again.

In my mind it was settled but instead of feeling a sense of relief I was feeling a sense of unease. Because of Carolina's bodyguards I had stopped worrying about being followed but now, on my own, I needed to be more cautious. There was, of course, no proof I had ever been followed. On the other hand, I had never seen the bodyguards who had been keeping Carolina under surveillance either. And, what if I were being followed?

Would I be putting Reverend Hoffmann in any danger? I quickly decided I was becoming paranoid. I had to stop thinking like this.

I went back to the computer to check my email. Bingo! There was a message from Carolina. She was simply confirming that I'd be there tomorrow at eleven directly outside the entrance to the Ambrosia Gourmet Shop as if that were necessary. I was guessing she did not want her security detail to notice she was leaving the university grounds, although it was hard to believe they just waited around for her all day outside the front entrance. Probably they just monitored the homing device attached to her Honda. Anyway, I was glad they wouldn't be following us. And, if being free of her security guards weren't enough, she ended her message by saying how anxious she was to see me again. Tomorrow couldn't get here fast enough.

I finally reached Reverend Hoffmann about four that afternoon, explaining how I came to be calling him.

"Ah, Erich, I haven't seen him for quite a while; is he well," Reverend Hoffmann asked.

"Quite well," I answered, "and he wanted me to say he'd be attending Sunday service soon."

"He's been telling me that for months," the reverend chuckled. "Now, what may I do for you Mr. Henrick?"

I decided almost instantly that I liked Reverend Hoffmann; I had been expecting someone more formal, more serious.

"I'm in possession of several pages of a book written, unfortunately for me, in German script," I explained. "I called the German School to inquire whether there might be someone down there who could translate it for me and that's when I ended up speaking with Erich; it was he who suggested I contact you. It's about eight handwritten pages and I don't need a precise translation. What I really need to know is the subject matter of these pages. I realize I'm being a bit presumptuous as I'm sure you're a busy man, but do you think you could do this for me? I'd be willing to reimburse you for your time, though I suspect it's something that won't take you long."

"I'd be happy to translate it for you and I wouldn't dream of accepting payment, of course, you could always make a contribution to the church," he laughed good-naturedly. "So, Mr. Henrick, do you have any idea what the book is about?"

It was a logical enough question but I felt a little embarrassed telling him the little bit I knew.

"The person who owns the book refers to it as a diary and suspects it has something to do with Atahualpa's gold. Personally, I'm not certain it does, though I'm not certain why I say this. But, there is one thing; it has a date, April 1945, or at least, I think it's April; it's definitely 1945 though. That's all I could translate. It's probably a waste of everyone's time but I promised a friend I'd get it translated for him."

"Atahualpa's gold, huh? I haven't heard any mention of that for years; now you really have my curiosity aroused. You can bring the materials over whenever it's convenient. Do you know where I'm located?"

He seemed genuinely enthusiastic so I felt a little better about my request.

"I'll have them to you within the hour. I live on Avenida Gonzales Suarez so I'm just a short walk from your church," I responded.

Hanging up the phone I went directly to where I had hidden the papers in my bedroom, then went in search of an envelope of some kind, which I found in one of the drawers in Adam's desk. I tucked the papers into the envelope and wrote my name, address and phone number on it. I did it without thinking; only later would I come to wish I'd simply said I'd get back to him.

Coming out of the apartment building I was momentarily blinded by the bright sunlight. Fortunately, I had brought my sunglasses with me and as I stopped to put them on, I noticed a black Range rover quickly pull away from the curb and head up the street. The driver had looked directly at me, and in that second before he drove away I felt he looked vaguely familiar, though I couldn't be certain since I had caught only the briefest glimpse of him. Could it have been one of Carolina's security guards? He was driving a black Range Rover like the one Carolina and I had ridden in, though there was no shortage of black SUVs in Quito. But, why would he be checking up on me? Maybe her father had decided to confirm if I actually was who I claimed to be. I guess I couldn't blame him, especially since my reasons for being in Quito had probably never been very adequately explained. I decided I should probably feel a little flattered. Did he know something I didn't? I'd be curious to learn what Carolina might have said to her father about us, though I was pretty sure she hadn't confided that she was in love with me, or that I was in love with her. Stop, I suddenly said to myself, once again I was letting my imagination get way out ahead of me.

It was a beautiful late afternoon as I walked over to the Lutheran Church; in fact, by Quito standards it was actually quite hot. There was barely a cloud in the sky and whichever way one glanced there was a range of mountains. Why didn't more Americans retire down here, I wondered. The weather was great, the people were laid back and polite, the prices of most things were lower and, to top it all off, Ecuador's currency was the American dollar. For that matter, why were there so few American tourists down here. Perhaps, I thought, when I got back to New York I should open a travel office devoted exclusively to arranging vacations to South America.

The Lutheran Church was directly across the street from the American ambassador's residence. A low white-stucco wall surrounded the grounds with an odd sky-blue colored fence running along the top. As for the church, it was anything but traditional—a pyramid-shaped building of white stucco with a reddish terra cotta roof. A similarly painted extension with the same sky-blue trim extended towards the street. The metal gate was locked so I rang the bell. A moment later a voice asked something in Spanish; I assumed it was either who was I, or what did I want. I explained I was delivering some papers to Reverend Hoffmann. My answer was followed by several seconds of silence.

Just as I was about to ring again, I saw a door open in what I guessed was probably the pastor's living quarters. A casually dressed young man stepped out and walked towards me along a path that threaded its way between stately palm trees and well-manicured flowerbeds.

"Reverend Hoffmann apologizes for not being able to speak with you right now," the young man explained as he approached me. His speech was heavily accented though I couldn't quite decide if it were European or Latin American. And, he didn't open the gate. "He asked me to bring the papers you wanted translated to him. He promised to contact you as soon as he has the chance to read them. Did you include your name and a phone number where you can be reached?"

"Yes, I did," I replied, handing him the material through the metal bars. "I've written my name, address and phone number on the envelope. Please thank him for me and tell him to call at his convenience."

The young man nodded and without another word turned and returned the way he had come.

I watched him until he disappeared from sight, feeling just a bit disappointed not to have had the opportunity to speak directly with Reverend Hoffmann; I would have liked to explain a little more about the materials I had given him to translate. In any case, I'd know soon enough whether the diary contained anything of importance. Deep down, and in spite of what had happened to Francisco, I suspected the whole thing about Atahualpa's gold was complete nonsense.

As I turned away and headed back towards the apartment, I found myself wondering about the young man who had taken the papers from me. He certainly didn't appear to be a clergyman of any kind, though to be honest, there was no particular reason why he had to be. The guy probably just worked for Reverend Hoffmann. At the corner I stopped to buy a package of chewing gum from two young boys. By this time I had forgotten the papers completely, my mind already occupied with thoughts of my luncheon date with Carolina. What, I kept wondering, was this surprise she had for me.

Eighteen

I pulled up in front of the Ambrosia Gourmet Shop at precisely eleven o'clock; it was just as Carolina had described. Almost instantly she came racing out the door carrying a small purse in one hand and a wide-brimmed hat in the other. I reached over and quickly opened the door without shutting off the motor. Carolina jumped in, flipping her hat onto the backseat as she did so. She then leaned over and gave me a surprisingly long kiss for someone who only a second before had seemed in such a hurry. But, I was the last person who was going to complain.

"Now, go," she said, with that incredible smile of hers. "Take a left up ahead and we'll head back the way you came; I'm pretty sure even if the security guards see us they won't recognize your car."

Carolina could not have just come from class, not the way she was dressed. She was wearing a bright yellow dress with a breathtaking V-neck that displayed ample cleavage, which she had further accentuated with a stylish amber necklace. I could also detect the subtle fragrance of her perfume that smelled to me of apple blossoms, though it was probably something far more exotic. I quickly found just having her there next to me was making it hard to concentrate on my driving, a task that became even more difficult when she gently placed her hand on my thigh. Looking down I couldn't help noticing her fingernails; they were long, smooth, and painted with a clear polish. If at that moment I had been asked to choose just one word to describe Carolina, I would have unhesitatingly responded with the term, exquisite.

"All right, where are we going," I asked, finding myself becoming aroused from just the feeling of her hand on my thigh.

"Today, we're going to Mitad del Mundo, the middle of the world. Don't worry; it's not deep underground like in some Jules Verne novel. It's a delightful spot; there are fun little shops there and an excellent restaurant, where you're going to take me for lunch," she replied, laughing softly. "And, it's not that far; it should take us no more than half an hour to get there."

As I reached the outskirts of Quito, Carolina directed me to turn north and after a few minutes driving we began to leave the city behind. Very quickly the landscape began to change becoming more open and much drier, almost desert-like. Many of the surrounding hillsides were totally barren of vegetation and the dust blown about by the wind colored the atmosphere an unhealthy brown. The only greenery was found in some of the deeper ravines that crisscrossed the region. When I commented on the near absence of trees, Carolina pointed to what at first glance appeared to be a barren hilltop where only a single tree was visible; it was tiny tree but a tree nevertheless.

"That's it, that one tree," I laughed.

"I wouldn't make fun of that tree if I were you," Carolina admonished me. "That tree is supposed to bring good health and happiness to anyone who sees it. After all, any tree that can survive in this dry climate must surely be imbued with special powers."

I was still smiling when it suddenly occurred to me just how much I could use a little good luck right now so I took a long look at the tree. The Lord only knew what the future held for me; I clearly had no idea. I wasn't even certain what I'd be doing tomorrow, but I was determined to seize the day.

"Mitad del Mundo is just ahead on the left, but you'll have to go right around the traffic circle," Carolina explained, in a manner that was at once both charming and professorial.

I drove into the parking lot and pulled up as close to the entrance as I could. Shutting off the engine, I turned to take my first full look at Carolina since she'd jumped into the car. My expression at that moment must have said it all for she unhesitatingly leaned over and gave me another of her long, passionate kisses. Between the kiss and the smell of her perfume, I decided I couldn't have cared less if we ever got out of the car. Carolina, however, had other plans, gently reaching for the door handle.

"Come on, it's a beautiful day, let's walk around a bit and work up an appetite before we have lunch," she gushed, getting out of the car.

It was a beautiful day. There was barely a cloud in the sky and to my surprise it was hot, much hotter than it had been back in Quito. Carolina immediately put on her hat when she stepped out into the sun.

"And, of course, you didn't bring a hat with you," she gently scolded. "You're not going to walk around without one; the sun is far too bright and there's no shade whatsoever around here. I knew I should have insisted on buying you that one when we were in Otavalo."

"What did I tell you then, that I never wear one, that I don't even own one. If you must know I look absolutely ridiculous in a hat."

"Michael, this isn't New York, it's Quito, elevation over 2500 meters. There's no thick layer of atmosphere here to screen out the ultra-violet radiation. A hat is more than a fashion accessory; skin cancer is extremely common here in Ecuador. So, this time I'm not going to let you talk me out of it; I'm buying you a hat, and that's final," she said emphatically. "Come on, I know just the place."

Carolina took my hand and literally pulled me in the direction of a narrow alleyway that was crammed with tiny shops selling all manner of clothing and jewelry. She seemed to know exactly where she was going for in no time at all we were standing in front of a shop selling hats of all kinds. Almost immediately an older woman appeared greeting Carolina warmly. Glancing about, Carolina walked over and picked up a hat that looked vaguely like her own, although with a shorter brim for a man.

"Try this on and see if it fits," she ordered, handing the hat to me with a bemused expression.

I could hardly refuse so I took it and placed it on my head without comment.

It seemed to fit perfectly, and when the older woman pointed to a mirror, I found myself reluctantly admitting that it did look rather good on me. Carolina must have felt the same since she promptly told the woman we'd take it, handing her the money before I could reconsider.

We spent the next half hour or so wandering about. She took me over to the monument that marked the equator where we acted like a couple of school children on a fieldtrip—straddling the line, each of us on either side of the line, laughing and joking the entire time. Then, we stopped to examine the work of a number of artisans. Many of the items for sale were similar to what we had seen at Otavalo, but it was fun nonetheless. We held hands, found ample excuses to kiss and seemed to find humor in everything the other person said. To anyone overhearing us it must have appeared as if we had known each other for years instead of only a single week. For that matter I was finding it a little hard to believe myself. Of course, the fact that my stay in Ecuador would be soon ending wasn't making the situation any easier and it wasn't one of those things I could easily push from my mind. It was becoming increasingly clear that I couldn't simply walk away as if she were nothing more than a casual one-night stand. Not for the first time, I found myself wondering if it might just be possible for Carolina to come back to New York with me; she certainly was old enough to be making her own decisions in spite of what Adam had said.

"Let's have lunch," Carolina suddenly announced, pulling me mercifully out of my reverie. "The restaurant is right over there."

We approached an arch painted a garish blue with the name Equinoccio appearing in yellow above the entrance. I couldn't help wondering what kind of restaurant to expect though I knew from experience that Carolina's taste in such things was impeccable. And, it was! Once through the gate we walked along a pathway edged by well-maintained lawns and shrubbery, putting me at ease. As for the restaurant, once we were inside, it proved an unexpected surprise. The dining area was in what must have once been the inner courtyard to the building. While entirely enclosed now by a glass roof, trees had been left to grow along the inside walls and their branches now interlocked overhead to create the illusion one was sitting outside. There was even a fountain in the center of the room whose splashing waters fed pots of brightly colored flowers.

"So, what do you think," Carolina asked, as we were seated by a smiling indigenous woman, dressed similarly to the women I had seen in Otavalo.

"I don't know what to say; it's absolutely charming....and quite romantic," I replied, taking in the ambience of the place.

The woman had seated us in the corner so we could enjoy a view of the whole dining area. The chairs were heavy and made from some dark wood while the table, probably similarly made, was covered with a reddish colored tablecloth. In the center of the table was a vase with a single pink rose; ferns were growing next to us. As if to reinforce the feeling of sitting out-of-doors several small birds flitted about in the branches overhead.

This time it was my turn to lean over and give Carolina a kiss.

"I can't remember ever feeling as happy as I do right now," I whispered, giving her hand a gentle squeeze.

We ordered a pitcher of Sangria and a plate of *morochos*, totally oblivious to other patrons who began filtering in to the restaurant. We talked, exchanged smiles, held hands and even managed to finish the entire pitcher of sangria. All the while I kept thinking how I didn't want this day to end. But, inevitably, Carolina spoke the words I had been dreading, "We really have to go now."

I could tell she was in a hurry so I didn't try to convince her to stay longer. Walking back to the car, Carolina glanced at me and smiled.

"Don't be so sad, Michael, the day is far from over. I still have that surprise I promised you."

"I thought having lunch here was the surprise," I replied, feeling like I had just been given a reprieve. "I can't imagine whatever you have in store can be any more delightful than this."

"I'm fairly certain it will be," she replied with a twinkle in her eye. "Or perhaps I should say, I sincerely hope it will be."

Exiting the parking lot, I was about to turn right in the direction of Quito when Carolina said, "Go around the circle to your left. We're going to continue north, just a little way further."

"And that's where the surprise will be," I laughed, my curiosity growing by the minute.

"Yes, that's where the surprise will be; you've just got to be a little more patient."

The road we took was paved and wound serpent-like up a very steep hill. At the base there were numerous houses and roadside food stands but they gradually thinned out as we climbed in elevation. By the time we reached the summit the terrain had become more rugged, and heavily wooded.

"Those are cloud forests," she explained, pointing to a series of forest-covered peaks partially obscured by a low-lying bank of clouds. "But, slow down, we'll be making a right turn in a minute. That's it just ahead. Now, let me warn you, the driving is not going to be easy and I suspect when this little excursion is over you may need to get Adam's car washed."

I turned onto a narrow gravel road that was lined on both sides by an impenetrable wall of vegetation. In places it actually extended over the roadway giving the feeling one was driving through a lush, green tunnel. Of course, I couldn't help thinking about what I'd do if I met another vehicle; there was no place to pull over. Fortunately, it didn't happen and before I knew it the road began to widen and Carolina was saying, "Here we go so be careful now." As if I hadn't been driving carefully.

The road had made a sharp turn to the left and instantly began to pitch steeply downward. At the same time the roadbed became a mass of large boulders and potholes causing the car to bounce wildly; it took all my strength just to hold onto the steering wheel. If it were possible, the road became even narrower and I found myself confronted with a series of hairpin curves. Carolina suggested it might be a good idea to start honking the horn to warn anyone coming up the road of our approach since there would be no place to quickly pull over. Immediately to our left was an impenetrable wall of vegetation, largely bamboo interspersed with giant orchid plants that hung down over the road and added the only bright colors to this eerie world; to our right there was literally nothing but a frightening drop straight down to the valley floor, though the valley itself was all but invisible beneath a thick, swirling mass of clouds.

Our ride continued like this for what seemed like an eternity though it was, in fact, only about twenty minutes, when to my immense relief the road leveled out and the valley floor magically appeared before us bathed in bright sunlight. The view was as incredible as it was sudden.

"This is the crater of the Pululahua volcano; it's been inactive for centuries," she explained. "And, that's the tiny town of Nublin. This valley has a fascinating history. It was settled first by the Incas over a thousand years ago, then later by Dominican monks. The government confiscated the land early in this century and about thirty years ago gave it back to farmers making it a National Park at the same time."

"What a gorgeous spot; I just can't believe people actually live down here. Is the road we just came down the only way in and out?"

"That's it, most people who live here probably only go to town once a week or so. But you do have to admit this valley is spectacular, isn't it? Look at that wall of mountains surrounding us; we're definitely in the very center of the old crater."

"So, if this is the surprise you had for me, I don't know what to say other than it's amazing and I thank you."

"Oh, no, this is only a small part of the surprise. See those building down there?" She pointed to one of the larger farms. "That's where we're going; it's our farm, or *quinta* as we refer to it, and that's more or less where your surprise awaits you."

There was a twinkle in her eyes that served to only further mystify me, or perhaps excite me would be the more appropriate term.

Every square inch of the valley floor appeared to be in use; there were huge vegetable gardens, cornfields and acres of pastureland for the grazing of cattle. We drove slowly passing several small farms houses before Carolina indicated I was to turn into the next driveway. At first glance the house looked similar to many of those we had just driven by, but upon closer inspection I began to notice a number of subtle differences. It was definitely larger and now I could see in much better condition; a sprawling, single-level structure of an ochre-colored stucco with a terra cotta roof that appeared new. The windows and doors were covered with wrought-iron gratings and the porch at the front held a series of trellises displaying a profusion of flowering hibiscus and roses. And, everything was so lush and well maintained—the lawns, the flower gardens, and at least the portion I could see of a vegetable garden in the back.

"I love being down here," Carolina whispered, wistfully. "When I was young we usually stayed here when we came to Quito; however, after we bought the house in Cumbaya we more or less stopped coming. On more than one occasion my father has suggested selling this place but I've refused to let him."

"It's really beautiful, so who takes care of it," I inquired admiringly.

"Oh, there's a family that lives on the farm; they basically run it as their own. I gave them the day off; that's what I had to arrange before we came out here. Shall we go in?"

One step inside and I had fallen in love with the place. I decided I could easily live here for the rest of my life. The interior was completely done in a dark, rich wood—floors, exposed ceilings, window frames and doors. The living room, which was the only room I could see from where I was standing, had a huge fieldstone fireplace at the far end. And, I loved the way it was furnished with large couches, overstuffed chairs and several antique-looking tables of various sizes. Though the furniture was heavy and dark, the room itself was brightened by the use of lively colored pillows, drapes and handwoven rugs. And, unlike Adam's rather austere approach to decorating, this room was filled with books, vases, table lamps, family pictures, woodcarvings, and figures made of stone, everywhere. The effect was comfortable and casual, a place where you could readily imagine a person relaxing or working if need be; it had life to it. The style was quite different from anything I had experienced in Ecuador so far.

As I continued my inspection I could see through one of the open doors a rather modern-looking kitchen and through another a hallway that apparently led to a set of bedrooms. And, what had once probably been the dining room had been converted into a study; there was a large desk strewn with sheathes of papers, a floor-to-ceiling bookcase crammed to overflowing with books and family pictures, and in the corner to my left stood a huge, antique-looking globe.

"Is this you," I asked, picking up a framed picture of a little girl holding the hand of a very stern looking man.

"Yes, that's me with my grandfather; he died a couple of years ago, though my grandmother is still alive."

"And, this is also you?" It was a picture of a young girl riding a pony.

"Yes, that's me riding Isabella; don't ask me why I named her that," she replied with just a hint of embarrassment. I placed the picture down carefully.

"What wouldn't I give to live in a place like this," I thought to myself, looking around approvingly.

"If you'll excuse me for a moment, I'll be right back." She disappeared down the hallway that led to the bedrooms.

When she returned she asked with that playful smile of hers, "So, what do you think?"

"Incredible," I responded, eagerly taking her in my arms and kissing her delicious lips.

"I mean about the place," she mumbled, trying not to seriously interrupt what were we doing.

By this time our kissing had begun to take on an almost desperate quality to it as we excitedly explored each other's mouth and tongue. Somehow she managed to convey we were to head down the hallway.

I didn't resist as she hurriedly pulled me into one of the bedrooms where we tumbled onto a huge double bed. Frantically, we began stripping off our clothes all the while attempting to continue our kissing. At one point we had to laugh at our efforts but finally we succeeded, falling lustily into each other's arms and igniting an afternoon of lovemaking that in my view could only be described as incredible. While I recently I had become obsessed with the idea of making love to her, the reality of it far exceeded my wildest fantasies. Carolina made love with an intensity that amazed me. Where did such passion come from? Moreover, she was tender and warm and almost disconcertingly imaginative. I tried not to think about where she had learned to make love like this.

I don't know how long we kept at it but there came a point when I desperately needed to catch my breath. Rolling over onto my back, Carolina nestle herself under my arm, simultaneously draping her arm across my chest and a leg across my stomach.

"My leg's not too heavy for you, is it?" she whispered, kissing my ear lightly.

"Not at all," I replied, hugging her even more tightly. "I love lying here like this with you. And, I have an admission to make, Carolina; I think I've fallen in love with you. No, let me take that back. The truth of the matter is I have fallen in love with you; in fact, I've fallen madly, passionately, head-over-heels in love with you. I've never met anyone quite like you in my whole life. I find you the most incredible woman, not to mention, by the way, the most wonderful lover."

"Oh, Michael, Michael, I'm so happy you said that because that's exactly the way I feel. And, would you believe it, I actually wanted to tell you I loved you the day we went to Otavalo, but I didn't have the courage. I was so worried how you might react; after all, we barely knew each other. But, I knew how I felt though I couldn't help continually asking myself if it was truly possible to fall in love with someone so quickly. Now, I know that it is. Oh, Michael, Michael, I can't begin to describe how much I adore being with you."

As she snuggled up against me, I began to gently stroke her hair. We stayed like that for the longest time, not saying very much, just enjoying the post-coital haze that engulfed us.

Suddenly, I felt Carolina unwrap herself from around me; a second later she was slipping hurriedly out of bed.

"Michael," she whispered, apologetically. "We must have fallen asleep; it's almost four o'clock. I'm sorry, but we really have to go. I need to be back at the university by five at the latest or the security guards may come looking for me."

She leaned over and kissed me. I wanted desperately to pull her back into bed but I fought the urge; I knew we had to leave. It's just that there was something about her that excited me so, especially when she was standing naked directly in front of me. So, it was with incredible reluctance I pulled myself out of bed.

We dressed quickly, though not without interrupting our activities to steal an occasional kiss. And, each time we kissed we had to restrain ourselves from dropping back onto the bed to make love again. Amazingly, I was the one who literally dragged us out of that bedroom. Under no circumstance did I want her to get into trouble over me.

The drive up and out of the valley went so quickly I was barely aware of it. Even when we met took a sharp corner and nearly ran into a battered white pickup truck I simply swung over to the right letting the driver worry about slipping over the edge. Finally we reached the main road at which time I took her hand, then leaned over and kissed her, something I continued to do all the way back to the university. We were both feeling just a little desperate and dreaded the thought of saying goodbye. At that moment if either one of us had suggested we commit right there to spending our lives together, the other would have concurred unhesitatingly. Later, I would look back on that moment and wish we had.

When I dropped her off at the university she appeared on the edge of tears.

"Could we please have lunch on Wednesday? I won't be able to see you at the end of the week or this weekend. My father's going to be away and I have to be around for my mother," she explained dejectedly.

"Not to worry, I'll be here," I replied, trying to cheer her up. "I need to see you, too."

We kissed, not as long as we would have liked, and she quickly climbed out of the car. I watched as she disappeared into the restaurant. I was hoping she would look back and wave. I was surprised how hurt I felt when she didn't.

Nineteen

"You're in love?" Adam exclaimed in surprise, as he poured a Makers Mark for the two of us. He'd come home late, working he said, though I suspected he had gone out for a drink and a quick dinner with Jennifer. Adam was really strange in that respect. While he seemingly had no difficulty finding dates, he was extremely reluctant to ever talk about them to the point where he'd often deny he had even been on one. To the best of my knowledge he had never become serious with anyone and I was fairly certain he wasn't serious about Jennifer. At least from my perspective his dates were always this great mystery. That was very different from me; I wanted to tell Adam everything about Carolina. Well, maybe not everything; I was not about to say anything of our afternoon together at her farm near Mitad del Mundo.

"Yes, I'm in love with her," I confessed with undisguised pleasure. "I even told her so."

"Now let me get this straight, you, Michael Henrick, actually said, 'Carolina, I love you'?"

Adam handed me my drink; he made them strong, a couple ice cubes and lots of Makers Mark. He was right when he teased me about not handling my liquor, but I suspected it might be Adam who actually had the drinking problem. I seldom saw him at home or in a social situation without a drink in his hand, and he never had just one. And, while he never appeared drunk I still worried about him for he had once let slip that both his father and mother liked their martinis in the evening. The word alcoholic was never mentioned but I got the impression they also tended to drink fairly heavily. I couldn't help thinking this was precisely the direction that Adam was headed.

"Yes, I actually said it," I answered, returning to our conversation. I took a sip of my drink, letting it slowly burn its way down my throat. "And, what you may find even more surprising, she made it very clear she loved me too. How about that!"

"What do you mean she made it very clear," Adam responded, looking at me curiously.

"What I mean is, she came right out and told me directly that she loved me, too. Furthermore, she claims she had actually wanted to tell me that as early as the day we went to Otavalo, but apparently she wasn't able to summon the courage to do so. As for me, I think I fell in love with her the very first moment we met; it just never occurred to me she might have felt the same way, until today, of course."

"My God, Michael, how you've changed since our years at business school; you weren't like this at all. Think of it, you've been here in Quito for what, three weeks, and in the brief span of time the most eligible young woman in this country has fallen madly in love with you. What, may I ask, is this secret charm you possess, and how come it didn't work on Rachel?

His mention of Rachel jolted me for a second as it served to remind me how seldom she had entered my mind in the past few days. It was truly amazing; a week ago I couldn't have gone five minutes without thinking about her. I would have been wondering what she was doing or I would have been fantasizing about her, about kissing her or making love to her. Now, I was doing exactly the same thing about Carolina.

"So, then, what are you going to do about Carolina? This isn't just some rebound affair, some infatuation, is it," Adam asked in his typically straightforward manner.

By this time he had taken off his suit jacket, loosened his tie, kicked off his loafers, and had shuffled over to refill his drink.

Adam's question had definitely gotten to the heart of the matter. What was I going to do about Carolina? One thing I was certain of, my feelings towards her were not just some childish infatuation. I was deeply in love with her. I had already concluded I had never felt this way about Rachel. And, yes, it was crazy how suddenly this had all occurred.

"At the moment," I replied, "the only thing I know is that I'm going to have lunch with her on Wednesday. Beyond that I haven't really thought about it."

But, in fact, I was not being entirely honest when I said it. What to do about Carolina was literally the only thing I ever thought about these days. Unfortunately, the one option I had been able to come up with, that she come back to New York with me, did not appear to stand much chance of success. I realized full well that it would be a very difficult, if not impossible, decision for Carolina to make. For one thing, her mother was seriously ill and she probably wouldn't want to leave her. And, then, there was the issue of her participation in her father's political campaign. So, it was difficult imagining her coming with me under these circumstances, I just didn't see any alternative. Out of desperation I decided to try the idea out on Adam to see what he thought of it.

"Go back with you to New York," he exclaimed, when I told him. "You must be out of your mind. I know you honestly believe you're in love with her, and maybe she's actually in love with you, but the truth is, you barely know each other. Tell me, you don't really think she's going to simply pack up and go off to New York with you? To begin with, her family would never allow it. I explained to you, things are very different with young women down here; they don't have the same freedom to do things that American women do. Now, if you two were married that would be different, but you're not and I'm pretty certain you won't be for a good long time, if ever."

"Yeah, you're probably right," I mumbled, reluctantly acknowledging the truth of what he was saying. "But, what choice do I have, either I can stay here, which is impossible in the short run, or she can come to New York with me; that's it. You do have to admit she'd love the place and you also know she'd fit in perfectly. She speaks English beautifully, whereas I barely know a word of Spanish; she also went to college in the United States. And, she's what, twenty-eight years old for God's sake."

"Listen, I'm not trying to entirely dash your hopes about Carolina," Adam explained, sympathetically. "I just want you to be very realistic about your chances of getting her to agree to all this, especially when there's no long-term commitment between you two. You know, her father really depends on her; she's a very intelligent young woman and he knows it. She's actually one of his greatest assets, so he's not going to let her go anywhere before the election. After that, well, maybe things will be different, though there's still going to be this marriage issue."

"So, what do you honestly think her father's chances are of winning the election," I asked, hoping they weren't too good.

"If the election were held today, I'd say sixty-forty. It's not going to be easy; he has enemies. And, unfortunately, one of his best friends, the US, can do nothing openly to help him."

"I've been trying to figure out whether it would be easier for Carolina to leave the country if her father won the election or if he lost it."

We talked about that for a while until it became clear we were both becoming drowsy from the alcohol.

"I think I'd better go to bed," Adam responded, draining his glass and getting up from the couch on which he had been sprawled. "I've got a long, boring day ahead of me tomorrow."

"Yeah, I guess I should go to bed, too. I'm completely worn out from thinking about what I should do. And, I suspect you're right about Carolina. Without our being married there's little chance she'd ever agree to come to New York with me. Oh, well, maybe I'll come up with something; it's just that time is not on my side."

At the door of the kitchen, Adam stopped and remarked, "Whatever happens, you're really a lucky guy to have met someone like Carolina. Believe me, she beats finding Atahualpa's gold any day of the week. And, not to worry, I'm certain you'll think of something."

At the mention of the gold, I was suddenly reminded of the materials I had left for Reverend Hoffmann to translate; I had totally forgotten about them in all my excitement surrounding Carolina. Why hadn't he phoned, I wondered. Or, maybe he had. I went into Adam's study to check the answering machine, but there were no messages. It couldn't have taken him long to read those few pages. Well, there wasn't much I could do about it at this hour; I'd just have to wait until morning.

As usual, I was awakened around six by the roar of aircraft landing at Mariscal Airport, but since it was too early to call Reverend Hoffmann, I continued to just lie in bed. While I probably should have been wondering what was in the pages of the diary I had given him, I found myself instead worrying about what was to become of Carolina and me. I found the idea of her coming to New York exciting even as I realized how difficult it would be for her. Slowly, I had begun to entertain the idea that Carolina might be destined to belong only to my imagination, not to my real life. More like a fantasy, a dream. Perhaps it was my misfortune to have met her in the wrong place under the worst of circumstances. Just thinking about it made me depressed.

A little later I heard Adam moving about somewhere in the other room, followed by his greeting Consuelo. It was impossible not to know she was around because she made so much noise. And, she spoke as if she thought the louder she did so, the easier it would be for us to understand her Spanish. I decided I might as well get up; at least Consuelo would have something waiting for me to eat.

By ten o'clock I had dressed and devoured a huge breakfast during which I had done my best to carry on a conversation with her. I also checked my email; there was a very brief message from Carolina which she must have sent just before she went to bed. It said simply, "I love you, Michael, sweet dreams." I quickly answered her in kind, annoyed with myself that I had not written to her last evening. I ended my message with an "until tomorrow." My excuses for not calling Pastor Hoffmann had now been exhausted.

Punching in the number I had called before, I listened to it ring several times before it was finally answered by a man who spoke to me in Spanish. When I asked for Reverend Hoffmann he did not switch to English as I had expected but asked, as best I could understand, what my name was; he seemed insistent. There was something in his tone that made me uneasy. I hung up quickly, then, wondered if I had done the right thing. I concluded I had; there was something in that voice that unnerved me.

I wandered over to the large picture window that looked down over Guapulo. Usually, the scene from the window served to relax me, but not this time. I was feeling anxious and my hands, I noticed, were trembling ever so slightly. I had no idea what to do next. I was definitely not going to call the pastor's residence again. Maybe, I thought, I should pay a visit to Carlos, even though I had told myself it was not wise to be seen going in and out of his place. On the other hand, I couldn't just hang around here; I had to go out. I finally made a decision. I would wander over by the Lutheran Church; I'd be discreet and if everything seemed all right I'd call at the front gate. For the life of me I couldn't think of anything else to do.

Twenty

Before leaving the apartment I slipped on a pair of dark glasses and grabbed an old Boston Red Sox baseball cap of Adam's, pulling it low over my eyes. Catching my reflection in the gleaming brass of the elevator taking me down to the lobby, I realized how absolutely silly I looked. I'd probably draw more attention to myself now than had I simply gone out dressed normally. An undercover agent I was not!

Exiting the elevator I noticed the security guard deep in conversation with some guy I had never seen around the apartment building before; I decided not to interrupt. I was a bit surprised, then, when I heard him call out, *"Buenos días*, Mr. Henrich." My hat and sunglasses had certainly not fooled him.

"Buenos días," I replied, quickly. I didn't bother to look at the man with whom he was speaking, though out of the corner of my eye I noticed he had turned to face me.

Stepping out onto the sidewalk, I sensed instantly that someone had come up behind me. I turned my head just enough to recognize the guy who had been speaking with the security guard.

"Just keep walking straight ahead towards that black Ford Explorer," he ordered. He spoke quietly but with authority. "Don't say a word or try anything stupid, please; we have no desire to hurt you though I will if necessary."

I couldn't believe it, all the talk about kidnapping down here and now it was happening to me, and in broad daylight. Even more frightening, it appeared that the security guard working in Adam's building was a party to it. I glanced around desperately hoping there might be someone who could come to my aid but my abductor was way ahead of me.

"Don't even think about it," he hissed, grasping my arm so tightly it hurt. "To repeat, I don't want to hurt you so don't even think of trying anything."

For the moment I decided it would be best if I did exactly as he said. It turned out to be an excellent idea since as I approached the car a short heavy-set man with a shaved head jumped out of the passenger seat and opened the door for me. As he guided me into the back seat I couldn't help but notice a huge scar on the side of his head made even more obvious by the fact the rest of his head was so deeply tanned.

"Now, just sit there quietly," he growled, in heavily accented English.

The door was then slammed shut and the two men quickly climbed into the front. I felt a little relieved they thought it unnecessary to have someone sit in back with me. But, then, the stocky one tossed something into my lap that looked like a black Halloween mask though without the slits for the eyes.

"Put it on; we don't want you to see where we're taking you, though to be honest you'd probably never find the place anyway. Just the same, it would be best to humor us and slip that thing on."

The driver waited until I had placed the mask over my face and sat back before starting the motor and pulling the Explorer away from the curb. Until now I had remained silent. For some strange reason I wasn't feeling as frightened as the situation would seem to warrant. It reminded me a little of a late November afternoon in Boston's Public Garden when I was accosted by two men demanding money. Since one flashed a knife I didn't hesitate a second emptying my wallet of cash, but it was not until the two had walked away that I actually experienced any fear. I suspected it would be similar here except these guys gave every indication of being potentially far more dangerous than the two who had robbed me. Worse, I had no idea what they wanted from me; it clearly wasn't a robbery. As for their continued assurances they had no desire to harm me, I took those with a grain-of-salt. On the other hand, having no reasonable alternative I decided to simply take them at their word.

"OK," I exclaimed, feeling a bit more confident, "I've done what you asked and have come along without raising a fuss, so could you now please tell me who you are and why you've kidnapped me."

"When we get to where we're going, and we'll be there in a few minutes, we have a number of questions for you," replied a voice I took to be that of the driver. "If you answer these questions to our satisfaction, we'll answer whatever questions you might have, within reason, of course."

I accepted his response for the moment and didn't say another word.

After that we drove in total silence for what seemed like about twenty minutes, at which point I felt the car slow, take a couple of sharp turns and come to a stop; the engine was quickly turned off and almost immediately I could hear a garage door closing behind us.

"You can take the mask off, now," said the voice I was coming to recognize as the leader of this little operation.

I was relieved for I felt as if I were beginning to suffocate. We stepped out into a garage with plain white sheetrock walls, a concrete floor and absolutely no evidence whatsoever that anyone lived here—no tools, no paint cans, no boxes, not even a broom. There was a door leading into what I guessed was a house and the swarthy one unlocked it with a key he had taken from his pocket. He stepped back and ushered me in. I couldn't help glancing at his scar again; there was something intimidating about it.

I stepped into a kitchen only slightly less bare than the garage. The cabinets were cheap and made of some kind of light-colored wood. There was a badly scarred wooden table with three chairs placed around it; none of them matched. The place also had a faint smell of coffee, which probably wasn't surprising since the only kitchen item visible was an old automatic coffeemaker.

"Let's go into the other room," suggested the driver, whom I now had my first opportunity to have a good look at. He was at least six-feet tall and had the kind of rugged build that one could only get from working out regularly. On the other hand, he didn't spend all his time in the gym since his face was well tanned. He also had the most piercing blue eyes and sandy-colored hair, which he wore close-cropped. I suspected with his looks he had no trouble finding women.

As I followed him into the living room, he called back," Jacob, see if you can find any coffee grounds for that machine; look in the refrigerator. We'll probably all be needing some before we finish here."

The living room must have been designed by the same interior decorator for it was just as austere as the kitchen---a well-worn couch, a couple of old chairs, a standing lamp and a coffee table. That was it; there was nothing on the walls while the windows were made of frosted glass that let in some light but otherwise made it impossible to see either in or out. Clearly, no one called this place home.

"Have a seat, Mr. Henrick," he said, indicating that I should sit on the couch. "My name is Frank and that's Jacob out in the kitchen. For your information they're not our real names; in fact, none of this is real.

Understand, Michael, that reality is nothing more than a state of mind; it can be anything you want it to be."

"So, what you're saying is I'm to pretend this isn't really happening to me," I replied sarcastically.

He smiled but there was no warmth to it.

"OK, I'll play your game; now will you please tell me, why I'm here," I asked. By this time I had come to the realization I had been taken to some kind of a safe-house, which I recognized from my John Le Carre' novels was the place spies were hidden away to be interrogated, or was it tortured.

"So, Mr. Henrick, may I assume you're going to make this easy for us and, of course, for yourself?"

He had completely ignored my question but instead stared at me as if trying to will my cooperation; I returned his stare.

"Look, we've done some checking on you and you appear to be a nice enough guy, but somehow you've gotten yourself caught up in the middle of a very dangerous situation. Even worse, I suspect you don't have the faintest idea just how dangerous it really is. So, what I need to do is ask you some questions for which I desperately need answers, and I need those answers quickly. We're racing against time here. Now, first question, do you have any idea what was in those papers that you left for Reverend Hoffmann to translate? "

"How do you know about those papers," I asked in amazement.

"Just answer my question, do you know what information those papers contained? I haven't time to play any games here."

"I have absolutely no idea what was written on those pages I gave Reverend Hoffmann. Why do you think I gave them to him; they were written in German script. But, I don't understand, if you know he has them, wouldn't it be more to the point to simply ask him? He's the one who purportedly knows how to read German script. So, tell me, how do you know about the papers?"

The expression on Frank's face made me suddenly uneasy.

"For your information, Mr. Henrick, Reverend Hoffmann is dead."

The words seemed to hang suspended in the air between us. Too stunned to respond I simply stared blankly at Frank trying desperately to absorb what I had just heard. When finally I regained my voice, all I could utter was a weak, "Reverend Hoffmann is dead? Please, please, tell me you're not serious."

"Oh, I'm perfectly serious," Frank sneered. "He was murdered in his study at the church."

"But, why," I stammered, recognizing instantly the answer to my own question, and also why these guys were holding me.

"Someone wanted the papers I left with him, right?"

"You catch on fast," Frank grunted.

"I simply can't believe it."

Frank turned to Jacob and asked, "Do you have that copy of today's Miami *Herald*?"

"I think it must be in the car, do you want me to go get it?"

"Yeah, I think it would be a good idea. It might just impress on our friend here the kind of people he's dealing with out there."

We waited silently as Jacob went in search of the newspaper. I knew Frank was watching me but I couldn't bear to return his gaze, not at the moment anyway. When a minute or so later Jacob returned Frank grabbed the newspaper and thrust it at me.

"Turn to page three." It came out less as a request than an order.

It was the Latin American edition of the Miami *Herald*. I did as Frank had ordered and turned to page three; I couldn't miss the article he obviously wanted me to see. In bold print it proclaimed, Lutheran Minister Murdered in Quito! I simply scanned the rest of the articled knowing Frank had every intention of filling me in on every last grisly detail whether I wanted to hear it or not.

"So, now do you believe it?"

"Yes, yes, I believe it," I sighed. "Now can you tell me what happened since I suspect you guys probably know a lot more than what appears here in the paper."

"Well, we don't know as much as we'd like but what we do know is that the killer or killers worked him over with a blunt instrument of some kind though the weapon wasn't found; he probably died of a fractured skull," Frank explained in an almost clinical manner. "In all probability he tried to resist turning over the papers. Had he done so, of course, he only would have died more quickly though probably less painfully. As for the individuals involved, they definitely knew what they were doing since they were able to gain access to his living quarters, beat him mercilessly, and then escape apparently without anyone hearing a thing. You do understand, then, why it is imperative we find out what was in those papers."

At that moment all I could think about was Reverend Hoffmann's murder. What had I gotten him into that made it necessary for someone to kill the poor man just to get hold of those papers? What kind of monsters would do such a thing anyway? I suddenly felt as if I were going to be sick. It quickly passed but not so the feeling of guilt that had now overwhelmed me. And, needless to say, it came as no consolation to think had I not given him the papers it might well have been me who was murdered; I might well be murdered yet, for that matter, and I still didn't have a clue who was after me and neither apparently did Frank and Jacob.

"The only thing I remember is a date," I finally responded to Frank's question. "One of the pages began with the year 1945. There may also have been a month, possibly April, though I'm not entirely certain, but I do know it was 1945. Beyond that the whole thing is a complete mystery to me."

"And, you're absolutely sure you can't remember anything else, not even a couple of words?" Frank persisted.

"No, just the date; that was it!"

Anxiety, guilt, and now frustration, what would I be feeling next?

"All right, all right, so what do we actually know then? That the papers were almost certainly written by a German, an older German, one who would have learned German script in school, and that this person began writing something in April 1945, or at least sometime in 1945. If it was April that would be when the war was nearing its end, so this person may have been recording what was going on around him during Germany's collapse. He might have been worried what was going to happen to him after the surrender. On the other hand, maybe the person was keeping a diary of his new life here in Ecuador. But, if that were the case, what would he be writing that someone did not want to get out? While it could be most anything I wouldn't be surprised if it had something to do with the writer's Nazi past."

"Well, whatever the content of that diary, you still haven't explained how you knew about the papers I had given to Reverend Hoffmann; or about me for that matter. I was the only one who could possibly have known about those papers. Wait a minute there was one other person, an Erich Kessler, a teacher down at the German School who recommended Reverend Hoffmann to me."

"Erich Kessler, that's a new name. I don't imagine you know anything about this guy?"

"Not a thing," I replied. "But, if he had been involved in some way, wouldn't he have suggested translating the documents himself rather than having Reverend Hoffmann do it?"

"Possibly. Still, we need to talk to him. Maybe he told someone about the papers; he may have even mentioned Reverend Hoffmann was going to translate them. Yes, we'd better have a talk with him just in case. Now, for just a moment let's get back to the papers. What did you think they were about," Frank continued. "I mean, let's face it, you must have considered them sufficiently important to go to all this trouble."

"The more I think about what's happened, the more stupid and guilty I feel." I was leaning forward, my arms resting on my knees. Frank was sitting across from me while Jacob stood quietly in the doorway to the kitchen. I hadn't quite figured out his role yet but it certainly wasn't just to make coffee.

"At the beginning," I explained, "I actually thought these papers might have something to do with the location of Atahualpa's gold. At least that's the only thing anyone ever mentioned to me. On the other hand, I didn't even take the whole thing seriously until Francisco was murdered. It was only then that I began to realize the diary had to be important if people were so willing to kill for it. But, even with all this I still thought it had to do with Atahualpa's gold, or at least Inca gold of some kind."

"Wait a minute, now, who is this Francisco? You've never mentioned him before; the number of people who might be involved just keeps growing. So, what did this Francisco have to do with this diary?" Frank was leaning forward and I could see he was watching me intently.

"Francisco was the person who originally claimed to possess the secret to the location of Atahualpa's gold. He was this old man, a peasant farmer or something, who used to come into this bar for lunch everyday and whenever he couldn't pay, which was like everyday, he would always tell the owner, 'Don't worry, I know where Atahualpa's gold can be found.' I just thought it was some kind of a joke until one day he apparently came in very frightened, claiming that someone was after him and he handed the owner of this bar, a guy named Carlos, an antique box for safekeeping."

"So, after this guy was killed Carlos opened the box and allegedly found the diary inside. Do you trust this guy, Carlos? Isn't it possible he's lying to you, that he may have his own agenda, that he's simply using you?"

"Believe me, I completely trust Carlos and I'd bet my life on the fact he's been telling me the truth," I replied, wondering if I honestly believed what I was saying. "Look, it was only when Carlos read in the newspaper that Francisco had been murdered, that, like you suggested, he apparently opened the box and found this diary; he showed it to me. I was the one who explained to him that it was written in German script and that's why he asked me to see if I could find someone to translate it. After I agreed, he had a few pages of the diary reproduced and gave them to me. Those were the papers I gave to Reverend Hoffmann. There was a moment, however, when I felt I was being followed so I stopped going to Carlos' place for several days, but when I never actually saw anyone I decided I was just being paranoid. Maybe there was someone and this person followed me to the church. Oh, man, you can't begin to believe how badly I feel about what's happened."

"You understand, then, how incredibly lucky you are that we found you before the people who killed Reverend Hoffmann, and probably this Francisco, too, were able to do so," Frank exclaimed. "We found out about the papers, the pages from the diary, because Reverend Hoffmann called the Israeli Embassy to report he had some information they might find extremely interesting. But, even you must now realize, whatever he wanted to tell us, it almost certainly had nothing to do with Atahualpa's gold. He would have had no reason to call the Israeli Embassy if they had, don't you agree?"

"I do," I replied dejectedly.

"Well, anyway, Reverend Hoffmann explained that this American had brought in these papers and by some good fortune he gave the person who took the call your name. When a couple representatives from the embassy went there the next morning to speak with him, they found the police swarming all over the place. That's when we were called in and we were given your name though, of course, we hadn't a clue how to find you since he hadn't given us your address or phone number. The only option that immediately came to mind was to call the American Embassy where we have, shall we say, 'good friends.' One of them discretely checked around and to his amazement found not only who you were but that you were staying with an employee of the embassy, one Adam Winthrop."

"But, didn't Adam become suspicious when you began asking about me," I asked, not certain how much of all this I actually believed.

"We did a little research on you before contacting Adam and one of the things we uncovered was that you flew to Quito on American Airlines. So, the woman we had call Adam simply identified herself as working for American Airlines and she informed him she needed to speak with you about your return ticket. Adam gave her both the address and the telephone number of his apartment, which turned out to be fortunate for you, but he'll have to be reminded not to do that quite so readily in the future."

Frank was not finished, however.

"You do understand, then, how much better it was that it was we, and not the police, who got your name, because the police would have brought you in for questioning; almost certainly you'd be their prime suspect. Of course, the main reason you're not a suspect is thanks to the killers; they took whatever materials you had given him and if your name was on them, they took that too since it would make their job of finding you just that much easier. Though it remains a mystery what's in that diary, we do know it has to be something someone wants to keep secret!"

"So, you think whoever these killers are, they're looking for me at this very moment," I asked, not really wanting to hear his answer.

"I'm certain of it, that's why we wanted to grab you first; these guys are getting desperate," exclaimed Frank. "Killing the pastor of the largest Protestant church in Quito? That gives you some indication of just how high the stakes have become."

"So, who may I ask are you, the Mossad or something?"

I was truly becoming anxious now, realizing there were people out there looking to kill me.

"Or something," he replied, referring to my last question. I heard Jacob snicker

"Obviously, we need to get our hands on this diary; it's certainly going to be the only way you can breathe easier, or even just keep breathing. So, you think there's a good possibility this Carlos still has it?"

"Oh, I'm sure he has, that is, if they haven't stolen it from him," I replied, suddenly realizing Carlos had to be in even greater danger than me. "Someone had broken into his bar shortly after Francisco's murder so he knew he was under surveillance. He had asked his brother, a former boxer, and some of his brother's friends, who by the way are pretty mean-looking dudes, to keep watch over the bar, though obviously they didn't do an especially good job of it."

"So, tell me honestly, do you think this Carlos character has any better knowledge of what's in the diary than you?"

"No, definitely not. He didn't even recognize that the diary was written in German. On the other hand, I don't think he believes it holds the key to Atahualpa's gold; he's too smart for that."

"Well, I want to talk to him immediately to find out if he does still have the diary," Frank declared. "Now, what did you say was the name of his place?"

"It's called *El Café de Los Toreros*. And, promise me, if you do talk to him, let him know I'm all right, though I'm not certain I'm high on his list of concerns. Just don't let anything happen to him, not after the murder of Reverend Hoffmann."

The last thing I needed was Carlos' death on my conscience. I was feeling guilty enough as it was already.

"Look, you've got to remember who we are. We are not the police and we're in no real position to protect him," Frank reminded me.

"Wait a minute, aren't you supposedly protecting me? Why not him, then?"

"Because we don't have the manpower to look after everyone," Frank replied. "As for you, you're going to stay here with Jacob; I'm going to have a drink at the ah….what was the name again?

"*El Café de Los Toreros.*"

"Yes, there. If you need anything Jacob will get it for you. But, under no circumstances are you to try to leave; Jacob is here to make sure you don't and, believe me, he may look like a pussy-cat but he can also be very persuasive when he sets his mind to it."

I glanced over at Jacob just in time to catch his wry smile. As it was, the nasty scar on his face provided all the incentive I needed to keep from angering him. For the moment I had every intention of remaining right where I was.

Twenty-One

No sooner had Frank gone out the door than Jacob seemed to noticeably relax. It had become obvious that whatever organization they worked for Frank was Jacob's boss and just as obviously it was not an easy relationship. When Jacob chose to come into the living room and sit down in one of the chairs opposite me, I decided this might be my only opportunity to find out exactly what was going on. The question was, how to get Jacob talking. Up to this point, at least, he had not showed himself to be much of a conversationalist.

"So, Jacob, tell me about the scar on your face," I began, assuming it was a logical question given that one couldn't help noticing it.

"I cut myself shaving," he responded curtly.

I had to smile; it was a tactful way of telling me some things were none of my business. I decided to try another approach, which proved far more successful.

"All right, then, how long are you planning to keep me here? Are we talking hours, or days? I mean you didn't even let me grab a toothbrush or a change of clothes."

"Probably a couple of days, unless by some stroke of luck we're able to quickly get our hands on that diary. Since I assume you've given us most of the information we're going to get from you, which certainly wasn't much by the way, once we have it you will no longer be our responsibility; you'll be on your own. In the meantime, don't worry, we'll see to it you get a toothbrush."

"I'm not particularly worried about the toothbrush, what I am worried about is what happens if you don't find the diary that quickly? Will I have to remain here indefinitely?"

This really frightened me, the possibility that it might take days or even weeks to find it; and what, if they never did? How long would they keep me under those circumstances? Of course, if the killers found the diary first, there'd be no reason to look for me; they'd have what they wanted. Then, again, if they thought I might know what was in the diary, well, I didn't even want to contemplate that possibility.

"We'll find it, don't worry. But, for the moment you're better off right here where we can keep an eye on you. The people looking for you out there are very nasty. Believe me, you do not want to fall into their hands."

"At least that's one thing I can't disagree with you on," I replied, remembering what they had done to poor Reverend Hoffmann.

Suddenly, Adam popped into mind. Until this moment I hadn't given him a thought, yet I now realized how much danger he could be in. It was entirely possible the people after me didn't even know what I looked like; they might easily confuse Adam with me and grab him by mistake. And even if they did know who he was, they still might kidnap him as a way of getting to me.

"Look, Jacob, you've got to let me contact Adam, the guy at whose apartment I'm staying; he could be in real danger, too. Not only that but if I don't show up at the apartment, Lord knows whom he might contact. Please," I begged, "you have to let me give him a call or something. I know you have a cell phone; just let me make one call, one call and you can even listen in to it. I promise, I won't try anything."

"Take it easy," Jacob said, calmly. I had already concluded that Jacob was at heart a much nicer guy than Frank. He couldn't help that he looked the part of a heavy, and Frank clearly used that fact to intimidate people. However, once you began talking to him just one-on-one he wasn't like that at all. He really did seem like a decent guy. I just hoped he was what he seemed.

"I thought Frank was going to explain," Jacob continued, "but he raced out of here so quickly I guess he just forgot. Anyway, your friend Adam is being looked after, at least for a couple days. A group of American businessmen from Miami requested the embassy to have Adam join them on a trip to Guayaquil, where they're looking into several investment opportunities. I suspect he's already there. It was a little last minute but they were able to make a good case for his accompanying them."

"A little coincidental, isn't it; this trip I mean. Coming right after you kidnapped me, or as you would say, placed me in protective custody." I had to give these guys credit they thought of everything, though clearly there were more people involved in this enterprise than just the two of them.

"Let's just say these businessmen occasionally help us out, like now, for instance. They are American, they just have allegiances that extend beyond the borders of the US," he explained.

"To Israel?" It was more a rhetorical question since I assumed he would not answer it directly. But, surprisingly, he did.

"Yes, to Israel," he replied with complete candor. "Frank wouldn't have probably answered you so directly, but you're a smart guy, college-educated. There's no point in playing around on something like this, especially when two guys have been killed already. On the other hand, I should remind you that no one is ever going to officially admit to it so as we suggested at the beginning, think of it as a dream, the memory of which will fade once you wake up in the morning."

"OK, OK, I get the point, but tell me, if you're not Mossad then who are you?" I knew I was pushing his willingness to be honest with me.

"Ah, the Mossad; that seems to be the only Israeli organization you Americans are familiar with. But in answer to your question, we don't work for the Mossad. Who we do actually work for is probably irrelevant. Why don't you just think of us as private contractors," he said, with a surprisingly disarming smile.

I was still a little worried about Adam; to think I had been responsible for Reverend Hoffmann's death was bad enough, but if anything happened to Adam I could never forgive myself. I was already worried about what I might be doing to Adam's professional career.

"Can you tell me about these businessmen? I mean, you can trust them completely, right? "

"You don't have to worry about Adam; these guys will see to it he's well taken care of," Jacob explained. "As I said, they're legitimate businessmen. The fact they were willing to drop what they were doing and fly over here on such short notice should tell you volumes about the kind of men they are."

His response put me at ease, at least for the moment. But now I realized I was hungry; famished would be an even better term to describe my condition. I hadn't eaten for hours. Thank God Consuelo had fed me well at breakfast. Unfortunately, that was several hours ago and now my stomach was beginning to growl; in a minute even Jacob would be able to hear it.

"Jacob, is there anything to eat around here; I'm really starving," I asked out of desperation.

"There's nothing; I checked when we first got here. Hopefully, Frank will remember to bring something. In the meantime there's no way I'm going to let you go out alone, and it's not a good idea to have us both go out. Though this place is secure, once we're out there, somebody might spot us. Whomever they are, they don't seem to worry too much about having to kill people who get in their way."

I slumped back on the couch. Why hadn't I brought my iPod at least? Some music right now would go a long way towards relieving my boredom, and possibly my hunger. The answer, of course, was that I hadn't exactly planned on being here.

"Are you absolutely sure there's nothing to eat in this place? Maybe there's a can of soup or something. You know, Jacob, if your organization asks me to write an evaluation of how well you two carried out your little mission here, I'm going to have no choice but to grade you down on the food end of things; you've really screwed up there."

For the first time Jacob smiled a honest-to-goodness smile, then shoved himself out of the chair and wandered into the kitchen. I heard the refrigerator open and then detected the slight clink of bottles hitting against one another. He came back with two Club beers.

"The best I could do," he announced; clearly my comment about the food had amused him.

"Thanks, it's better than nothing," I replied, relieved just to have something to do. In fact, the beer tasted great; I had become dehydrated. I finished it quickly, too quickly, and because my stomach was so empty, I actually began to feel a little light-headed. On one beer! It was just one more indication of how poorly I handled my alcohol.

It suddenly dawned on me that tomorrow was Wednesday and I had promised Carolina I'd meet her for lunch. Not only was it becoming increasingly obvious that I'd be unable to do that, I was almost certain now they were not about to let me get in touch with her to explain why. What was she going to think? After our passionate lovemaking, the last thing I wanted her to think was that I was only in this relationship for the sex. I had to get in touch with her some way, but how?

"Jacob, are you sure I can't use your cell phone? One call and it's not to Adam. I really need to make a call, to tell someone I won't be making lunch tomorrow."

"Sorry, my orders are to make sure you contact no one," he responded.

As I was trying to figure out some other way to get a message to her, I heard the garage door open, then close a few seconds later. Frank came bursting through the door and into the room where Jacob and I were sitting. The first thing I noticed was that he had no food with him, the second, that he was clearly upset about something.

"They got to him; your friend, Carlos? He's in the hospital," Frank burst out. "Those guys you said were supposed to be looking out for him, well they didn't do a very good job of it."

Why was I not surprised, the fact is, those guys had always appeared too stupid to me to be especially good at anything, even fighting.

"Please tell me he's not been hurt too badly," I asked, trying to control my emotions. "He always seemed like the kind of guy who could take care of himself."

This whole thing was becoming a war and like a war the casualties were mounting—Reverend Hoffmann, Francisco, and now Carlos. What possibly could be in that diary that could lead to so much bloodshed? It didn't make any sense, though I had now concluded that the diary had nothing to do with Atahualpa's gold. But, if it didn't, what secrets did it contain that someone was prepared to do anything to keep from being revealed? They had to be incredibly damaging to somebody.

"He's in pretty bad shape though it looks like he's going to survive. I couldn't really get close to him; probably the same guys who couldn't protect him earlier are now standing guard outside his hospital room. Let's hope they do a better job this time. Anyway, they wouldn't let me get near and I was not about to argue with them, not at this point. But, by chance, I did get to speak with his doctor. He reported that in addition to his many cuts and bruises, Carlos has a rather serious concussion. And you're right, Carlos is one very tough guy; apparently he was conscious when they brought him in although they're keeping him sedated at the moment. I'm hoping that maybe by tomorrow I'll get a chance to talk with him."

"I still can't believe all this is happening, and over a stupid diary, though to someone whatever it contains must be dynamite," I remarked angrily. "And, by the way, does anyone know if the people, who did this to Carlos, did in fact get the diary?"

"Since I wasn't able to speak directly with Carlos, I can't answer that but it's a good question," Frank replied, a bit calmer now than when he first stormed in. "As for those guys hanging around outside his hospital room, they were not about to tell me anything. But, there is one thing that leads me to suspect they couldn't get the diary; Carlos wasn't killed. I hope tomorrow I'll have the opportunity to talk with him. I have to be extremely careful since that may be exactly what the killers are now waiting for, someone to lead them to the diary."

"So, what are you trying to tell me," I asked, worried more than ever that I was not going to get out of here anytime soon.

"That we're onto something really big here," Frank replied. "I just wish I had some indication of what it was. One of the things, that has been bothering me from the beginning, is why the police seem to have done so little. It can't help but make you wonder if perhaps they're involved somehow. Of course, it's also possible someone is pressuring them not to push the investigation. I mean, this should be big news, or at least bigger than it is, yet there's surprisingly little in any of the newspapers about it."

Twenty-Two

The day seemed to crawl by; I barely moved from the couch. Of course, there was no place to go and even less to do. Since Frank and Jacob had both assured me that Adam would be fine, that left me basically free to worry about Carolina. What, I asked myself repeatedly, could she possibly be thinking? She had probably emailed me, several times in fact, and had obviously received no answers to any of them. So, what could she conclude? That I had used her? That I saw her as a one-night stand, a one-afternoon stand, whatever? How would I ever be able to explain to her what had happened? For that matter even if I had the chance, she'd never believe me; I'd never believe a story like this. The more I thought about her the more miserable I became, even more miserable than when Rachel had unceremoniously told me "to take a hike," though she hadn't used that phrase exactly. Why was it, I wondered, that every time I fell in love with a woman our relationship not only ended suddenly but disastrously, at least for me?

At some point Frank sent Jacob out to get us something to eat. He came back with a large pizza and a couple six-packs of beer. As hungry as I been earlier, I now found it impossible to eat anything; the pizza just didn't look particularly appetizing. Naturally, that turned out to be fine with Jacob who happily devoured my share along with his own. I sipped on a beer and wondered how I was going to survive if I had to spend several more days like this? I almost preferred taking a chance with the guys out there looking for me than remain cooped up like this.

As Jacob cleaned up from dinner, Frank disappeared for a moment, then, returned with a book in his hand.

"Here," he said, "I brought something for you. It was the only book in English I could find. Hope you haven't read it."

"Ah, *The English Patient*; I can never remember the author's name. Oh, yes, Michael Andaatje, he's a Canadian if I'm not mistaken. Anyway, I've never read the book, though I have seen the movie, several times, in fact. I thought it was superb—Ralph Fiennes, Juliette Binoche as the nurse who takes care of him after he's so badly burned. I think I fell in love with her every time I saw it."

"*The English Patient* is a much better book than the movie. To be honest, I've seldom seen a movie that I thought was superior to the book on which it was based," Frank asserted. I was beginning to think this was his manner; he didn't offer an opinion, he simply stated things as if they were facts. I found it annoying, which is probably why I couldn't help challenging his assertions.

"How about Tom Clancy's *The Hunt for Red October*? Now, that movie was unquestionably better than the book," I declared smugly.

"The movie was very good," he admitted reluctantly. "Of course, if I were going to pick one movie about submarine warfare it would have to be *Das Boot*."

"I'd probably agree with you," I responded, "but that wasn't my point. My point was that the movie, *The Hunt for Red October*, was far better than the book, something you said you'd seldom found."

"OK, so you're a real movie fan," Frank answered, refusing to concede my point.

We continued to talk movies for a little while longer but there's a limit to everything and in time we exhausted the subject. I was really getting tired, though from what I was not sure. Frank directed me to a small bedroom that was as bare as the rest of the house—a single bed, a chair, and a night table. It was then I also remembered I had no spare clothes and they still hadn't brought me a toothbrush. I decided I could do without clean clothes for a day or so, but I had to get a toothbrush; I couldn't stand not brushing my teeth. I couldn't help wonder what other things I was about to learn about myself; it was a little scary.

Sprawled on the bed, I tried my best to fall asleep, but it proved impossible; my mind was far too active for that. And, while I consciously tried not to think about Carolina knowing it would drive me crazy, it proved impossible. I became obsessed with the memory of that afternoon we spent together at her farm, replaying over and over every exciting moment of our lovemaking. Carolina had amazed me with her passion and now suddenly I couldn't help but wonder if I'd ever experience it again. Just the thought that I might not was already becoming painful.

As images of Carolina flashed one after another through my mind I gradually became conscious of Frank and Jacob conversing in the other room; unfortunately, I couldn't quite make out what they were saying. At some point I heard the sound of the garage door opening, then closing. I assumed it was Frank going out, leaving Jacob to look after me. That made me wonder what would actually happen if the guys looking for me tried to enter the house. Would Jacob be capable of protecting me? He was definitely one tough guy and could probably take on anybody one-on-one but I was certain whoever came after me would not come alone; he'd bring plenty of help. Then, amazingly, I dozed off to sleep.

In the middle of the night I was suddenly awakened by the sound of a car door slamming. Could it be the killers coming after me, I wondered? I lay there barely breathing for what seemed like eternity but nothing further happened. Gradually I began to relax, though I still found it impossible to sleep. To my surprise, I began thinking about Rachel, though not with any great affection. Oddly, I found myself blaming her for my being in this predicament. Had she not left me so suddenly, I'd be in New York right now. I'd be sleeping in my own bed in my own apartment thinking about what I'd be doing the next day at my new job. I certainly wouldn't have come down here and therefore I wouldn't be trapped like this. I might someday forgive her for breaking up with me, but I'd never forgive her for this. And, yet, without this there'd be no Carolina.

I must have drifted off again because the next thing I knew Jacob was shaking me.

"Come out and get some breakfast," he said. "You have to be hungry since you ate next to nothing last night. Come on."

As he headed out to the kitchen, I forced myself to sit up. Man, did I need a shower; I smelled simply awful. But, Jacob was right, I was starved, so my shower would just have to wait. And, if my body odor offended them, it would serve them right.

Frank was leaning against the kitchen counter when I entered the room, holding a cigarette in one hand, a cup of coffee in easy reach.

"Well, well, if it isn't sleeping beauty. Do you know what time it is?" he laughed. It was strange but that was the first time he'd actually laughed in the past two days.

"I haven't the slightest idea," I replied, still trying to clear the cobwebs from my brain.

"It's nearly ten o'clock; you slept for twelve hours!"

"I beg to differ with you," I answered. "I stared at the ceiling for seven hours, I slept for five, or maybe it was eight and four. Anyway, that's quite a difference."

I helped myself to a huge cup of coffee and grabbed a couple of pan de yuccas, then walked over and sat down at the table with Jacob.

"Cheers, " I said to him, raising my coffee cup in a mock toast.

He nodded in response.

"Ouch, that's hot," I yelled, spilling some of my coffee on the only pair of pants I currently possessed. "Why didn't you warn me?"

They both laughed in the same perverse way most people laugh when some guy unexpectedly spills scalding coffee in his lap.

"Sorry about that," Frank replied, trying unsuccessfully to wipe the grin from his face.

The sun was shining through the window above the curtain, which was meant to keep anyone from looking in, or out. It reminded me that other people were going about their daily lives out there while I was stuck here in this depressing house. Adam was probably at this very moment escorting his American businessmen around Guayaquil. How I envied him. As for Carolina, she was undoubtedly getting ready to drive to the university in her Honda Pilot, where she would deliver her day's lecture and perhaps even worry a little over why I hadn't been in touch with her. I certainly hoped so, anyway.

"Look, you've got to let me out of here," I begged suddenly. " I'm going stir crazy. Can't you speak to your superiors or someone in the embassy? Tell them I'm more than capable of looking after myself, really. I won't leave my apartment, I promise. Just let me out of here"

"Reverend Hoffmann was killed because someone out there does not want the contents of those papers to be made public. That same someone may think you have the diary from which the pages came, or at the least, may think you have an idea what's in them. If that's the case, how long do you think it will take them to find you? Right now, we're about the only protection you have, and that goes for your roommate Adam, as well. So, just be patient and, please, don't act as if you don't care whether you live or die."

"But, I don't even know what I'm to be patient about," I replied, feeling more than a little desperate now. "I mean, am I supposed to wait for the police to do something? And, don't worry, I'm not anxious to die."

"No, not the police, they don't have a clue," Frank explained. "They don't even know where to start looking because there's no way they'll be able to come up with a motive. You know what their motive was and I know what their motive was, but if the killers managed to locate and take with them all the papers you gave Reverend Hoffmann, the police will never figure it out. Of course, there's the additional complication that when it comes to investigating homicides, Ecuador's National Police is not known for being an especially efficient organization."

"So, what then? What exactly am I waiting here for," I screamed in frustration.

"You're waiting for me. I'm going back to the hospital to see if I can talk to your friend, Carlos. If I can get that diary from him, you're free to go. We won't have to protect you because the people out there searching for the diary will be on the run, at least once they find out we have it."

"Do you think Carlos will be well enough to talk to you?" For the first time in the past twenty-four hours I was beginning to feel optimistic about getting out of this place.

"Well, that's what I'm about to find out right now. Cheer up, you could be out of here in a couple hours if all goes well," he responded with a smile.

"And, if all doesn't go well," I asked.

"You don't even want to think about it. Do yourself a favor and try to think positively."

He and Jacob disappeared through the door leading to the garage; I assumed he was giving Jacob his orders. A few minutes later I could hear the garage door open, then close. Jacob returned closing the kitchen door behind him.

"So, Jacob, how are we going to spend the day?" My question was at best rhetorical, but the sarcasm in my voice was obvious.

Jacob gave me a look that made clear he didn't appreciate my tone. I suddenly felt like a jerk. If I were to believe them, and nothing they had done suggested otherwise, they very possibly had saved my life. Now, admittedly, they had initially wanted to find out what I knew about the diary, or the pages from the diary, but once they found out I knew next to nothing, they could have sent me on my way. Instead, they had forced me, though force seemed for some reason to be an inappropriate term, to remain here under their protection. Even now when I had begged them to let me go they had refused, asking me only to be patient. Well, I was not going to apologize to Jacob, but neither would I hassle him; he was an all right guy and, I guessed, Frank probably was, as well.

Since Jacob did not seem inclined to engage in conversation at that moment, I went in search of *The English Patient*; I couldn't think of a single thing else to do since there was neither a radio nor TV in the place. Finding the book on the table next to my bed, I decided to read it there. But, as much as I tried, reading proved impossible; I couldn't concentrate for more than a few minutes at a time. I would read a page or two and then I'd put the book down. Almost instantly these incredible images of Carolina would take shape in my mind: Carolina struggling to unfasten her bra, freeing her full, luscious breasts; Carolina slipping her panties down with my help and rolling over on top of me: Carolina giving me that smile so filled with love and desire, just the thought of it aroused me. Though we had made love only once, every detail of that experience was burned indelibly into my brain. I found it impossible to stop thinking about her. I was missing her so badly.

Twenty-Three

I spent most of the day sprawled on the couch, my copy of *The English Patient* lying unopened next to me. But, if my body remained largely inactive, my mind more than made up for it. At one time or another I thought about Carolina, Adam, Rachel, and amazingly even my parents, which did nothing to help my mental state though it did serve to relieve my boredom. More importantly, it had the effect of calming me and I found myself gradually feeling less afraid and more annoyed. It wasn't that I doubted the fact I could be in some kind of physical danger, after all, everything these guys had told me seemed to make perfect sense. And, I suspected there was probably far more to the story than what they had revealed. Yet, I was still more or less hoping I would suddenly wake up to find this whole thing had all been nothing more than a bad dream.

I barely saw Jacob for most of the day. He appeared to be doing something out in the kitchen although for the life of me I couldn't figure out what it was. Very possibly Frank had suggested he stay away from me, or just maybe he didn't have anything much to talk to me about. At one point I did hear his cell-phone ring; unfortunately, when he answered he spoke so softly it was impossible for me to make out what he was saying. But, the fact he possessed a cell-phone made me think perhaps he did live here in Quito; on the other hand, it was just as possible the Israeli Embassy or someone had loaned him a phone for the duration of this operation. Why I even thought about such a thing was beyond me since it really didn't matter one way or the other.

My stomach began growling again and I cursed myself for letting Jacob have my share of last night's pizza. I decided I had just learned lesson number one for surviving captivity, if you're offered food and it's even marginally edible, eat it! You never know when your next opportunity will arise. Right now even a cold leftover piece of pizza would taste deliciously. It was impossible not to wonder if this was kind of thing these guys actually did for a living, and if so, how they could survive eating like this.

At some point probably from a combination of hunger and boredom I must have dozed off for I was suddenly awakened by the sound of Frank's voice. He was in the kitchen talking animatedly with Jacob though what must have penetrated my unconscious mind was that he was speaking in a language I didn't recognize. I suspected that meant he did not want me to hear what he was saying, which so annoyed me I swung off the couch and walked directly into the kitchen; it was my life after all. If I surprised him, Frank didn't show it; he simply shifted over to speaking English without a second's hesitation.

"We're going to take you back to your apartment," he announced. "There's no longer any need for you to stay here."

I should have been ecstatic since that was precisely the news I'd been hoping for, but instead I immediately became suspicious. There were any number of things I thought he might say; that I could leave was not one of them. When finally I got over my initial surprise, it occurred to me that he must have gotten the diary from Carlos. Yet, there was something in his manner that made me begin to wonder if the contents of the diary had been a lot less important than everybody had expected.

"So, you do have the diary, right," I ventured. I automatically assumed that if he did, he'd have no reason not to say so, which is why I became suspicious again when he proceeded to ignore my question.

"I have an airline ticket here for you; it's for tomorrow. You'll be returning to the United States on an American Airlines flight that leaves at 7:30 in the morning; Jacob will pick you up from your apartment at six o'clock and drive you to the airport. Not only would it be in your best interest to be on that flight, we're going to insist you be on it."

The manner in which he spoke to me annoyed the hell out of me and I didn't hesitate to let him know it.

"Where do you guys get off ordering me around the way you do," I shouted. "I don't care if you do have my best interests at heart, which by the way, I doubt you do, I just want you to leave me alone, do you understand?"

"Oh, we understand," Frank replied testily, "it just isn't going to happen. Jacob will be there in the morning and you are going back to New York, now do you understand?"

Frank had not raised his voice in any of this but I could tell he was not about to argue the matter with me; his mind was made up. I harbored not the slightest doubt that if it became necessary, they would bodily transport me from the terminal to the plane.

"All right, all right, I'll go but can you at least tell me if you found the diary?"

If they had, there was no logical reason for me to return to New York so quickly. And, I desperately needed to see Carolina. How could I possibly leave the country without having the opportunity to explain to her what had happened?

"To be honest with you," Frank replied, "we still haven't been able to find the it, nor do we yet know the identity of the people looking for it. That means they're still out there and clearly they remain extremely dangerous. It's, in fact, because we have no idea how long it may take us to obtain the diary that it would be safer for you back to New York; it's also one less worry for us. You can always come back here when everything calms down, as it will in time."

I couldn't argue with Frank's logic; it probably was best if I went home for a while. By staying here not only would I remain in danger, I would also be placing Adam and Carolina in danger and I clearly wanted to avoid that. They were both very vulnerable in large part because they knew so little of what was going on.

"So, whom am I too thank for this ticket," I asked, curious to discover whether the Israeli Embassy was behind it.

"Yourself," Frank answered with a wry smile. "We suspected you came down here on a roundtrip ticket, or at least an open-ended one, so we used our contacts at American Airlines to set-up your return for tomorrow. We did upgrade you to business class to compensate you for some of your troubles, which I need not remind you, were of your own making. But, now, let me give you some advice, stay out of things that are no concern of yours; you're way in over your head on this one! Now, just maybe if you listen to us you may get out of here safely."

"I appreciate your concern," I answered, trying not to give in to his obvious good sense, "but can we get out of this place? I don't wish to appear ungrateful, however, as I'm certain you'll be the first to admit, the accommodations here are hardly Club Med."

We were standing there in the kitchen and I could feel my impatience increasing almost as fast as my annoyance. I needed to contact Carolina and to do that I had to get back to the apartment. Everything else, a hot shower, clean clothes, a decent meal, was secondary. Of course, if I hadn't left my Blackberry back in New York I could have been in touch with her right along. She had probably sent me a flurry of emails in a desperate effort to find out what had happened. But, now, not only would I be required to explain my whereabouts for the past couple of days, I was going to have to break the news to her that I was being forced to leave the country as early as tomorrow. I suspected she knew my leaving was inevitable, she simply would not be expecting it quite so soon. I'd still have to think about whether this would be the right time to invite her to come up to New York. But, I would have to do something to assure her I wasn't simply walking out of her life; I had to make her believe somehow or somewhere we'd be together again.

"All right, let's get out of here," Frank ordered, turning and heading towards the door to the garage. "I don't think much of this place either."

I hurried after Frank while Jacob made sure the house was secure. Once in the car Frank explained I'd have to put my blindfold on again.

"Is it really necessary," I asked, feeling I was playing a part in some B movie. "What's the point if you're shipping me back to the US tomorrow."

"Regulations," Frank growled, but I didn't believe him for a second. I was certain he was going out of his way to be perverse, probably for being stupid enough to have caused Reverend Hoffmann's death. I guess I couldn't blame him for being angry with me about that; it was something I was going to have to live with the rest of my life.

Slipping into the car I didn't object when Jacob checked to be certain my blindfold was in place. Almost immediately I heard the rumbling of the garage door opening and our car began to move. I felt a wave of relief sweep over me; I was going home. Well, I was going back to Adam's apartment, but it felt like I was going home. And, in the morning, when I actually would be leaving for home, how was I going to feel then? For the moment, I tried to put it out of my mind.

The trip back to the apartment was conducted in silence, which was fine with me since the only thing I could think about was checking my email to see what messages I had received from Carolina. That she might not write me never once crossed my mind

"You may remove your blindfold now," he said quietly. "Remember, Jacob will pick you up right here at six o'clock tomorrow morning; your flight leaves at eight. Take care of yourself until then and by that I mean don't go wandering around the streets."

I opened the car door quickly and stepped out. I couldn't think of a thing to say to either of them so I said nothing. I was hardly about to thank them for kidnapping me and holding me incommunicado; I was not suffering from Stockholm syndrome, or whatever it's called when you begin to sympathize with your captors. I hadn't been a captive long enough for that. If anything, I was feeling resentful for their keeping me from contacting Carolina. So, I simply nodded to the two of them and walked casually into the apartment building. For some reason, probably stupid pride, I didn't want them to think the ordeal had been anything other than an inconvenience for me.

The moment I was inside the building, where neither Frank nor Jacob could see me, I sprinted for the elevator. To my annoyance the elevator was in use so I had to wait for it to come back down. And, though the trip back up could not have lasted more that a minute, it seemed to take forever. When finally the elevator door opened, I raced into the apartment nearly trampling Consuelo in the process.

"Mister Michael, I so worry for you," she cried with obvious concern. "I thought you go, no say goodbye."

I gave her a big hug and mumbled, "*Un momento.*" I hurried into Adam's study and turned on his computer. As I was waiting Consuelo came to the door and said, "You eat?"

I assumed it was a question so I nodded my head and replied, "*Si, por favor.*"

She disappeared and I could hear her busying herself in the kitchen.

Quickly accessing my email account I was relieved to see there were several messages waiting for me. As I scanned down the list I found to my dismay there was none from Carolina; I then checked the Spam file just in case it had been diverted there. That can't be, I murmured to myself, there has to be at least one; I had expected several. What could have happened? Why hadn't she at least inquired about our Wednesday lunch date, although naturally I should have been the one writing her. But, when I didn't, shouldn't she have double-checked with me? Now, suddenly, I was more worried about her than I was before. It never occurred to me to be hurt or angry. All I could think was that the same people looking for the diary had done something to her? They could have been following me and learned about our relationship. Now, I was becoming frantic, especially after what had happened to Francisco and Reverend Hoffmann.

There simply wasn't time to write her even a condensed version of what had happened to me since we had last seen one another so I just dashed off a short message asking her to contact me immediately and sent it. Please, please, be at your computer so you get my email immediately. Time is running out and I desperately need to hear from you.

"Mister Michael," I heard Consuelo call out, "eat, eat."

I dragged myself out to the kitchen where Consuelo had a huge meal ready for me; she must have been cooking for hours. There was a *ceviche* with the usual plantain chips and popcorn, a beet and carrot salad, a huge plate of rice and *trucha*, as Consuelo called it, and a glass of *jugo de mora*. After the little I had eaten in past two days the food looked out-of-this-world; in fact, I had dreamed about sitting down to just such a meal. And yet, once again my appetite deserted me; I had absolutely no interest in food at this moment. The only thing I could think about was Carolina. Why hadn't she emailed me? I was on the verge of panic.

I was about to push my plate aside when I noticed Consuelo looking at me inquisitively. It was clear she was feeling hurt because I wasn't eating anything. I picked up my spoon and tasted the *ceviche*; it was delicious and under normal circumstances I would have wolfed it down with great enthusiasm. I tried a mouthful or two of rice and fish, but it was no use. The best I could do was to push the food about my plate to make it appear I had eaten more than I actually had, the way I had done when I was a child. But, it was apparent from the way Consuelo kept glancing over at me that I wasn't fooling her for a second.

"*Lo siento*, I'm sorry, " I mumbled, using one of the few terms in Spanish I had picked up from Adam. Pushing my chair away from the table, I walked guiltily out of the kitchen and into the living room. For once the view down the valley held no interest for me. Instead I slumped down in Adam's favorite chair, next to his private bar. Why not, I thought, and got up and poured myself a Maker's Mark, no ice, no water, just a very healthy shot of bourbon. Sitting back down I couldn't help but marvel how a single seemingly unimportant decision, to enter *El Café de Los Toreros* in search of a bathroom, had set in motion a chain of events that would have such tragic consequences. Had I only chosen a different bar, or simply waited to use the bathroom back at the apartment, I wouldn't be in the situation I found myself now. And, to make matters worse, I was taking the coward's way out by running back to New York leaving Carolina and Adam to face the consequences of my stupidity. I wondered if maybe I should just tell Jacob when he came to pick me up in the morning that I simply couldn't leave Quito for a few more days, that I needed the time to straighten some things out. The problem was I couldn't come up with one good reason why my staying would improve the situation. The sooner I accepted the fact I'd be on that plane in the morning. I decided, the easier it would make it on everybody.

Twenty-Four

Much of the afternoon I spent running back and forth to Adam's computer hoping to find that Carolina had answered my email. I was at wit's end worrying that she had been threatened or kidnapped by the same people who had murdered Reverend Hoffmann. I even tried to phone her. Unfortunately, the only telephone number listed on her business card was for her office at the university where repeated calls went unanswered. My attempts to obtain a home phone number likewise proved useless. I concluded her father had an unlisted number, which was probably understandable given his prominence in the country and the threats such prominence generated.

I was also facing another problem, not as serious as Carolina, but a problem nevertheless. It was Consuelo; I couldn't decide whether I should tell her I was leaving or not. It wasn't as if we had established any kind of a close relationship; we couldn't even communicate very effectively. And, anyway, Adam was in a better position than I to explain whatever it was that needed explaining. But, no sooner had I settled on this option than I began to feel guilty about it; Consuelo had been very sweet with me.

So, later that afternoon when I heard Consuelo open the closet in the kitchen where she always hung her sweater I walked out into the foyer. As best I could, I explained that I'd be leaving in the morning and probably wouldn't be seeing her again. She must have been expecting it; probably Adam had said something to her for she showed no great surprise. She gave me a long affectionate embrace and as she did so I could see tears in her eyes. She let go quickly as the elevator door opened, getting in without looking back. And, then, she was gone.

Standing there, I gradually became aware of just how quiet the apartment had become. I felt strangely alone, as if I no longer had any business even being in Ecuador. I wandered back to the computer but there was still nothing from Carolina; I was certain by this time that I was not going to hear from her. It was as if Carolina, like Consuelo, had simply stepped into an elevator and vanished from my life. Of course, in Carolina's case I was desperate to learn the reason for her doing so. My only thought was that something horrible had happened. As I was wrestling with the question of what I should do, I heard someone out in the other room. Walking into the kitchen, I saw Adam entering from the foyer.

"Michael," he said, looking at me with surprise. My initial reaction was that someone must told him about what had been happening in Quito while he had been away, but as it turned out this wasn't so.

"Welcome back," I responded, trying my best to sound normal when, in fact, I was feeling increasingly frustrated at the situation in which I now found myself.

He must have detected something in my tone for he answered with a quick, "Let me drop my stuff in the bedroom then I'll come back and get us a drink."

When he returned a few minutes later I had moved only as far as the large picture window from which I could look down the valley in the direction of where Carolina lived. The scene only served to frustrate me even more. Why couldn't I get in touch with her? It occurred to me I should ask Adam if I could borrow his car and actually drive down to her house. I honestly couldn't think of anything else to do.

Adam poured two large tumblers of bourbon over ice and handed one to me. "*Salud*," he offered, touching his glass to mine. "Now, for God's sake, tell me what's been happening? I've never seen you look so upset."

"I've probably never been this upset," I replied, letting out a long sigh. "So much has happened in the last couple days and it seems none of it's been good."

"I'm assuming this has do with Carolina? Did she break up with you," Adam asked with audible concern.

It was funny, but there were moments, and this seemed to be one of them, when I sensed that Adam would be perfectly happy if Carolina and I were to become serious, and I decided to stay in Ecuador. Obviously he would not want me to live with him but he'd certainly help me get my own place in Quito.

"Well, it is Carolina, but, no, she didn't break up with me or, at least, I don't think she has. My problem is I haven't been able to contact her and I'm beginning to fear for her safety."

"Her safety, what are you talking about? She's probably just out of town," Adam suggested. "It was you, wasn't it, who told me her father likes to have her accompany him when he travels around the country campaigning for the presidency. The election is not that far away and while he appears to be the leading candidate, it's going to be a close race; he's probably trying to reach as many people as he can in these last few weeks."

"You may be right, but listen, Adam, I think there's something I'd better explain, especially since, I'm sorry to say, you're a part of it, too."

Adam looked at me quizzically. "Me? Yes, please do explain. I'm curious to know what I might be involved in?"

"Do you remember me telling you about this old man who claimed to have knowledge of where Atahualpa's gold is buried? Well, it turns out he had a diary, which he gave to this bartender, Carlos, for safekeeping; the old man was murdered shortly afterwards. The diary, as it turns out, was written in German script so Carlos had several pages of it reproduced and asked me to find someone who might be able to translate it."

I was talking so hurriedly I knew Adam was having trouble keeping up but I continued on.

So anyway, I was directed to the minister of the Lutheran Church, the one over there by the American ambassador's residence, where a Reverend Hoffmann agreed to translate it for me. And then, unbelievably, he was murdered, too!"

"You mean, all this has been going on and you haven't said a word to me about it until now," Adam exclaimed.

I could see he was becoming angry and he had every reason to be.

"Look, I only just found out myself so please give me a minute to explain. However, I should warn you you're probably not going to believe everything I tell you, maybe none of it, but it is the truth, at least as I know it. First, I was kidnapped! Yes, kidnapped right outside this building by two guys who claimed they were actually taking me into protective custody. It was they who told me about Reverend Hoffmann's murder; apparently he was tortured or something. Whomever did it, wanted the diary, or at least the pages of it I had given him to translate."

"Michael, are you losing your mind? You're actually asking me to believe you were kidnapped by two guys who took you where? No, forget that, by two guys who kidnapped you for what reason?"

I couldn't blame him for thinking I was crazy; I was beginning to think that myself.

"OK, would you believe me if I told you the two guys who kidnapped me were Israelis, or at the very least they were working for the Israelis. No, I'm pretty sure they were Israeli themselves."

"Israelis," Adam exclaimed in astonishment. "Clearly, I'm having trouble with this but continue anyway and explain what on earth the Israelis have to do in all of this?"

By this time Adam was shaking his head and looking at me as if I were certifiably insane. I did have to admit my story was more than a little bizarre. Talk about the truth being stranger than fiction, this was definitely one of those instances.

"The Israelis became involved because apparently Reverend Hoffmann called the Israeli Embassy after reading the pages I had given him to report that he'd found something they'd be very interested in; he didn't give them any clue as to what it was at that moment but suggested someone stop by to see him in the morning. When the person or persons from the embassy arrived at his residence the next morning they found the police there. Sometime during the night Reverend Hoffmann had been murdered. What makes his death so difficult for me to accept is that whoever killed him may have followed me there."

"Wait a minute, wait a minute," Adam implored. "What you're implying is that whatever was in that diary was something of great interest to the Israelis? What on earth could it be? I'm assuming now it had nothing to do with Atahualpa?"

"Even the guys who kidnapped me had no idea what was in the diary or so they said. That's one reason they took me to one of their 'safe-houses' so they could interrogate me. I mean, they were not protecting me out of altruism; they wanted information. Oh, and that sudden trip you took to Guayaquil, they set that up too, or so they claimed. They didn't want you sounding the alarm when I went missing."

"What do you mean, they set up my trip to Guayaquil," Adam asked looking confused. "I admit it was last minute but everything seemed legit, though I did wonder why they specifically asked for me; on the other hand, they were incredibly professional and business-like. Now, you're telling me this trip was set up by the Israelis just to get me out of town? Come on, Michael, I find that a little hard to believe; actually, I find just about everything you've told me a little hard to believe. But, you did warn me."

"Look, I no longer know what to believe either. All I do know is what they told me, that they have this group of businessmen, I assume they're Jewish, who are prepared at a drop-of-the-hat to come to their aid in an emergency. I think these guys flew over from Miami and clearly they did so because they were told it was an emergency. But, I still don't understand exactly what the emergency is."

"I guess it all comes down to what kind of information is in the diary. Clearly it has to be important since people are willing to kill to keep whatever it is a secret. And, if it's not too much to ask, who has the diary now?"

"That's a very good question," I replied. "Carlos did have it, oh, I guess I forgot to explain that Carlos was badly beaten by the people who are after the diary; he's in the hospital. But, whether he told the guys who were holding me where the diary was hidden, I have no idea. They certainly wouldn't confirm they have it."

"My God, Michael, so this guy, Carlos, has been beaten, too. You do realize how serious this all is? What have you gotten yourself into? At the very least I can see why these Israeli guys took you into protective custody. My question now is what are you going to do? You are in a heap of trouble and for the moment I'm not sure what I can do to help you."

I could sense that even Adam was beginning to get anxious now.

"Not to worry, you won't have to do anything. I'm leaving for New York in the morning. I'm sorry, I should have mentioned that right up front but there was so much else to explain. These Israeli guys have scheduled me to leave here at six in the morning; one of them will pick me up and look after me until I'm safely on the plane. I admit, it's rather abrupt but with everything that's been happening, there's probably no other choice."

"And you're absolutely sure these guys are Israelis?"

"I'm sure, well, I'm pretty sure. To be perfectly honest I'm no longer sure of anything," I responded.

"And what about Carolina, does she know you're leaving in the morning? I can't believe you'd go without saying goodbye or something. Aren't you two supposed to be in love?"

"I'm afraid she doesn't know. And, the strange thing is, and here's that word strange again, I was supposed to have lunch with her yesterday. Obviously, I couldn't make it since I was in 'protective custody'. However, I assumed when I wasn't able to contact her, she would try to contact me to find out what happened, but she didn't. And, now she hasn't responded to my emails. I'm incredibly worried because it's quite possible the same people, who are after me, or the diary, might have done something to her. My only consolation, I guess, is knowing she has good security around her."

"So, do you want to borrow my car and run down to her house; at least, you can make sure she's all right. And, you can tell her you're leaving."

"I've thought about it, in fact I was actually thinking about it when you walked through the door. Unfortunately, the Israelis, or whomever they are, advised me not to go out just in case Reverend Hoffmann's killers are watching the place. And, I certainly don't want them following me down to her house; I'm already worried they know about us. But, tell me, is there anyway you can have someone at the embassy try to contact her, or at least her father? That way, at least, I'd know she was all right."

"There's no one there right now who'd know how to reach Carolina's father but I'll have someone who does call first thing in the morning. Maybe I can even get the ambassador to do it; your story is going to fascinate her; she'll be sorry you're leaving."

Adam was sprawled on the couch still looking the part of a successful businessman though he had removed his jacket and tie. At that moment I envied him; his life seemed so orderly whereas mine, on the other hand, appeared to be heading in the direction of chaos. How ironic, I thought, that I had come down here to get away from my personal problems—my breakup with Rachel, the loss of my job-- now I had even more serious problems, including a possible threat to my life. And, there wasn't enough time to resolve any of them. It was maddening to think once again I'd be running away, though admittedly this time I honestly didn't seem to have much of a choice since other people were involved who could get hurt if I stayed.

"Let me freshen that," Adam proposed, getting up and taking my empty glass. I must have downed it quickly though I barely remembered even taking a sip. What the hell, I had too much to drink the first night I got here, I might just as well have too much to drink on the last.

Walking over to where I had finally taken a seat, Adam said, "You know, I've been sitting here trying to absorb everything you've told me tonight and I must say I find the whole thing incomprehensible. You've barely been here two weeks yet in that time you've been involved in a couple of murders, your own kidnapping, and you've had an affair with one of the most eligible women in Ecuador, no, let me correct that, the most eligible woman in Ecuador. I can remember telling my parents when they were here visiting that I was enjoying my work but I was finding Quito the most boring city I had ever been in. Yes, I used the word boring. And, you've turned your stay here into this incredible adventure though admittedly a dangerous one. At this moment I can't figure out if I'm sorry you're leaving or whether I want you to go before you're responsible for some kind of international incident."

We both laughed nervously probably suspecting there was a certain truth to the statement.

Adam and I continued to talk well into the evening. At some point, I think it was after draining my fourth Maker's Mark, I reminded him I still had to pack. As I headed unsteadily to my bedroom Adam assured me he'd be up in time to see me off in the morning. When sometime later I tumbled into bed I found it impossible to fall asleep; my mind was continually assaulted by unsettling images of Carolina being held captive somewhere. Several times I sat up in bed in an attempt to calm myself. At some point it must have worked for the next thing I became conscious of was the sound of my alarm. It was time for me to go and I dreaded the very thought of it!

Twenty-Five

True to his word Adam was up well before me and had even laid out juice, coffee and a small plate of *pan de yucas* for the two of us. He was also completely dressed, casually for him in a navy-blue blazer and grey slacks, and quite ready to leave for work. As usual I looked like some down-and-out college student, on the other hand, why shouldn't I. It would certainly make it a lot easier for me to blend in with all the rest of the college students flying economy with me to Miami unless, of course, Frank and Jacob had been serious about upgrading me to business-class.

"So, what time is your friend coming to pick you up," Adam asked with an expression that suggested he still didn't completely understand everything that was happening. "If he doesn't show I can drive you to the airport. I'm in no rush to get to work, though I haven't forgotten about trying to contact Carolina's father; I'll probably end up doing it myself. Whatever I find out I'll try getting word to you before the plane takes off; I realize you don't have your cell-phone with you but I'll figure out a way to get through to you somehow. If for any reason you don't hear from me, don't assume the worst; I can always reach you at home in New York."

"OK, I just need to know she's all right, that she hasn't been kidnapped or something," I answered, startled by my own words.

We were both leaning on the counter, drinking our coffee. I was too nervous to sit; I always seemed to get that way before I was to fly. That was another thing I had always envied about Adam; he flew constantly and it never seemed to bother him, or at least outwardly it didn't. Of course, that was probably the reason; I didn't fly often enough to become comfortable doing it.

"Oh, I'm sure he's already down there; they seem very determined to get me on that plane," I responded with just a touch of irritation. I was anything but happy that I had to leave without saying something to Carolina, though I kept trying to convince myself it was for the best.

Taking a final sip of my coffee, I walked over to the sink and rinsed out my cup.

"Time to go," I said, walking reluctantly out into the foyer where I had left my luggage. Adam followed me out.

"Look, Adam, I really do want to thank for inviting me down here and for being so hospitable. I hope someday I'll be able to return the favor. In the meantime I'm truly sorry for the mess I'm leaving behind. I just hope I haven't done anything that will create any kind of problem for you, that is, over and above the little trip you were required to take to Guayaquil."

The elevator door opened and Adam stepped forward to hold it.

"And, Michael, just try not to worry too much; everything will get cleared up and I'm certain Carolina is in no way involved in any of this. I promise that somehow I'll get in touch with her and I'll let you know when I do."

"Thanks, Adam. You can't imagine how much I enjoyed my stay down here, that is, until all this happened. I mean wandering around Quito, meeting Carolina that was great! Of course, now I don't know what to think about her; I hate having to leave without talking to her but I have no choice. I've certainly tried: I just couldn't get in touch with her. On the other hand, she didn't try to contact me either and that's what really bothers me. I just hope you'll be able to get in touch with her and explain what happened. I guess I'd better get downstairs; I wouldn't want them coming up and kidnapping me again!"

"Have a safe trip back, Michael, and after all you've been through, I don't say that lightly," Adam said with a laugh.

"Thanks, again, I'll send you an email letting you know I got home safely."

The elevator door closed and I was on my way. And, for all I realized this would happen one day, to anticipate it is one thing, to actually be going through with it is quite another.

As I exited the elevator, I spotted Jacob, dressed casually in a navy-blue tracksuit with white trim, talking quietly to the security guard; he was obviously not about to take any chances with my safety, or was it simply that he wanted to make sure I got on that plane to Miami.

"Good morning, Michael," he greeted cheerfully. Since he hadn't been that friendly with me the last time we were together I decided he was eager to get me on the plane, or maybe he had come to like me, who knows.

I nodded a less than enthusiastic "hello" and headed for the front door, Jacob trailing after me. I wondered what was going on in his mind at this moment. Did he honestly think someone might try to get me before I made it onto the plane or was all this just show to scare me into leaving Ecuador.

"This way," he said, directing me towards a black Ford Explorer with the requisite tinted windows. He pushed his remote to unlock the doors.

"Here, let me take your suitcase, I'll put it in the back. Why don't you sit in the front seat."

His tone was not entirely business-like but just his being here made me nervous. I suddenly wondered if I'd have been better off having Adam drive me to the airport

Jacob got in a second later and started the car. Pulling quickly away from the curb he headed up Avenida Gonzalez Suarez. At this time of the morning there was little traffic so he was able to drive at a reasonable speed. I didn't feel much like talking and apparently Jacob took his cue from me for he remained silent as well. Since I suspected I might never see Quito again I tried my best to capture a few final images of the city: the architecture of the buildings; the way people were dressed; even the kinds of cars they drove. But, it proved impossible; my mind was so consumed with thoughts of Carolina I couldn't focus on anything else.

It took only about ten minutes to reach the airport. Passing the end of the runway I was surprised to see that even at this early hour there were a number of people lined up along the heavy chain-linked fence watching planes landing and taking off.

"It's like that every day," Jacob observed, when he noticed me staring at them. "And, it doesn't matter what the weather's like. I've seen them lined up there in rain so heavy that they've actually shut down the airport. But, still, they stand there and wait. Can you imagine an American doing that?"

"No, I can't," I said, caught by his comment. Clearly, then, he either lived in Quito or he'd spent considerable time here to notice such a thing. Before I could think anymore about it we were pulling up in front of the international terminal; now, it hit me, I was really leaving.

"I think you can take it from here," Jacob said. "Just enter through these doors and go straight ahead. Do you see that crowd of people in there? That's where security is. Those people are not waiting to get through security; they're just seeing someone off. Once you get through security you'll be fine."

By the time I had climbed out of the front seat Jacob had retrieved my suitcase for me, then, handed me my ticket.

"Yes, we did upgrade you to business-class. We decided it was the least we could do after what you've been through down here."

He smiled though even after all the time we'd spent together I couldn't help staring at his scar.

I wasn't exactly sure what to say so I offered Jacob my hand and simply mumbled a "thanks." To be honest, I still didn't understand exactly what he and Frank had been up to. Had they really been looking after me? I had my doubts, but what else could they have been doing. It occurred to me that I should probably board the plane as quickly as possible; at least I'd be safe there.

"Take care of yourself," Jacob called to me as I walked towards the terminal entrance. I turned and gave him a nod.

I followed Jacob's instructions and walked directly over to security. As he had predicted the people gathered there were not waiting to pass through, in fact, there was no one waiting. I simply walked up to the security official, handed him my passport and paper ticket, and was almost immediately admitted into the main part of the terminal. It was only then I noticed the long lines of people waiting to check-in, so much for my hope of boarding the plane quickly. The terminal appeared to serve about a dozen airlines and I had no trouble spotting American Airlines since it's lines were by far the longest of all. I immediately felt better when I looked at the waiting line for business class—six passengers! Adam was absolutely correct; why did I ever choose to fly economy? Anyway, I'd never do it again, that was for certain, though I also doubted I'd ever be going through this airport again.

As I waited to check in I studied the people standing in the economy-class line. Most of them appeared to be middle aged and American, probably members of some tour group. They were all dressed as if they had been out hiking and although probably total strangers a week ago they were now busy exchanging addresses and phone numbers while promising to get together again on another such tour. I couldn't get over how loud and animated they were; I found it almost embarrassing. Listening to them, I couldn't help wondering if someday I'd be that. I certainly hoped not!

Finally, my turn came and I found myself standing before a very business-like young man, whose name according to the silver bar on his chest was Antonio. He inspected my passport, checked in my suitcase and presented me with my boarding pass, all without anything that even remotely resembled a smile. What did he think I didn't belong in business-class? As I picked up my passport and ticket he instructed me to cross the terminal and pay my exit tax. Now, I felt I was actually on my way home and, in spite of the ticket agent's brusque manner, I found myself beginning to relax.

For some reason Carlos suddenly entered my mind, I guess because I had forgotten to ask how he'd been doing after his beating. Carlos had actually started the whole thing by agreeing to hold the wooden box for Francisco though, of course, at the time he hadn't had the slightest idea what the box contained. At least I didn't have to bear the guilt for his situation. Still, I felt badly about leaving Ecuador without visiting him at the hospital or somehow saying goodbye. I had to admit everything about my stay in this country had been bizarre.

As I was approaching the line to pay my exit tax a young man, dressed in the blue uniform of the airport's service personnel, walked up to me.

"Are you Mr. Henrick, a Mr. Michael Henrick," he asked politely. I noticed his English was heavily accented but I couldn't recognize it.

My immediate reaction was one of annoyance, especially after what I'd been going through. Then, it suddenly occurred to me that perhaps Carolina was trying to contact me, or maybe even Adam with some word about her.

"Yes, I'm Michael Henrick," I answered hesitatingly.

"Could I just see your passport, please?"

I thought this request was a little unusual but I had already made up my mind that someone was about to give me a message and that this guy was only making certain I was who I said I was. He took my passport and examined it carefully.

"Would you come this way, please? It's all right; you won't miss your plane. There's somebody who needs to speak with you before you leave."

"Could you please tell me who it is," I begged, desperately hoping it was Carolina. I even convinced myself she had chosen to see me like this as a way of escaping her security guards.

The agent was walking more quickly now, my passport still in his hand. At the very least I wanted to get my passport back. Directly ahead was a door marked Authorized Personnel Only; he opened it and motioned me ahead. I did as he suggested though by this time I was feeling increasingly uncomfortable about the situation; I was even beginning to doubt that Carolina was waiting for me somewhere up ahead. Passport or not, I had to get out of here, and quickly, but the agent must have sensed my hesitation.

"Just around the corner," he indicated with a nod of his head.

His words provided just the assurance I needed to continue on when my instincts were screaming for me to get out. And, for all I had been suspecting trouble from the moment I had walked through that door, when it came it still took me by surprise. Turning a corner I came face-to-face with two tough-looking characters dressed in the coveralls favored by aircraft mechanics. Before I had a chance to react one of the men grabbed me and clamped a beefy hand over my mouth while the other pulled a hypodermic needle out of nowhere and jabbed it in my neck. I had no doubt as to its purpose and within seconds I began to lose consciousness. The last sound I heard was someone shouting "*Vamonos de aqui.*"

Twenty-Six

Gradually I began to awaken from my drug-induced nap, an experience similar to someone desperately trying to swim up to the surface of the ocean in order to get air. When finally I regained consciousness, I almost wished I hadn't; my head was throbbing unbearably. I was also having trouble getting my eyes to focus properly; everything was swirling around and around in a gray blur. But, I was able to recognize, at least, that I was alive. I next tried to move my arms and legs and when nothing happened I panicked. Only, then, did I realize I was bound spread-eagle on a bed wearing only my boxers, a t-shirt and my socks. I struggled to free myself but the rope used to bind me cut into my wrists; whoever had done this was clearly a serious professional.

Adding to my growing sense of isolation was the absence of any sound. It was so still the only thing I could hear was the rapid thumping of my heart. I felt myself becoming panicky again but did my best not to let it overwhelm me. I commanded myself to relax and consciously slowed my breathing; it seemed to work. So, what had happened and how did I get here?

As my head slowly cleared, my memory returned as well. I remembered checking in at the airport and almost immediately afterwards having some guy stop me to examine my passport. What happened after that was still a bit fuzzy though I seemed to recollect following him down a deserted hallway. Everything else remained a blank, including unfortunately what he looked like. I was sure he was wearing a uniform of some kind but I couldn't quite picture his face. It suddenly dawned on me that I had totally lost track of time; I had no idea whether I'd been out for minutes or hours, though it actually seemed like days.

My mouth, I now noticed, felt so parched it was as if it was filled with cotton and I became desperate for something to drink.

"Is anybody here?" I called out, startled by the sound of my own voice.

I instantly regretted doing it for my captors would now know I was awake and could begin interrogating me. And, what if they weren't satisfied with my answers, might they not very well do to me what they had done to Reverend Hoffmann? While I still didn't know who these people were I had a pretty good idea of what they wanted from me; they wanted the diary and they seemed pretty certain I knew where it was located.

My thoughts were suddenly interrupted by the sound of the bedroom door being opened. It didn't swing wide, just a crack, but it was enough for me to see a portion of a man's face before the door closed and I was left alone again to ponder my predicament. I found the whole thing unnerving, yet for some strange reason I seemed to be gradually gaining control over my fear. I concluded the whole point of this exercise was probably to unnerve me such that I'd readily answer their questions. I had no intention of being a coward about it, however. What was that line, the coward dies a thousand deaths, the brave but one? Of course, the author of those words in all probability did not envision a guy tied to a bed and dressed only in his underwear!

While waiting for the inevitable someone to come through the door I began to survey the room in which I was being held. I found something strangely familiar about it as if I'd been here before. But, how could that be? And, then, it struck me; I had been here before. This was the very bedroom where Carolina and I had made love, the very bed for that matter! They, whomever they were, must have brought me to Carolina's *quinta* in the crater of the old volcano out by Mitad del Mundo. But, why would they do that? Why here? Then, the craziest thought suddenly occurred to me, had Carolina's father somehow found out she had brought me here? It was entirely possible. We had been so certain we had outwitted her security guards, but it was more than possible we hadn't? What if, in fact, they had followed us and then reported back to her father just what we had been doing here? He might very well be orchestrating this thing as a way of making certain I would get out of her life once and for all. While I could think of better ways of handling the situation, I reluctantly found myself admitting that I couldn't actually blame him. In his mind I was anything but the perfect match for Carolina: I wasn't Ecuadorian, I wasn't Catholic, and I wasn't wealthy, at least, not in the way her father defined wealth. The more I thought about it, the more I could understand her father's point-of-view. I just wished he hadn't felt the need to humiliate me. Why hadn't he been more macho about it, I mean, couldn't we have just talked things out man-to-man? I intended to make certain this approach would prove to be a huge mistake on his part.

Yet, as I started thinking about it something about this whole scenario didn't add up. For one thing her father had honestly seemed to like me, or at the least, he had been pleasant enough to me the couple times we met. So, was it possible that maybe he didn't know anything about this, that being brought here was pure coincidence? Or, at least it was if one believed in the Easter bunny and Santa Claus. Unfortunately I didn't and, therefore, it was quite a logical question to ask why I had been brought here of all places.

Lying stretched out as I was, my muscles were beginning to ache. I tried shifting the position of my body but I was bound so tightly I couldn't move an inch. Unfortunately, though my body remained inactive my mind was anything but. All I could think about was what torture might be awaiting me. At the same time I was anxious to see who would be coming through the door. Might it actually be Carolina's father? And, if it were, was there even the possibility that Carolina might be with him? Perhaps, he'd even make her watch as a couple of his security guards beat me senseless. At this point I knew my imagination was getting the best of me. Yet there was still this nagging question: if he knew I was in the process of leaving the country, why didn't he just let me go? Of course, that also raised another question. How did they know I was going to be at the airport? The only people who knew other than Adam were my trusted bodyguards, Frank and Jacob. Adam didn't have time to tell anyone, and anyway, whom would he tell? So, that left Frank and Jacob. But, why would they tell anyone? I had so many questions, and so few answers. If I were becoming paranoid, I decided, I had every reason in the world to become so.

My only hope was to get word to Adam, but how? And anyway, by this time he probably assumed I was on my way to Miami. As for Jacob, forget it? Wasn't he supposed to be looking after me until I boarded the aircraft? Clearly, then, there was nobody who could help me; I was completely alone. And, to think only a few days ago I was making love to Carolina on this very bed. Carolina, yes, maybe she could do something? But, she had no idea where I was and very possibly didn't care since she had never tried to contact me. Whatever fear I had been experiencing was now beginning to feel more like panic. I could in all likelihood be killed and buried out here someplace and there'd be no one to even report me missing for days, maybe weeks. How could this be happening; it was crazy. It was beyond crazy.

Just then I heard the door open. A man I was pretty sure I had never seen before entered the room and walked over to the bed; he looked down at me without visible expression. My first thought was, he didn't seem like the killer type, though my knowledge of killers was pretty limited. Most of what I knew was drawn from television and the movies. Still, he didn't fit the image--medium build, brown thinning hair, and a remarkably average-looking face. In his light tan suit with a matching tie, most people would probably take him for an accountant.

"So, Mr. Henrick," he said, with a pronounced accent that seemed more Central European than Spanish, "I'm glad to see you're awake and well."

"No thanks to your thugs who brought me here," I responded, doing my best to sound tough. "I really don't appreciate being treated like some common criminal. You can bet the American Embassy is going to hear about this. You can't just kidnap an American citizen and expect to get away with it. And, anyway, if you had wanted to ask me something, why didn't you just do it at the airport; there was no need to kidnap me."

"Yes, well I suppose I should apologize for the rather crude manner in which we brought you here; we simply didn't want to create a scene at the airport on the chance you refused to come with us," he explained matter-of-factly. "You see, we need you to confirm something for us before you can be allowed to leave the country. Confirm it to our satisfaction and you will be free to go."

"I've heard that line before, cooperate and you can go home. I've never been in a country that's so difficult to leave. All I want to do is get out of here. Is that really too much to ask?"

"Excuse me, Mr. Henrick," he interrupted. "Did I hear you correctly? You did say, 'I've heard that line before,' referring to my comment about asking you to confirm something before you are allowed to leave. So, tell me, who else has said that to you?"

Was it possible they knew nothing about Frank and Jacob? If that were the case it would probably be in my best interest to keep it that way, I quickly decided. I would have to draw his attention away from my last comment; I was fairly certain my next comment would do it.

"Look," I blurted out, "Is Eduard Mayer behind all this? I happen to know this is his farm; it is isn't it?"

"Eduard Mayer?" he exclaimed. "Why possibly would you think he has anything to do with this or that this place belongs to him?"

His surprise was genuine and I knew instantly I had hit the right button just by the tone of his voice. But if that were not enough his face showed even further how close I had come to confirming the truth for if looks could kill, I had little time to live.

"Let me tell you something, you arrogant little piece of shit," he hissed threateningly. "Eduard Mayer is going to be the next president of Ecuador. So, why on earth would he be interested in someone like you? You're a nothing, some American student who comes down here and sticks his nose into something he has no business being involved in."

His outburst could have been genuinely directed at an arrogant American who knew little about Ecuador, but I doubted it. And, it was possible that Edward Mayer may not have sent him and he may not have known who actually owned the place, but after seeing the expression on his face I seriously doubted that, too. What I suspected was that my captor's outburst sprang from my recognizing where I was being held. It now appeared clear they really didn't know I'd been here before. Carolina had apparently planned it right; by having me pick her up from the university's restaurant her security detail never did see her leave campus. Just in case, I decided I'd be better off if I said nothing more. I had already complicated my situation by stupidly letting on that I knew where I was being held, an admission that was almost certain to make my situation more precarious.

"What I need from you, Mr. Henrick, is to learn whether you have any idea what was in those papers you gave that Lutheran minister?"

He was literally snarling now and the way he looked down at me was enough to send a shiver up my spine. There was something about him now that truly scared me, and this was the man only a few minutes ago I had decided had the harmless look of an accountant.

"So, Mr. Henrick, you haven't answered me. Do you know what was in those papers?"

I could tell by the tone of his voice that he was deadly serious and that if I didn't answer he might just kill me, although to this point he hadn't threatened me with any kind of weapon. Yet, it was obvious my options were limited and I'd be better off if I told him the truth; my problem was, it was probably not going to be enough for him.

"If I had been able to read what was written on those pages why would I have even bothered to take them to Reverend Hoffmann? And, furthermore, I never would have taken them to him if I had known I was placing his life in danger by doing so. Can you imagine how I feel about what happened to him? No, of course, you don't since either you or one of your associates was responsible for killing him," I sneered. "I can't believe you did that and for what? Nothing in those papers could be so important that it was worth taking the life of a totally innocent person. You guys are insane!"

"Believe me, Mr. Henrick, what's in those papers is more important than you'll ever know, but I must say if you hadn't foolishly become involved much of this would never have happened. Certainly the good reverend would still be alive."

"No, you can't shift the blame on this to me. It appears you'll stop at absolutely nothing to get back those papers, which begs the question, what do you plan to do with me?"

Before he had a chance to answer my question, if he had even intended to, we were both startled by the sound of shouting coming from somewhere just outside the house. My interrogator turned quickly and rushed out of the bedroom in the direction of the front door; unfortunately for me, he slammed the bedroom door shut as he raced out so I could only imagine what was happening out there.

Several minutes passed during which I heard nothing. Then came the sound of doors slamming and a car, or maybe two, driving out of the yard. Had I been abandoned?

Why hadn't someone come inside looking for me? Concluding I was now alone in the house I was shocked when the bedroom door unexpectedly opened and I caught sight of a familiar face.

"You! What are you doing here?" I exclaimed, staring up at Jacob in amazement.

Twenty-Seven

"How did you know I was here," I asked, amazed to find him standing there.

Jacob, who was wasting no time untying my hands and feet, responded simply, "We followed you."

"What do you mean you followed me? How did you even know I'd been kidnapped?"

My initial sense of relief was almost instantly replaced by a feeling of anger at the way I was being shoved around by people who saw me as nothing more than a pawn in their stupid games.

"Here, put these on," he ordered, throwing me my clothes that had been lying on a nearby chair. "We've got to get out of here, and we've got to do it quickly."

"Look, I'm not going anywhere until you tell me how you were able to follow me here. I have a lot more questions than that but for the moment I'll be satisfied with an answer to this one."

"Come on, I'll answer your questions on the way. Right now we're going to get out of here just in case other people show up. We've already explained we're not operating here in Ecuador in any legal capacity and the people you've managed to stir up are very powerful or at the least they have very powerful friends, either way we have to be extremely careful. So, please, can we get going now?"

He hadn't answered my question but I followed him anyway, frantically stuffing my shirt into my jeans as I stumbled out of the house.

"What happened to the guy who was questioning me, and for that matter who the hell was he anyway?"

"There were actually three of them and I have no idea who they are. Right now they're all taking rides with a couple of my colleagues. Hopefully, we'll know a lot more about this diary after we've had an opportunity to talk with them," Jacob replied.

"But, what if they refuse to talk," I asked naively. I should have anticipated Jacob's answer.

"Oh, they'll talk. My colleagues can be amazingly persuasive when necessary," he laughed.

"And, you have no idea who these guys are working for? Could they be working for Eduard Mayer?"

If I had expected Jacob to react in some way at the mention of Eduard Mayer's name, I was sadly disappointed for his face remained impassive. Ahead of us in the driveway was an old silver Volvo. Jacob opened the driver's side door and motioned impatiently for me to get in the other side.

"Don't I rate one of those big, black SUVs that all you guys seem to drive," I asked sarcastically.

"Buckle up," Jacob snapped at me. "I wouldn't want you to get hurt, not at this point."

With that he started the engine and backed hastily out of the driveway. As we headed for the rocky, twisting road that represented our only way out of the valley, Jacob looked over at me curiously.

"Why did you mention Eduard Mayer back there?"

It was just at that point we began our ascent and Jacob so quickly found himself trying to keep the wildly bouncing car on the road that I decided he had forgotten what he had just asked. But, once again, I underestimated the man.

"Of course," he blurted out, "you're dating Eduard Mayer's daughter, or at least you were before you got yourself in this mess."

Jacob had such a strange manner about him I could never tell whether he was being sarcastic or just matter-of-fact.

"I would like to think we still are dating," I replied glumly, "but thanks to you guys I'm not sure anymore."

"What do you mean thanks to us? What have we done other than save your precious skin so you'll be able to see her again? But, let's get back to my original question, which was why you think Eduard Mayer might have something to do with your kidnapping. Does he object that much to your dating his daughter? For an American you don't seem like such a bad a guy but, hey, what do I know."

Jacob was clearly needling me but I suspected he was also trying to pry actually information out of me, which didn't bother me in the least since I was just as eager as they were to discover who was behind all this.

"That was his farm back there, where they were holding me. Carolina brought me there once though I had always assumed her father never knew about it, that is, until today; now, I suspect, he had us followed. And, one thing I know, he'd do anything to protect his daughter. So, if he had found out about our being here together he would be furious and not above having me kidnapped. The problem with this theory naturally is Reverend Hoffmann; his death just doesn't fit in to any of this."

Jacob said nothing, seemingly concentrating on his driving, but I knew he was thinking about what I had just told him. By the time we reached the main road, the overcast that had covered our escape had miraculously given way to bright sunlight. For the first mile or so the road stretched perfectly straight before suddenly descending in a series of sweeping s-shaped curves. Jacob had little choice but to slow as we passed through a village of poorly constructed mud-brick houses with a maze of narrow, dusty streets extending off in all directions. The side streets teemed with fruit and vegetable sellers, playing children, and the usual emaciated–looking dogs on the search for something to eat. A few minutes later we reached the traffic circle at Mitad del Mundo where Jacob took a sharp right and headed for Quito twenty minutes away.

"You know," I said, breaking the silence, "you never did answer my question about how you were able to follow me. I can only assume you had someone keeping me under surveillance at the airport, am I right?"

Jacob looked at me with an expression that was difficult to read. I decided he was thinking I was probably the most naïve guy he had ever met. And, he was probably correct. Still, I found myself becoming annoyed as hell with his attitude.

"So why, then, didn't you rescue me at the airport? Whoever was watching me must have just stood there twiddling his thumbs as they drugged me and smuggled me out to their car. But, of course, that's it; you guys set me up, didn't you? I should have known. You used me as bait to draw these people out? In fact, you probably even leaked the news I was leaving this morning. You sons-of-bitches, I could have been killed just like Reverend Hoffmann and that poor guy who started all this, Francisco. On the other hand, if it enabled you to find the papers you so badly want, you would have just shrugged it off as a cost of doing whatever business you're in."

I was really getting upset now but I had every right to be. Anyone, who had just gone through what I had, would have felt the same way.

"Don't you ever shut-up," Jacob growled angrily. "Let me remind you of the role you played in helping to create this mess. We were simply contacted to come in and clear it up. And, we didn't place you in a situation that was any more dangerous than the one we found you in when we got here. These are the very same people who have been after you from the beginning. Anyway, we wouldn't have let you get hurt. So, would you please stop whining! I never thought of Americans as whiners, that is, until I had the pleasure of meeting you."

Ouch! Jacob really stung me with his comment about me being a whiner. I'd been called many things in my life but to the best of my knowledge never a whiner.

"So, where are you taking me, and please, don't tell me to shut up or stop whining because I have at least the right to know that." I was really feeling pissed now, only I wasn't sure whether it was because of Jacob's comment or because he refused to tell me anything. It was, after all, my life that was being kicked around like a soccer ball.

We were approaching the outskirts of Quito, and when we came to a traffic circle, I noticed Jacob took the road directing us to the airport.

"Give me a break, are you taking me to the airport again," I asked in exasperation.

"Yes," Jacob replied, "only his time we are truly going to get you out of here. I suspect we've had all we can take of one another."

I couldn't argue with that.

"But, wait a minute. I thought that flights to Miami only left early in the morning; what airline do you have me booked on?" Now, I was getting a little suspicious.

"You're not going to Miami, you're going to Guayaquil," Jacob explained. "We have a plane waiting for you; it's a private plane so it will be leaving as soon as we get there."

"And, what happens to me when I get to Guayaquil," I asked anxiously.

"We've booked you on an American Airlines flight to New York via Dallas. No more games on your part, or ours. You're outta here."

"But, what about my luggage, I had checked it in to Miami?" I realized I was beginning to sound whiney even to myself.

"Don't worry for God's sake, we've taken care of it. It's probably already stowed on the plane to Guayaquil, but if it isn't you can have it sent up from Miami." Jacob was clearly becoming annoyed with me.

We were in Quito now driving through a part of the city with which I had little familiarity. t was a typical working-class neighborhood; the buildings were mostly three floors with shops selling every imaginable item on the ground level and residences above. The narrow streets were heavily congested not only with automobiles but shoppers as well. Several times we were forced to stop because people were walking in the middle of the street. Jacob would honk impatiently but it did little to move people out of the way. Finally, I caught a glimpse of the airport runway between several buildings; a few seconds later we were driving past the terminal entrance.

"Where are we going," I asked nervously.

A second later Jacob pulled into a parking space along the street.

"Come on, let's go," he ordered.

As we started walking up the sidewalk towards one of the large hangars that served the airport, Jacob pulled out his cell-phone and called someone. It quickly became obvious why he did so. Surrounding the hangar area, there was an imposing heavy wire fence, and the only way in was through a gate that was securely padlocked. As we approached the gate, a side door to the hangar opened and a short, swarthy man with a thick head of hair and an equally thick moustache walked over to the gate and unlocked it. Jacob herded me through.

"Let's get into that hangar quickly," Jacob snapped. "Almost certainly they have more people watching the airport."

The interior of the hangar was huge. There were at least four small aircraft inside and a single-engine plane just outside the main hangar door. A couple of the planes were in the process of being serviced, other than that the only people I saw were standing around the plane outside. Jacob strode directly over towards them while I began to feel just a little sick to my stomach. I suspected that was the plane that would be transporting me to Guayaquil, that tiny, fragile-looking, single-engine aircraft.

The three men standing by the plane obviously knew Jacob for they greeted him warmly. He introduced me to them but so hurriedly I didn't catch anyone's name. Probably intentional, I decided. They briefly spoke among themselves and only afterwards did I realize it was in a language I didn't recognize.

Turning away from them, Jacob said, "Unfortunately, your luggage is already on its way to Miami so you'll be traveling light. Robert here will be your pilot. And, don't worry, he flies often to Guayaquil so he knows the route and the weather intimately."

There was some subdued laughter, which left me to wonder, if Jacob was being honest or just his usual sarcastic self. The men were moving now so I guess it didn't really matter.

Robert opened the cabin door and slipped in. I was directed around the other side where I was given the choice of sitting up with Robert in the copilot's seat or in one of the two seats behind. I chose the latter. I had no need to look at the sky around me, especially when the only thing separating me from the outside was a frighteningly thin layer of metal.

After a few more words with his colleagues Robert taxied out to the runway where we sat for several minutes before he received word from the control tower he was cleared to take off. Revving the engine we began racing down the runway. The plane jounced noisily and I found myself holding on for dear life. Just when I thought we'd reached the end of the runway, the aircraft lifted off and I was suddenly given an extraordinary view of Quito out the side window. And, then, just as quickly it was gone as we entered a layer of swirling clouds. I sat back and did my best to relax but I realized only too well I was in for an agonizing couple of hours, that is, if I really were being flown to Guayaquil! When it dawned on me they could have been taking me anywhere, I decided it just didn't matter since there was nothing I could do about it at this point.

Twenty-Eight

The flight to Guayaquil seemed to take forever though in fact it actually lasted just over an hour. As luck would have it we ran into a succession of severe thunderstorms and while the pilot did everything possible to avoid them, it still made for an extremely rough ride. More than once the violent pitching of the aircraft made me certain I was about to be sick but by some miracle it didn't happen. Other than occasionally asking how much longer the flight was going to take, to which he would inevitably grunt "just a little longer," I left the pilot alone. He clearly had his hands full trying to keep the aircraft steady. Of course, it didn't help much that I could hear him constantly muttering to himself. I couldn't quite make out what he was saying; I just hoped he wasn't praying. What I desperately needed from him was to display a little more confidence that we were going to make it.

If there were one consolation to the rough weather, it was that it left me no time to dwell on the fact there were people out there looking to kill me. After all, if I didn't make it to Guayaquil, the whole thing was a moot point. Except in a James Bond film you couldn't die twice. I couldn't believe I was thinking like this. There was nothing funny about the situation in which I now found myself. In fact, the whole thing was crazy! Here I was being whisked out of the country in order to keep me from being killed when all I did was to try to help out a friend by delivering some documents that needed to be translated! How on earth had my quiet almost boring life been so suddenly turned upside down? Ironically, I had come to Quito to get away from my personal problems for a few days, nothing more. And, now, I found myself in a small plane, flying through the kind of weather that should have grounded us, trying to get out of Ecuador in one piece.

At long last, I felt the aircraft begin its descent into Guayaquil. Glancing out the window I could see nothing but a mass of white clouds rushing past. As I was blankly staring at them the aircraft suddenly broke through the cloudbank and there was the city of Guayaquil spread out below me. On any other occasion I might have been looking forward to visiting the place but not today when I had no idea what to expect once we landed. Hopefully, the people waiting for me were friends of Jacob's, though past experience had shown I could not completely trust him either. Still, when the plane touched down I couldn't help but feel a sense of relief if for no other reason than we had survived.

As we taxied in the direction of a distant hangar I reached over and tapped the pilot's shoulder.

"Thanks," I said. "The weather was pretty bad but you did a great job getting us here safely."

"That's what they pay me for," the pilot mumbled.

I had the urge to ask him who "they" were but if I'd learned anything in the past few days it was not to expect anyone to explain what was going on so I said nothing.

As we were approaching the hangar, two men appeared to be waiting for us. They were dressed as mechanics or some kind of airport personnel though I assumed they worked with Jacob. On the other hand, I remembered the guys who had kidnapped me; they were wearing airport uniforms of some kind too. Didn't these airports have any security?

As we pulled up and the pilot cut the engine they approached the aircraft and placed chocks against the wheels. Apparently they were whom they appeared to be, which made me just a little apprehensive. Where, I wondered, were the guys who were supposed to take care of me and see that I got safely on my plane.

"End of the line," growled the pilot, climbing out of the plane.

I pushed the front seat forward and clambered out onto the tarmac. Since I had no luggage to retrieve I found myself just standing there waiting for someone to fetch me. The pilot basically ignored me, choosing instead to speak with the two mechanics. I gathered they were talking about readying the aircraft for the pilot's return flight to Quito.

It was then that I spotted a dark-haired man standing in the shadows just inside the open hangar door. From a distance he looked like a businessman; he was wearing a dark suit, pale blue shirt and striped tie. But, as he began walking towards me I noticed he was tall, easily six feet two or three, with a well-proportioned build. Clearly, if he were a businessman he spent a lot of time working out at the company gym. However, I suspected he had a military background and the way he carried himself in a self-assured, almost arrogant manner only further strengthened my suspicions.

"Mr. Henrick," he asked quietly. It was only then that I realized while he possessed what some might consider rugged good looks, his face had been badly scarred or burned. What was it about these guys?

"Yes, I'm Michael Henrick," I replied cautiously. After all, I had expected a couple of tough-looking guys waiting to escort me to my plane, not that this guy didn't look as if he could take care of himself, and me too if necessary.

He must have guessed what I was thinking because he replied, "Not to worry, I'll see that you safely board your flight back to the States. You'll be flying American Airlines. The flight will take you to Dallas where you'll change planes and then fly on to New York. Once I get you on board, however, you'll be on your own."

He gave me what for him was probably a smile though it was so brief it hardly qualified as one. And that was it; he didn't introduce himself, show me any kind of identification, or make any move to shake my hand. It was weird and once again I began to feel a bit anxious; there was definitely something unnerving about the guy.

"I trust you have your passport," he said matter-of-factly and for the first time I detected a slight accent in his voice though not one I could place. "I've taken care of everything else, including paying the exit tax," he continued, "so, stay right with me and I'll get you on the plane."

I followed him past several hangars and administrative buildings until we came to the terminal itself. The terminal building was not especially large and in no time we arrived at the first security checkpoint where he handed me my boarding pass. With no luggage I simply had to show the boarding pass and my passport and I was through. I saw him flash some kind of identification and he was waved through as well. Who, I wondered, was this guy? What I would have given to see his identification.

"Come on, we have to go to gate 6B. If you check your ticket you'll see we've booked you business class so you can be one of the first to board. They should begin the boarding process in the next fifteen minutes or so."

We passed a couple of waiting areas before coming to our gate. Spotting a men's room I said, "If you don't mind too much I'd really like to use the bathroom; I've been needing to go almost since my flight took off from Quito."

"And, if you don't mind too much I'll come in there with you. I was told of your adventure at the airport in Quito," he replied with a touch of sarcasm.

I really detested this guy. I had found nothing amusing about the incident at the airport since I could have very possibly been killed. And then, of course, there was that little issue of my kidnapping having been encouraged by the very people for whom I assumed he was working. They had done everything but send out an invitation to grab me, and they may even have done that. But here in Guayaquil my kidnapping did not appear to be a part of their agenda; this time they really did seem intent on getting me safely out of the country.

Exiting the men's room I could see people were already lining up to board the plane.

"Why don't you go ahead over there and get on board as quickly as you can. I'll stay here until I actually see you go through the gate. Oh, yes, and may I give you a little advice, Mr. Henrick? Stay out of Ecuador; you managed to make some pretty nasty enemies in the short time you were here.

He gave me that annoying smile.

"I'll remember that," I snapped, wondering how it was possible to come to dislike someone so quickly. Turning my back on him I walked over to join the line. When a few minutes later I presented my boarding pass and headed down the ramp towards the plane, I never glanced back. It was depressing enough to leave Ecuador without having his the last face I would see.

However upset I may have been with my Israeli "friends," if that's who in fact they were, my anger was substantially lessened by their booking me home business class, although I suspected I'd actually be paying for it myself. Still, I relished the large comfortable seat and the attentive stewardess who even before take-off served me my first bourbon. And, if that were not enough, the seat next to me remained unoccupied. I had absolutely no desire to carry on a conversation with anyone; I wanted only to be left alone. I was utterly exhausted emotionally and physically. All I could think about was getting some sleep once the plane took-off.

But, of course, I couldn't, though it certainly wasn't for lack of trying. I stretched out, plugged in my earphones to the soft music channel and closed my eyes. There may have been a moment when I began to slip off but the next thing I knew the stewardess was asking me what I wanted for dinner. It was only then I realized how long it had been since I had eaten. When my meal was served I amazed myself by devouring everything on the tray along with a couple of mini-bottles of red wine. The food was actually pretty good, unlike the meal I was served on the flight from Miami to Quito. That one I had found utterly inedible; ah, the pleasures of flying business class.

No sooner had everything been cleared from dinner than the movie came on. Unfortunately, it was one I had seen already, *The Hurt Locker*, and though it was an excellent movie I just wasn't in the mood for that kind of intensity, not at this particular moment. What I needed more than anything was to relax and get some sleep. I was almost certain the bourbon and the several glasses of wine would help me do both.

As I closed my eyes my mind wandered once again to Carolina. Everything had been going so beautifully. How could this have all happened, and so suddenly that I never even had the chance to offer her an explanation? I tried to imagine what she was thinking. Could she possibly believe I'd just walk out on her? Of course, she could for in a sense that's exactly what I did. Admittedly, I didn't do it voluntarily, but she didn't know that? On the other hand, she had promised to email me, yet for some unexplained reason she never did. The whole thing was so strange. Could it really be linked with the diary and my taking those pages to Reverend Hoffmann? But, how could it, I'd never even told Carolina about any of it. As I slipped off to sleep the image of a smiling Carolina crept into my consciousness. I couldn't help but wonder if I'd ever see her again. Perhaps Adam could somehow smooth things out for me; he was good at that sort of thing and he was a diplomat, wasn't he?

Twenty-Nine

As my taxi pulled away from the American Airlines terminal at JFK, I slouched back in my seat and let out an audible sigh of relief; I was on the final leg of my trip home. The past several days had unquestionably been the most stressful of my life. In fact, I was still having trouble accepting everything that had happened. For the moment though, I just wanted to forget about it and enjoy the rush of heading back into the city with its dissonant symphony of honking horns, wailing sirens and cursing drivers. It was also reassuring to realize I could speak English and have people understand me. Ironically, glancing at the picture of my driver, I was not certain I could count him among them.

"There's no place quite like New York City," I sighed, wondering if I really believed that to be true.

It took nearly an hour with the traffic to actually reach my apartment building and as we pulled up in front of the bleached-brick structure I found to my surprise my euphoria at being home was already beginning to ebb; in its place I discovered an almost painful sense of loneliness setting in. One didn't require a doctorate in psychology to understand I was already missing Quito, and it wasn't just the beautiful weather or the laidback lifestyle of the Ecuadorians. Obviously, what I was really missing was Carolina, who was now separated from me by nearly three thousand miles depending upon where she actually was at the moment. And, making it only worse was the gnawing realization I might never see her again. For some strange reason, or maybe not so strange, the final scene from the movie, *Casablanca*, flashed through my mind, the scene where Humphrey Bogart is watching the plane carrying Ingrid Bergman take off into the foggy Moroccan night. I guess I was thinking how about how stoical he appeared.

Handing the driver his fifty-five dollars to pay for my trip from JFK I couldn't help but remind myself how the same ride would have cost me less than fifteen dollars in Quito. How long, I wondered, would it take for me to stop comparing whatever I did in New York with Ecuador? I exited the cab and walked slowly up the front steps to my apartment building oblivious to everything going on around me. Entering the lobby I was quickly brought back to reality by a familiar voice.

"Welcome back, Mr. Henrick, I wasn't sure whether I'd be seeing you again or not. I was just beginning to wonder what to do with all your mail. By the way, don't you have any luggage?"

Bernie Katz had worked at the front desk literally since the building had opened. He had been born in Lithuania, his parents escaping first to Germany, then Holland, before finally making it to New York. Bernie was seven years old when his parents moved to a tiny apartment in the Village. They were both dead now but Bernie still lived in that same apartment. He claimed he had never been away from the Village for more than a day or so at a time and had every intention of dying in the Village. I couldn't for the life of me imagine why anyone would be so proud of such a fact but I had never felt the need to question him about it.

"Why don't you give me my mail since I'm not carrying anything. My luggage unfortunately is at the airport in Miami. I'll have to call American Airlines to have it sent up here."

Handing it to me he said, "Nothing really important in there, mostly just catalogues and a couple of bills."

"Thanks," I replied, feeling depressed by his comment. I don't know why it bothered me. I knew there wouldn't be anything from Carolina, she didn't even know my New York address, and if she did and had written me it wouldn't have had time to arrive. But, I knew there'd be nothing from her, not after having been unwilling to even email me when I was still in Quito.

I headed for the open elevator and stepped in; it reeked of cleaning fluid or disinfectant. I suspected someone's dog had gotten sick in there and the elevator had been recently cleaned; ah, welcome back to New York! I quickly pushed the button for the fourth floor and impatiently watched the numbers change as the elevator climbed: I was desperate to get away from the disgusting smell. When finally it reached my floor I stepped out into a carpeted hallway that was well lighted and spotlessly clean though definitely not the gleaming marble entryway leading to Adam's apartment. The hallway, however, was probably good preparation for what was to come next. Opening the door to my apartment I was shocked by how tiny it suddenly looked. My studio apartment, of which I had always been so proud, could not have been much larger that Adam's entryway and living room. And, I certainly didn't have a view like the one looking down the valley towards Cumbaya. On the other hand, it was New York, not Quito, and if I were going to be miserable, I'd probably get over it a lot more quickly here than I would down there, or at least I hoped I would.

I slumped down into my favorite leather chair and glanced around. The room by New York standards was relatively large and easily held my desk on which sat my laptop, a couple of expensive but very comfortable Italian-leather chairs, my Swedish-designed couch/bed, and my flat-screen television, not quite as large as Adam's but it did have a Bose sound system into which I could plug my iPod when I wanted to listen to music. I even had room for a tall, narrow bookcase that unfortunately was not nearly sufficient for all the books I owned; the overflow I had simply piled up on the floor for now.

So, while my apartment was small, at least compared to Adam's, I grudgingly decided it was comfortable, affordable, and it had a great location. Admittedly, Greenwich Village was no longer the center of bohemianism that it had been in the Twenties or later during the 1950s when the Beat Generation gathered here and the neighborhood provided the setting for stories by Jack Kerouac, Allen Ginsburg, and Dylan Thomas. It wasn't even the same place as in the 1960s when it became a sanctuary for the Weathermen, the most notorious of the radical anti-war movements. Still, the Village remained unique even within New York for its rich array of Off-Broadway theaters, jazz clubs, and comedy centers and I loved the area's ambiance and its liberal live-and-let-live attitudes. One thing was certain, there was no neighborhood quite like Greenwich Village in Quito; for that matter, there was probably no place quite like it anywhere in the world.

So, here I sat feeling suddenly alone and depressed even though I was back in New York where I belonged. Or did I belong here? At this moment I wasn't certain. All I knew was that I was really missing Carolina, something only made worse by the fact I had been forced to leave without ever having a chance to explain why I was doing it. Not, I had to now admit, that I'd tried very hard to get in touch with her. So, should I do something, but what? I could try to call her only I had no phone number.

Probably what I should do was call or email Adam to see if he could get her number for me. In the meantime I decided I'd try to email her again though I suspected it wouldn't do much good. Either my previous emails had not gotten through, though I'd never received an error message or any kind of notification they hadn't, or whatever had happened was so serious she was unable to respond to me.

The whole thing was really strange. What possibly could have happened? Had her father found out about our being together at the farm that afternoon and forbade her from having any further contact with me? I didn't believe that because I knew she'd contact me anyway. The more I thought of my leaving Ecuador the more upset with myself I got. Why hadn't I stayed and tried to find out what happened to her. What a coward I had been letting Frank and Jacob shove me out of the country.

Angrily I picked up my mail and began thumbing through it. To my surprise I spotted a small manila envelope addressed to me in handwriting I recognized immediately. The return address sticker in the upper left corner only confirmed the obvious; it was from Rachel. I tore open the envelope trying to imagine what reason she might have for writing me. I don't know what I was expecting; I guess I was hoping it would at least be something to brighten what had been a very depressing day. Unfortunately, it proved just the opposite. The envelope contained the apartment key I had given Rachel when we had started dating seriously; there was also a brief note explaining that since we were no longer going together she was returning it. Why, I thought angrily, hadn't she just thrown it away; why make such a big issue about it. Was she trying to rub it in? And, I couldn't believe her sense of timing; it was almost as if she knew what had happened between Carolina and me.

Even more distressed now, I slumped back and stared out the window at the building next door. I must have sat like that for what seemed like ages when my computer suddenly caught my attention. I jumped up and went over to my desk. As I turned the computer on, I thought just possibly there was an email from Carolina. After getting my key back from Rachel, I knew I was setting myself up for another huge disappointment. There were plenty of messages waiting for me but they were much like my mail--junk; advertisers had clearly learned how to slip things through spam filters. But, of course, there was nothing there from Carolina. Yet, I still checked the trash on the tiniest of chances my spam filter had somehow blocked out her messages; there was nothing there either.

Staring at the screen, I couldn't help wondering if I really had taken a trip to Ecuador. Was Carolina a real person or just some imaginary figure I had dreamed up to take Rachel's place? Had I really made love to her that afternoon at her family's farmhouse or was I imagining that, too? And what about Carlos, the diary, the murder of the minister, even my kidnapping, had those things really happened? I had an overwhelming urge to call Adam and ask him if I'd, in fact, been down there, but I was just a little nervous about what he might say. I truly began to wonder if I might just be going crazy. I almost hoped it was all a dream, that way I wouldn't have to deal with it, which seemed to be the way I handled most unpleasant events.

Over the next few days I did my best to restore some semblance of a life, that is, by trying to pretend none of this had happened. I called my parents to let them know I was back, I got together with a couple of old friends for drinks, and I even began to look for a new job though I was in no great hurry for that. Partly, it was because I continued to feel unsettled. It was as if I was unconsciously planning to leave New York soon and didn't want to get tied down to anything. But, I was sure this wasn't the case, at least I didn't think it was. I suspected what was eating away at me was that I still hadn't heard anything from Carolina and it didn't make sense. How could this woman who secretly took me to her farm outside of Quito to make love to me in the most surprisingly passionate manner and who continually told me how much she loved me, just drop me? What had I done? I mean, first Rachel, and now Carolina? No, it had to be more than that; something else had to have happened, and that's what was worrying me.

To top it all off, Adam hadn't contacted me either. I had sent him an email the very evening I had arrived home, thanking him for putting up with me, and everything else associated with my visit. I had expected an immediate response but as yet I'd heard nothing. Now, I truly began to wonder if Adam was upset with me because of what happened? But even if it had caused problems for him at work I would have expected at least a brief note acknowledging that I had gotten home without further incident. Something wasn't right.

Returning from a job interview at Morgan Stanley one afternoon, Bernie, the doorman, startled me by reporting that someone had stopped by to ask about me. He explained that the guy obviously knew me; he had mentioned my trip to Ecuador and asked when exactly I had returned home. He had not, however, left any message saying only he'd get in touch with me later. When I asked Bernie what the guy looked like his description did not appear to match anyone I knew, though to be honest it probably could have fit half the men in New York. Who could it have been, I wondered, and what did he want? My first thought was he was probably someone working for the Israelis, though if Bernie's description of the guy was even half close it definitely wasn't either Frank or Jacob. Of course, there was no shortage of people right here in New York the Israelis could call on. But, what if it weren't someone working for them. What if it had been one of the kidnappers or at least someone working for them? And, were they taking their orders from Carolina's father? Again, Carolina's father, but why on earth would he send someone to check up on me? The whole thing was weird, and also just a little frightening; someone was definitely keeping me under surveillance. I decided, whomever it was wanted to be able to find me if it became necessary. Oh, God, what kind of a mess had I gotten myself into? More importantly, how was I ever going to get out of it?

Thirty

I had just stepped out of the shower when I heard the phone ringing above the hum of the bathroom exhaust fan. Quickly wrapping my towel around me, and leaving a trail of wet footprints in my wake, I raced to pick up the receiver before the answering system kicked in.

"Hello," I said, noticing by the clock on my desk it was only eight-fifteen.

I was both surprised and delighted when the voice at the other end said, "Michael, this is Adam." It was the first time I had heard from him since my return.

But, it quickly dawned on me there was something in the tone of his voice that suggested this was more than just a social call.

"Adam," I replied cautiously, "I'm glad to hear from you. To be honest, I had expected to hear from you sooner. Is everything all right down there in Quito? You are calling from Quito aren't you?"

"Oh, yes, and as a matter of fact that's what I'm calling you about. Let's just say that all hell has broken loose down here, at least here at the embassy, and I thought just possibly you could shed some light on what's been happening. You do know, right; it's been all over the evening news, or on CNN anyway. Maybe someone even has called you from Quito. Do you have any idea what I'm talking about? "

My first thought was to make some wise comment like how about a "Hello, Michael, how are you; I'm glad you made it home safely," but I quickly thought better of it. I could tell he was worried about something. I just hoped he was not in any kind of trouble because of me.

"No, I haven't the slightest idea what you're talking about and, no, no one has called me from Quito. And anyway, whom do you think would be calling me? Other than Carolina I didn't become close enough friends with anyone to exchange phone calls, and I can assure you I haven't heard a word from her. Furthermore, as if you didn't already know, I've heard nothing from you either, though I should point out I've called and left messages and even written you a couple of emails. So, if it would not be too much effort on your part please tell me what's going on in Quito that is so important you suddenly feel the necessity of calling me," I exclaimed, the sarcasm to obvious to miss.

Adam instantly softened his tone.

"I'm sorry, but it seems that Eduard Mayer, Carolina's father, has disappeared. No one seems to know anything of his whereabouts; he just suddenly disappeared into thin air. We're not even certain he's alive; no one has seen him. We're guessing he's left the country since he'd be recognized if he were still around. I just thought by chance you might have heard something from Carolina that might give us a clue as to his whereabouts and Carolina's as well."

"Carolina is missing, too?" I asked, with a mixture of concern and relief. If nothing else it helped explain why she hadn't been in touch with me, but where could she have gone? Almost immediately, Frank and Jacob came to mind. Could they have had something to do with Carolina and her father's disappearance? Try as I might, however, I couldn't think of a good reason why they would.

"I'm assuming she's missing, too, and probably with her father," I heard Adam saying, "though I don't know that for a fact. The concern around here has obviously been for her father. Washington is going crazy. As I had explained to you when you were down here, the White House had been counting heavily on him becoming the next president of Ecuador. I've even heard some of the president's advisors using the term 'axis of democracy' to describe the governments of Ecuador and Colombia. It's clearly their hope that this 'axis' might be able to counter the growing influence of Chavez. And, possibly even initiate a trend away from the sort of left-wing, populist governments that have been coming to dominate much of Latin America of late."

I wanted him to stop rambling and get back to the issue of Carolina.

"So, what do all you experts think happened to Carolina, and her father of course? I mean, Chavez or the other left-wing governments you've been referring to, they would never kidnap them to keep Carolina's father from being elected president, would they?"

"That's highly doubtful, although I'm beginning to suspect anything is possible in this world. The point is, we don't know a thing. Washington's position at the moment is to say absolutely nothing; there are already enough rumors swirling around out there. The consensus seems to be that he may have become caught up in some kind of scandal but if that's the case we have no idea at the moment what that scandal might be. Now, of course, there's this little issue of you and the alleged diary that purports to explain where Atahualpa's gold is buried. According to you, although it's proved impossible to corroborate, the minister of the Lutheran Church was murdered because he discovered what was in that diary. And, then also according to you, I was sent on a bogus mission to Guayaquil by a group of apparently American Jewish businessmen to keep me from learning you had been kidnapped or taken into protective custody, and to protect me. Have I got it right so far?"

"You have," I replied, realizing once again how ridiculous it sounded.

"So," he continued, "it might not surprise you if I told you the Israeli Embassy down here has denied everything, claiming the whole story is pure fiction. As for the business cards these guys handed me, they seemed to be legitimate though when we called them companies listed on them they claimed to know nothing about the trip. In light of all this I was hoping you might have some information that would help unravel these mysteries? You certainly know more than we do."

"But, I don't," I replied, wondering now if I'd been incorrect in assuming that Frank and Jacob had been working for the Israelis. They were the ones who had informed me that Reverend Hoffmann had called the Israeli Embassy to report what he had discovered in the diary, or at least the pages of the diary I had given him. Unfortunately, he never explained to anyone apparently what exactly he had found. So, was it possible that Frank and Jacob had just lied and, in fact, had followed me to the church whereupon they had murdered Reverend Hoffmann? But, if that were the case, why did they kidnap me? Was it just to find out if I knew what was in the diary? Then, why let me go? That didn't make sense; in fact, the more I thought about it, the less sense it made. And, then there was this guy who had stopped by my apartment building asking about me. Who was he working for?

"So, you can't tell me a thing that might help," I heard Adam asking. "Then may I ask you another question? I know it will sound crazy and you probably won't or can't answer it anyway, but do you, by any chance, work for the CIA or some such agency?"

I couldn't help laughing; I honestly thought he was kidding. As it turned out he was being entirely serious, or at least half serious.

"Are you out of your mind, Adam? Are you really asking me if I work for the CIA? Me? All I can say is things must be crazy around your embassy if that's the best you can come up with. And, anyway, shouldn't your CIA types at the embassy be using their sources to find Carolina's father? They are on your side, aren't they? And, if they are, just what do you think I would have been doing down there?"

"I'm sorry, Michael, but the fact is the Agency often runs operations in countries without informing the embassy and we only learn about them when something goes awry, like now. We simply can't come up with any plausible explanation for Mayer's disappearance. The diary, whose existence we know about only because of you, may provide the answer but no one seems to know anything about it. I mean, there really was a diary, right?"

"Jesus Christ, Adam, are you going to ask me next if Carolina really existed? You were the one who introduced me to her, you remember."

"I'm really sorry, I know I'm probably sounding paranoid, it's just that we have no idea what's happened to Carolina's father, or the rest of his family for that matter," Adam responded, the frustration clearly audible in his voice.

"OK, OK, so have you talked to my friend, Carlos, the guy who owns the *Café de Los Toreros*? As far as I know he's the one who has the diary, or at least, he had it. Although after all that's happened I can't be sure of that."

"Again, as you might expect, we had somebody check up on him. Unfortunately we discovered he was in the Metropolitan Hospital in a coma, or at least that's what we were told. And if it's true, see how paranoid I'm becoming, there's no telling how long it will be before we can get anything out of him."

"So, you haven't found out anything from Carlos?" I couldn't help wondering if Frank and Jacob were behind the coma story. "But that reminds me, Adam, there are a couple more things I haven't told you about and I'm afraid when I do it'll probably make you wonder about me even more."

"There's more? What can you possibly add that will be anymore bizarre than what you've already told me, but please, go ahead."

"You remember the morning I left for the apartment? I explained that Jacob, one of the two guys, who was 'babysitting' me as they called it, was to meet me downstairs and take me to the airport. Well, he did that, and I checked in and received my boarding pass. But, as I was walking towards the counter where you pay the exit tax, a guy dressed as one of the security guards came up to me, addressed me by name and asked me to follow him. He explained in perfect English there was someone who wanted to speak to me. I more-or-less assumed it was Carolina, or perhaps even you, so I went. As we were walking down this deserted corridor I was suddenly grabbed by two men, one of whom proceeded to stab me with a hypodermic needle. Whatever the needle contained it knocked me out almost immediately."

"Tell me your kidding," Adam gasped. "All this happened right at the airport here in Quito and you have never told me about it until now? I had just automatically assumed you got on the plane and flew back to Miami. So, what happened after you got to the farmhouse, or do I really want to know? They couldn't have hurt you, or at least not too badly, otherwise I wouldn't be talking to you now and you wouldn't have made it back to New York. Am I right?"

"Yes, you're right, but listen for I haven't told you the half of it."

I proceeded to explain about the afternoon I spent with Carolina at Mitad del Mundo, even about our lovemaking at her farmhouse.

"Now, the only reason I'm telling you all this is because these creeps, the ones who grabbed me at the airport, took me to this very farmhouse. They even tied me to the bed on which Carolina and I had made love. Now, whether that was done intentionally or just coincidentally I have no idea."

"So, are you suggesting it was Carolina's father who may have had you kidnapped," Adam asked in amazement. "But, what possible reason would he have to do that? He might not have wanted you for a son-in-law, but must be easier ways to get the point across than kidnapping you, though I do have to admit it was quite a dramatic one."

"As far as I can make out, it had nothing to do with my relationship to Carolina. What they really wanted was to find out exactly what I knew about the diary. But, what I have yet to conclude is whether these guys had any direct connection to Carolina's father. They might just have known that nobody would be using the place. On the other hand, the guy who was questioning me did seem surprised that I knew the place was owned by Carolina's family although that doesn't necessarily prove her father was behind the kidnapping. To be truthful, it seems rather farfetched even to me. But, the coincidence is still troubling."

"So, how did you get away from these guys if they had you tied up," Michael asked in a tone that suggested he was still having trouble believing what I was saying. Of course, I couldn't say I blamed him. It did stretch the imagination.

"Now, here's where it gets even more bizarre, if that's even possible. As I lay there being questioned, there was a commotion outside the farmhouse and who suddenly appears but Jacob, the guy that had taken me to the airport. Though he never came out and admitted it, my guess is they had set me up, that is, used me as bait to find out who was after the diary. He refused to confirm anything because, he explained, it was in my best interest to know as little as possible. He, then, drove me to the airport where I was flown to Guayaquil in this tiny, single-engine aircraft, and in Guayaquil a guy met me and put me on an American Airlines to New York. And I didn't tell you sooner because I haven't been able to get through to you."

"You do realize how unbelievable your story sounds, don't you, especially when you add you have no idea who all these people are that want that diary. And, no one has tried to contact you since you've been back in New York," Adam asked, still sounding incredulous.

"No one," I replied. "But, wait, the guy down at the front desk told me that some guy had been around asking about me. Apparently, he was checking to find out what day I had actually returned. As far as I know he hasn't been back since, though that doesn't mean I not still under surveillance of some kind."

"I don't know what to say, Michael. It's just that nothing seems to be making any sense right now. But, I promise if I hear anything about Carolina I'll let you know. Needless-to-say if anyone contacts you please give me a call or, at the least, email me. In the meantime, be careful."

"Oh, I will, believe me," I replied, wondering whatever happened to my quiet, uneventful life.

Thirty-One

In fact, Adam did begin to call regularly over the course of the next several weeks. Unfortunately, he had little news to pass along about Carolina's family; it was, he claimed, as if the earth had opened up and swallowed them. There were plenty of rumors, however. They were hiding out somewhere in the Oriente. They had fled the country and had been sighted in Santiago, in Bogotá, in Buenos Aires. But, the truth of it was that no one had actually seen them. Of course, Adam reported, this was exactly the kind of story the news media loved; no explanation for Eduard Mayer's sudden disappearance was too implausible for television talk shows or the front pages of even Ecuador's most respectable newspapers.

During one of our conversations Adam informed me, half in jest, that even I had been implicated in the Mayer's disappearance, though not specifically by name. According to him one of Quito's daily newspapers had reported that Carolina had been seen in the company of an unknown American who was rumored to have possible connections to the CIA. Adam claimed that without question I was the unknown American, and then added with a laugh, obviously he was not the only one who suspected I might be working with the Agency. On a more serious note he said that Washington was now concerned that the only candidates for the presidency remaining were representatives of the Left; Eduard Mayer had unfortunately been the only candidate the US had deemed capable of guiding Ecuador in a new direction.

For some reason I suspect Adam is holding back information, that he knows more than he's letting on. I find it very difficult to accept that an entire family, as well known as the Mayers, could just disappear without anyone having the slightest idea where they had gone. Clearly they had help; they couldn't have simply jumped in the family car and driven across the border. Yet, no one involved had apparently uttered a word about it. In this day and age such a thing appeared impossible. But, then, I thought about Atahualpa's gold; no one had ever revealed that secret either. Of course, Rumiñahui had seen to it that everyone involved in hiding the gold was killed. It flashed through my mind that something similar might have occurred in this instance though I quickly dismissed the thought as highly unlikely. While Eduard Mayer was widely known for being a ruthless businessman, there was nothing in his background to suggest under any circumstances could he be a cold-blooded killer.

My concern though was for Carolina; I couldn't care less what Eduard Mayer meant to Washington. They'd quickly forget about him anyway if he didn't win the election. Already, I was willing to bet, someone around the White House was suggesting the administration cut its losses and cozy up to whichever candidate now had the greatest chance of becoming the next president of Ecuador. This was just one more reason to be worried about Carolina; people would very soon be losing interest in the case and when that happened they'd stop looking for them.

With every day that went by without any word from her, my concern grew. I tried conjuring up a mental picture of where she might be or what she might be doing. Thanks to my own experience I understood only too well the stress she must be under if she were being held captive. To keep myself from becoming too stressed, I replayed in my mind literally every moment of our brief time together--our trip to Otavalo, our lunch at Mea Culpa, and, not surprisingly, our afternoon of passionate lovemaking at her family's farmhouse. I consciously fought to keep alive the little things that endeared her to me: her warm smile, the delicious smell of her hair, the adorable way she had of teasing me. I prayed she wasn't in any kind of danger, but deep down I suspected she was. Why else would she not have gotten in touch with me by now?

This uncertainty over Carolina was also making me restless, to the point where I was finding it impossible to get on with my life. Even sitting around the apartment was difficult; I felt claustrophobic. I decided if I got out and started looking for a job it might at least take my mind off her. So, I did, and to my surprise I was able to very quickly line up a number of interviews; even more surprisingly I received several job offers, a couple of which were extremely generous. I turned them down; I just wasn't certain that I wanted to return to the business world. There had to be something more to life. Ironically, while thinking about my options, I briefly considered contacting the CIA, though I never went through with it. I concluded that subconsciously what I really wanted was for Carolina to call and invite me to rendezvous with her in Rio or Buenos Aires or some such exotic location. And, while I realized perfectly well there was little chance of this happening, it was still comforting to know there was nothing to prevent me from doing so if the call ever came.

One morning as I sat at my computer checking on how the stock market was doing, I was suddenly startled by the sound of my phone ringing. I was so certain it was Adam that I was completely taken aback when a strange voice said, "Michael? This is Bernie down at the front desk."

"Oh, Bernie, hi there," I replied. "What can I do for you?"

If he detected the disappointment in my voice, he was gracious enough to ignore it.

"Michael, there's some bald guy down here who says he needs to speak to you; he won't give me his name, but says he knows you. He's a really mean-looking character with this huge scar on his face; does it ring any bells? Believe me, the scar is not anything you'd easily forget."

Jacob! He was only one person in the world I knew who could be described as a bald guy with a huge scar on his face. As for mean looking, I might dispute that.

"It's OK, I know him: tell him to stay put, I'll be right down," I yelled excitedly.

If after all this time Jacob had made the effort to find me, it had to be for something important. While I was certain he had news about the disappearance of Carolina and her family, whether that news was good was entirely another issue.

I raced out of my apartment and down the hallway. Taking the elevator to the lobby, I stepped out, immediately spotting Jacob sitting on a small settee reading a magazine. I could tell he wasn't impressed much by being in New York because he was dressed in his usual casual style: running shoes, tan chinos, and a pale blue polo shirt that showed just how hot it must be outside for it was spotted with sweat marks.

At my approach he quickly stood up, tossing the magazine onto a small table next to where he had been sitting.

"Jacob," I exclaimed exuberantly, forgetting for the moment he had personally kidnapped me once and presumably watched me get kidnapped a second time.

"Michael," he responded, giving me a bear hug. "It's good to see you again; you're certainly looking better than the last time I saw you."

"Well, I wish I could say I was feeling better," I responded. "But, I'm not. So, tell me, what brings you to New York. I'm sure you didn't come all this way just to say 'hello'; I'm at least hoping you have some information you want to pass along to me. You do, right? I'm desperate for news, any news, about Carolina; I haven't heard a single word from her since you guys escorted me out of Ecuador."

"OK, OK, slow down. Actually, I'm here in New York on business having nothing to do with you but, to be honest, I did hope to see you. And, I do have some information that should interest you though it may not be exactly what you were hoping to hear. Let's go for a walk; I don't want to talk here."

When we stepped out onto the sidewalk it was like entering an oven; the temperature had to be in the nineties, and with the humidity, it felt over a hundred degrees. Almost immediately the sweat began forming on my brow.

"There's a Starbuck's just up the street and it's air-conditioned; let's go there," I said. "But, please, what can you tell me about Carolina? At least tell me she's all right? I have to know."

Jacob gave me smile that was difficult to interpret. It was my first hint that he was probably correct I was not going to like what he had to tell me.

"To the best of my knowledge she's fine, though I must admit I don't know anything definitive about her. Eduard Mayer had to leave Ecuador hurriedly and Carolina accompanied him. Carolina's mother, I'm sorry to report, passed away about the same time. I guess you knew she had been ill for a long time. I'm sure the stress of suddenly having to face leaving her home and possibly never returning had something to do with it."

"But why did they have to flee the country," I asked worriedly. "I knew they had disappeared, and had been told there were rumors they might have left the country, but I'd never been given any explanation for why. They weren't kidnapped or anything, were they?"

Before he could reply we arrived at the Starbuck's. Like every other Starbucks, there were several small tables in front, but on this steamy day no one was sitting outside. As I was about to push the door open Jacob unexpectedly said, "If you don't mind too much, let's sit at the table over there; it has an umbrella so we won't be sitting in the sun? The chairs are very close together inside and, if it's all right with you, I'd just as soon not have anyone overhear our conversation."

"Fine, but in that case let's wait on the drinks," I replied impatiently. "I'm anxious to find out what happened to Carolina and her father. So, tell me, did it have anything to do with the diary?"

"It had everything to do with it, I'm afraid."

"I knew it," I said angrily. "I've suspected it for some time but never knew until now for certain. I gather you must have found the diary, then."

"We did, shortly after we got you out of the country. Carlos had it, though we had to wait until after he came out of his coma before he was able to tell us where he had hidden it; fortunately, he hadn't told another soul, including your friends in the American Embassy, so in that respect we were all lucky."

It was an immense relief to learn that Carlos had survived but that didn't stop me from thinking it would have been better for everyone concerned had the diary never been found.

"How is Carlos," I asked. "You mentioned that he came out of his coma but is he going to be all right?"

"Well, he was beaten pretty badly, and he's lost some of the mobility on one side of his body, but he's a pretty tough guy; he'll be fine," Jacob explained in a tone that made clear his respect for how Carlos had handled the whole incident.

"I hope the diary was worth it, then," I responded sarcastically. "By my count at least two people were killed and Carlos was badly injured. So, could you please tell me what was in the diary that could possibly have justified killing these people and forcing Carolina and her family to flee Ecuador?"

"All right, let me begin by saying the diary was not as informative as we might have liked, though that doesn't mean in didn't contain some pretty damaging material."

"To Eduard Mayer, I assume. Obviously it had to be very damaging if he was so willing to have Francisco and Reverend Hoffmann killed to get it back. And, when he couldn't get it back, I assume as well that's why he fled Ecuador in such a hurry?"

I couldn't believe I was saying this about Carolina's father.

"Exactly. But, I should point out that while we've all been referring to the material as a diary, technically that isn't so. Rather," Jacob explained, "it's a collection of notes, many of which we've had trouble making any sense of. The author, by the way, was definitely Eduard Mayer's father, but I must say, he was very careful not to use people's names. We're not even certain of his real name; it definitely wasn't Mayer."

"Anyway," he went on, "I suspect that Eduard Mayer's father was among the hundreds of Nazi officers who fled Germany in 1945 to avoid prosecution for war crimes. Many sought safe havens in South America, especially in the countries of Argentina and Paraguay. Eduard Mayer's father, however, was an exception in escaping to Ecuador. Typically, these Nazi officers took with them large quantities of what has become popularly referred to as 'Nazi gold.' It's a generic term, which is meant to include the billions of dollars in assets stolen from Jewish Holocaust victims."

Jacob stopped for second to wipe the sweat from his face.

"Anyway," he went on, "the term, 'Nazi gold,' refers not only to gold but also to bank deposits, jewelry, artworks, as well as non-monetary gold, which is the gold confiscated from victims of the death camps in the form of eye-glasses, jewelry, watches, coins, and even gold teeth. Much of this vast wealth would be used over the years to create various kinds of Nazi front organizations, not to mention legitimate business enterprises. The purpose of all this was to preserve and, if possible, increase the value of these assets until a new Third Reich could be established in Germany or even somewhere in South America."

Jacob hesitated a moment to catch his breath and let what he had been explaining to me sink in.

"Are you sure you don't want to go inside to at least cool off for a second?" I asked, feeling a little badly for him since he was constantly wiping perspiration from his face. On the other hand, I reminded myself, it was his idea to sit out here.

"No, I'm fine, and anyway, I'll have to be going very shortly. I do have other business to tend to today so I can get away from this wretched city," he smirked. "Just let me finish my story before I leave."

"Eduard Mayer's father was one of these Nazi officers. A member of the SS, he came to Ecuador, probably by U-boat, along with another SS officer and a substantial quantity of gold and foreign currency. The other officer died soon after arriving, apparently from wounds sustained in the war, but who knows, maybe the father had him killed."

"So he wouldn't be able to tell anyone where the gold was buried," I interjected, thinking again about Rumiñahui.

"Very possibly," Jacob replied. "Eduard's father went on to become a very successful businessman and one of the largest landowners in Ecuador.

He accomplished this, in part, by marrying into the Cordobes family, one of the country's most respectable and wealthy families, but he also invested very wisely, in time creating a financial empire that included textile and leather factories, several large banks, and Ecuador's largest supermarket chain. He and his wife had two sons, the younger of whom apparently died at a young age; that left Eduard to become the sole heir of his father's ever-growing financial empire. Accordingly, he was educated abroad, given incredible business opportunities of his own, and finally, pushed into politics. And, he might very well have made it all the way to the presidency had you not arrived on the scene just when you did. This Carlos individual would never have been able to make the diary as public an issue as you did, even though it was quite unintentional on your part."

"I'm still having difficulty understanding exactly why you and Frank were invited in, was it because of the gold they smuggled into Ecuador?" I asked, realizing how naïve I must be sounding.

"Yes. To put it simply, we're part of an ongoing effort to help recapture whatever of these assets we can. It's not an easy process and Eduard Mayer is a perfect example of why. While thanks to the diary, which you played no small part in bringing to our attention, we know how Eduard Mayer's father acquired his wealth, trying to trace where he invested it may take years. But, keep in mind that some significant part of what was smuggled in was almost certainly hidden or buried. Eduard's father was no fool; he knew only too well that bank deposits could be frozen, businesses confiscated. So, we're looking for those buried assets as well."

"Can you tell me one other thing," I asked, uncertain whether he actually would. "Did you guys kidnap Eduard Mayer and smuggle him out of the country? I don't necessarily mean you and Frank but people who work for the Israeli government."

"Off the record, no we didn't. But, someone did, and did it very professionally I might add. We suspect the government of Argentina was involved; of course, whatever part the government played has been kept very secret. It was only through contacts we have with individuals inside the Argentine government that we were able to track them down; the general public, however, seems to know absolutely nothing about it."

"Will you try to abduct him and transport him back to Israel for trial like you did Eichmann and that doctor, what was his name, Mengele or something?"

"Just to set the record straight, we did not abduct Dr. Mengele; unfortunately he was allowed to die of old age somewhere in Brazil. As for Adolf Eichmann, yes, he was abducted from Buenos Aires and returned to Israel where he was tried and executed. But, Eichmann was a Lieutenant Colonel in the SS and the man responsible for rounding up Jews all over Europe and transporting them to the death camps. Believe me, Eduard Mayer is small potatoes compared to Eichmann, and we have no interest in extraditing him, though I suspect the authorities in Ecuador will want to, once they find out he's in Buenos Aires; he is after all implicated in two murders. On the other hand, Eduard Mayer almost certainly has good friends in the Ecuadorian government so you can never be sure what will happen. As for us, what we want primarily is to acquire his financial assets, assets that belong primarily to the Jewish people. At this point in time it's the only way we have of bringing some measure of justice to Holocaust survivors and their heirs."

"You know, I'm still finding all this impossible to believe. I mean Carolina's father a Nazi, or whatever. I admit I only met the man a couple of times but he was so charming, so personable, and to suddenly have people tell you that he's a ruthless murderer. How can that be?"

"What is the old expression, 'like father, like son'? I guess it applies here," Jacob responded.

"So, what do you think about Carolina, then? You can't possibly think she was involved," I asserted testily. "She didn't even want him to be president; she actually told me that."

"I suspect she didn't know that much about it; it wouldn't have been in her father's best interest to tell her, especially if as you say he knew she didn't approve of his politics. As for her mother, who had to know something of her husband's background, she probably kept it from her daughter to protect her, though the cost of this knowledge may have been too great for her to bear."

"Then, you can imagine just how terrible I feel right now. It's not that I can't understand your side of it, I can, and if Carolina weren't involved, I'd probably be very pleased with the small part I played in all this, inadvertent as it might have been. But, unfortunately, Carolina is involved and my stupidity, in getting in the middle of this mess, has only served to destroy her family. I wish in a way you had never told me what happened. Perhaps I would have made up a story about her disappearance I could have lived with."

"Michael, believe me when I say you weren't responsible for what happened to Carolina's family; anyway, it would have been very difficult undergoing the scrutiny presidential candidates go through to keep the source of his wealth a secret forever. And, let's be honest, it was Reverend Hoffmann who actually contacted us about the diary. The main thing for you to remember is that the financial empire inherited by Eduard Mayer, not to mention his position in Ecuadorian society, was built upon the stolen wealth of Hitler's helpless victims. Don't for a second ever feel sorry for Eduard Mayer. In his own way he was as much a murderer as his father or any other member of the SS."

"I guess I understand, really, but it still hurts to think about how much Carolina must hate me."

"Look," Jacob replied, "if Carolina is the woman you say she is, the woman who didn't want her father to become president because she opposed many of his policies, you may be surprised how she'll react, though you're going to have to give her some time. I realize it isn't going to be easy for her to accept the fact she has no money but she will come to accept it knowing where her grandfather got that money. In fact, I suspect what will hurt her the most is not losing the money as much as knowing it underwrote her entire life up until now."

"I suspect you're right," I sighed. "I only wish it hadn't been me that had helped reveal the source of her family's money."

"Well, I can't say that I blame you there, but you do have to remind yourself that what happened isn't your fault. As I said, sooner or later Eduard Mayer would have been found out, and believe me, it's better for everyone that it was sooner. Don't beat yourself up over it."

"I'll try not to. On the other hand, I don't suppose you'd be willing tell me where I can find her," I asked, knowing full well he wouldn't.

"Michael, I've already given you far more information than I was told to. Just promise me you won't do anything to complicate what is already a delicate and potentially dangerous situation. Whatever you do, don't take it upon yourself to fly down to Buenos Aires to look for her. You won't find her anyway. The best advice I can give you is to be patient and let this thing play its way out. Once it has, Carolina may very well discover that she needs you, that you're now the only thing she has left in this world."

"Will you promise me, then, that you guys will leave Carolina alone? Please, Jacob, promise me."

But he was already on his feet, explaining that he had to go, that he was late for a meeting.

"Jacob, promise me; I'm begging you."

I desperately want to hear him say yes.

He stares expressionless at me for a second, then nods assent. After a final bear hug, he turns and without another word walks quickly away.

I stand watching him until he disappears around the corner at the end of the block. Strangely, and in spite of the heat, I experience a slight shiver; I'm feeling suddenly alone. All I can hope is that Jacob is right about Carolina.

Epilogue

It's been almost a year now since my meeting with Jacob at Starbucks, a year in which I've done a great deal of soul-searching. One thing I decided was that I didn't want to simply resume my old life so I applied and got accepted into Columbia's doctoral program in History. It was not an easy decision and I agonized over it for months before ultimately sending off my application. In retrospect it was the smartest decision I've ever made; I love the program. Oddly, I feel a lot older than my classmates though I know for a fact that I'm not. I suspect it has something to do with what happened in Ecuador. In short my experience there forced me to grow up in a hurry. I appreciate now, as never before, how suddenly and irretrievably one's life can change, and not always for the better.

I should probably mention I'm seriously thinking about majoring in Latin American History; I even wrote a paper on Atahualpa's gold! My professor was so impressed with it he suggested I try publishing it somewhere. He remarked he had been fascinated with my theory that Rumiñahui had buried Atahualpa's body along with the gold; he claimed he had never heard of it. I decided right then and there that Rumiñahui would make a perfect topic for my doctoral dissertation for, among other things, it would require me to return to Ecuador for research purposes.

I'm also taking intensive Spanish and, if I do say so, I'm making very good progress in comparison to my previous attempts to learn a foreign language. I've even hired a tutor, a Colombian woman who lives in my building, and we spend three or four hours a week just speaking in Spanish. The woman doesn't exactly remind me of Consuelo, but talking with her, I can't help remembering my hapless attempts to carry on a conversation with her. I'm pretty sure Consuelo would be impressed with just how much my Spanish has improved.

I guess it's only natural to assume I'm doing all this because of Carolina but I'd like to think it's more than just that. I've come to realize, that like Adam, I don't want a career in the financial world. Perhaps I'll go into college teaching, or apply to the Foreign Service. I wish I could say Carolina has contacted me but I still haven't heard a word from her since coming back here to New York. I do hear from Adam, though not as frequently as I used to. He recently informed me that he'd be leaving Quito; he was being transferred to the embassy in Lisbon. I congratulated him on the move though strangely I found myself upset at the thought of it. I guess I had come to see him as my last remaining link to Carolina. On the other hand, she almost certainly had not returned to Ecuador and it was highly unlikely she ever would.

I received an unexpected reminder of my visit to Ecuador one gray spring day when an official-looking envelope arrived for me from the Israeli Embassy in Washington. To my surprise and amusement it turned out to be an invitation to attend a small ceremony where I would be presented with an official citation from the Israeli government thanking me for my efforts in Ecuador "on behalf of the Israeli people". Thinking about it, I've convinced myself I've done nothing to deserve such an award. On the other hand, I know for certain now I'll never receive any award from the US government, especially after Ecuador's recent presidential election in which the candidate who won has begun to look suspiciously like a clone of Venezuela's Hugo Chavez. I can only imagine how Washington must have reacted, and Adam as well. But, hey, it's no longer any great concern of mine, and while I suspect there are no more than a handful of people who actually know of my role in all of this, I still think I'll take a pass on flying down to Washington to pick up my award from the Israeli government.

Yet, even with the invitation from the Israeli Embassy, I often find myself questioning whether this entire series of events really happened: the diary, the murders, my being kidnapped. But, then, I think about Carolina and I know it had to be real. After all this time I can still picture her face with such clarity, her eyes so full of love, her mouth at one moment so serious and the next breaking out into that delightful smile of hers. I do remind myself, and it's often, that with what she's had to endure there's a very good chance her love for me no longer exists. Yet I force myself to go on as if nothing could ever extinguish it. I occasionally date other women though I seldom invite them out a second time. I'm not certain this makes any sense, it's just for the moment I seem to prefer it that way. Of course, none of the women I've met can begin to compare with Carolina in looks, sophistication, or intelligence. That alone should prove how in love with her I am.

So what, you may ask, is the emotional situation I find myself in these days? First of all, I've had to constantly fight the urge to fly to Buenos Aires and look for Carolina. I remember Jacob's warning but I also rationalize that I'd probably never find her anyway. Perhaps the best way to describe my situation, then, is to explain what happens when my computer screen alerts me that I have mail. I tend to stare at the notification for several seconds whispering, "Please, Lord, let it be a message from Carolina." I then open the message with a combination of anticipation and trepidation. When I realize the message is not from her I'm momentarily crushed. But, I always snap back, reminding myself that I'm one day closer to receiving the message from her that says, "Michael, I love you, I need you, please don't give up on me."

About the Author

David Lindgren was born in Ipswich, Massachusetts, and educated at Boston University. For thirty-five years he was a member of the faculty of Dartmouth College from which he is now retired. Upon his retirement from Dartmouth Professor Lindgren moved to Ecuador where for four years he taught at San Francisco University in Quito. It was while living here he became inspired to write this book. The author is presently living in Washington, DC, where he is working on his latest novel.